A NAME

Catherine Dunne was born in Dublin in 1954. She studied English and Spanish at Trinity College and went on to teach at Greendale Community School. She lives on the north side of Dublin with her husband and son. Her first novel, *In the Beginning*, was published in 1997.

ALSO BY CATHERINE DUNNE

In the Beginning

Catherine Dunne

A NAME
FOR HIMSELF

V

VINTAGE

Published by Vintage 1999

2 4 6 8 10 9 7 5 3 1

Copyright © Catherine Dunne 1998

The right of Catherine Dunne to be identified as the author of this work has been asserted by her in accordance with the Copyright, Designs and Patents Act, 1988

First published in Great Britain in 1998 by
Jonathan Cape

Vintage
Random House, 20 Vauxhall Bridge Road,
London SW1V 2SA

Random House Australia (Pty) Limited
20 Alfred Street, Milsons Point, Sydney
New South Wales 2061, Australia

Random House New Zealand Limited
18 Poland Road, Glenfield, Auckland 10,
New Zealand

Random House South Africa (Pty) Limited
Endulini, 5A Jubilee Road, Parktown 2193,
South Africa

Random House UK Limited Reg. No. 954009

A CIP catalogue record for this book
is available from the British Library

ISBN 0 09 926854 X

Papers used by Random House UK Ltd are natural, recyclable products made from wood grown in sustainable forests. The manufacturing processes conform to the environmental regulations of the country of origin

Printed and bound in Great Britain by
Cox & Wyman Ltd, Reading, Berkshire

FOR EAMONN

Farrell is watching his sleeping wife.

Her small face is pale, framed by dark, glossy hair. In repose, her expression is trusting, childlike. He bends down and smoothes the hair away from her forehead. He feels the tug beginning just below his heart as he repeats this old, familiar gesture.

Reluctantly, he turns away. The room is oddly silent. No playful shrieks rise from the neighbouring gardens; no bedtime calls float on the quiet evening air.

He hangs up her clothes and straightens her shoes. Closing the curtains, he looks down into the garden, glowing and golden in late September sunshine.

He tucks the white cotton sheet up under her chin. He doesn't want to leave her, yet. But he has things to do.

The heavy bedroom air begins to oppress him. He turns away from her and closes the door quietly behind him.

His hands are shaking a little; he needs a drink.

He goes back downstairs to begin his preparations.

Chapter One

Farrell hated P.J. Browne on sight. He hated all men who were called by their initials. It was as though they *expected* everyone to know who they were. They didn't need names like everyone else; their uniqueness was proclaimed, arrogantly, by two full-stops.

From the very start, Farrell wished that Christy hadn't sent him on this job. He hated seeing the houses in Merrion Square transformed into little hovels, partitioned rat-runs for the men in suits. Steel lighting-frames hung from the ceilings, fireplaces were boarded up, cables strung everywhere. It offended his sense of what was proper.

'Come on, Christy, for fuck's sake. Send Gerry. He's good at that sort of thing.'

But Christy had shaken his head.

'No way, mate. There's a lot of fancy boardroom stuff they want done as well. It's your baby, all the way. And there's an end-of-contract bonus if we finish up early. Gerry'd be late for his own funeral.'

When Farrell reported for work at half eight on his first day, he was surprised to find someone already there, waiting.

The older man looked up as Farrell walked into Reception.

'I'm from Collins Construction,' Farrell offered as the other man said nothing.

'At least you're punctual. I'm P.J. Browne. I own this building, and I supervise everything personally.'

And fuck you, too, thought Farrell. He felt a stir of

3

anger. He caught all the implications. *At least?* He hadn't done anything yet and already the man was grudging.

'Where's what's his name? Dwyer?'

'O'Dwyer. Christy will be along with more materials at ten. He said there's enough four by twos for me to start the frames down in the basement.'

Farrell waited. P.J. brushed cigarette ash off his waistcoat. When he stood, Farrell noticed how small he was. Big-bellied, fat-handed. Farrell stood up straighter.

'This way.'

P.J. led the way into the wide hallway. He pointed through the arch.

'The materials are in the return. The stairs on the left lead directly to the basement.'

'I know where the basement is.'

Farrell's reply was soft. P.J. opened his mouth, about to speak sharply. Something in Farrell's face made him close it again. He ran his hand over oiled, thinning hair.

'Right, then.'

He turned abruptly and walked off.

Farrell watched as he tried to walk with dignity on his little short legs. He could see by the set of his shoulders that the man was furious.

He smiled to himself. It looked like being a long three months.

But the basement was large and airy and there was no one there to annoy him. The bars on the window were ugly but, apart from that, it was still a gracious room, its proportions not yet destroyed.

Farrell took out his radio and set the volume low. No point in tempting fate. *Mr* P.J. Browne was already on the look-out for something, anything, to complain about. Farrell wouldn't give him the pleasure. He unstrapped his toolbox and surveyed the contents, wiping his palms on the white cotton cloth he always carried with him. No

4

matter how many times he opened and closed it, the toolbox always brought him a rush of pleasure. His first major piece of work, a solid reminder that he'd served his time well. Poor old Casey was dead now, died the year after Farrell had finished serving his time. A perfectionist, he'd goaded and harried his apprentices for over four years. He'd go purple in the face if anyone left as much as a panel pin on the floor when they'd finished working.

'Dirty bastards!' he'd yell. 'Sweep up after yourselves! Leavin' muck behind yis is no part of this trade! Now get the brush!'

Sometimes they did it just to annoy him. Just to see his face flush from pink to beetroot. When they'd learned everything he could teach them, they presented him with a sweeping-brush, wrapped and beribboned, and sang a song suggesting where he could put it.

It was one of the few times Farrell had ever seen him smile. He'd called them a pack of guntherers, mullockers. But to Farrell he'd said: 'You're good, lad. You're a craftsman, not a tradesman. Remember that.'

Farrell remembered now. A big, white-haired, watery-eyed man, older than his years. The first good teacher Farrell had ever known. He'd grunted when Farrell had handed him the toolbox for his inspection. He'd run his hand over every joint, opening and closing the lid again and again. Twenty-odd years later, Farrell could still remember how nervous he'd felt. Finally, Casey had nodded.

'Not bad, lad, not at all bad.'

Farrell's heart had soared. Casey had been the only one in his whole nineteen years who had ever really praised him.

He oiled his saw and stuck his hammer into the loop at the side of his apron. It was nice to remember someone with affection.

Farrell measured, cut and nailed the rough timber frames for the rest of the morning. He always liked this process of transformation, of making something out of nothing. He enjoyed his own company. He was content.

He ate his sandwiches with Christy, sitting on a plastic wine crate, while Christy muttered about the ignorant old bollocks upstairs who wouldn't even supply a kettle.

Farrell didn't care. He had two flasks of tea, as usual. He'd long since stopped depending on people who expected you to eat your lunch in the garage, or out in the back garden, even in the pissing rain. After forty years, Christy still liked to grumble about it.

At half-past five, both men stopped work and strapped up their toolboxes. Christy's haphazardness still irritated Farrell. He constantly lost tools, leaving them behind him on building sites; then he'd want to borrow Farrell's. Or he'd forget to sharpen his plane, and his hand would stutter over the wood, spraying curled shavings everywhere. And he never swept up.

Tonight, he was in a hurry, as usual.

'Pint?' he asked Farrell.

Farrell shook his head.

'Naw. I'm goin' home to get cleaned up. You go ahead.'

Christy's eyebrows shot up.

'She must be somethin' else to make you pass up a pint.'

Farrell didn't reply.

'See ya tomorrow, then.'

''Night.'

When he was gone, Farrell stacked the timber neatly in the corner and brushed the floor. He left the shavings and the sawdust in a tidy little mound, picking out the nails that Christy had spewed everywhere. He looked around him for refuse sacks. Nothing. He'd ask old Browne for some. Seeing as how he supervised everything personally.

Farrell picked up his toolbox and walked up the wide staircase, stopping to look at some ornate plasterwork, damaged in the renovation. Egg and dart; life and death. He hoped someone was going to fix it, to bring it back to what it once was.

He knocked at the door marked Reception. No answer.

He was just about to turn away when the door was opened abruptly.

'Yes?'

Farrell felt a sudden lump in his throat as he looked at the woman standing in front of him. He was much taller, and she had to look up at him. He had a blinding impression of deep blue eyes, pale skin, mouth a perfect crimson arc.

He couldn't speak. Someone pushed past her from behind, racing for the front door. A man in a dark suit, Farrell noticed.

' 'Night, Gracie!' floated back as whoever it was slammed the heavy door behind him.

' 'Night, David!'

She was smiling at Farrell now, eyes all gentle amusement.

Farrell was immediately angry at the familiarity between them, jealous of the departing back.

'I'm sorry,' he managed, 'I was just lookin' for some black sacks. I'm cleanin' up downstairs.'

Christ. He was making himself sound like a common labourer. And the man who had just run out was wearing a suit. Farrell was suddenly, painfully conscious of his dark blue overalls and his Dublin accent. No matter how careful he tried to be, broad, unguarded vowels still slipped to the surface of his speech in moments of stress.

'I don't think there are any. I'll get P.J. to bring some tomorrow.' She was looking at him kindly.

7

He wanted to be gone. But more than that, he wanted to look at her. He was greedy for those eyes, that mouth.

'Right,' he mumbled, turning away suddenly and hitting his knee painfully off the corner of his toolbox. Let me out of here.

'Goodnight!' she called.

There was laughter in her voice.

Farrell couldn't reply. He pulled angrily at the door and stepped out into the September sunshine of Merrion Square.

He could do with a pint after all. He could do with forgetting what he had just seen. Christy's familiar conversation would drown the swirling of his gut.

But he knew. He felt panicked, elated.

He knew he had just met the only woman he would ever want.

★　★　★

Vinny was minding his family. In the morning, he had taken Eoin and Jody to school, leaving them at the corner in case Brother McCormack spotted him. Eoin was in High Babies, still too small to take care of Jody, who was only now finding his feet. Jody wasn't sure whether he liked school at all; Eoin only liked it as long as he was with Vinny. Baby Patrick cried as his two brothers waved goodbye, and tried to pull away, to cross the road with them.

Vinny was proud to be in charge. He had a lot to do, keeping everyone happy.

He waited until they'd crossed the road safely, stood there waving until they turned the corner out of sight. He could hear the roar from the playground. In ten minutes' time, everything would fall suddenly quiet; four hundred boys would stand silently in the yard in their line, while black-cassocked brothers swept up and down, hands crossed low behind their backs, making sure there was order, uniformity. The first time Vinny had seen the brothers, he'd thought they had no hands. He'd been frightened by their black flapping sleeves, reminded of crows swooping.

That morning, he didn't have to face them. He made Patrick chuckle all the way home. He was glad to be free, to be doing anything other than sitting under Brother McCormack's small, stern eyes.

His mother had told him that she thought the new baby would be a little girl. Vinny was glad; he had three brothers already.

When he got home, she was still asleep. He had heard them at it again, last night. Eoin and Jody hadn't woken up; neither had Patrick. But he had: the minute the front door slammed, he had been wide awake, his heart hammering. Usually, he couldn't hear what was said, could never make out the words they threw at each other. But the way it happened was always the same. Low voices at first, then a sudden shout or a noise that seemed to unlock a whole sea of sound. Vinny wondered why his mother didn't just go to bed. If she was asleep, then his father couldn't fight with her. He couldn't understand why she stayed on guard, sitting nervously in the kitchen, waiting for the same things to happen over and over again.

Just before the front door had slammed shut for the second time, Vinny had heard him shouting.

'I'll tear the bloody place apart if I have to!'

He had strained to put shape to his mother's shrill words, lifting his head from the pillow, not daring to get out of bed. But all he could catch was something about leaving the clock alone, that that was for the children. Vinny didn't understand; he was too tired to try. He'd waited until he heard her heavy step on the landing. Then he must have slept at once. He did not remember her coming in.

She always came in, every night, to make sure they were asleep. Vinny never let on; he always kept his eyes closed while she passed her hand over his forehead, straightened the blankets over Eoin and Jody, kissed baby Patrick in his cot and tiptoed out again, stepping carefully over the boards that creaked. She never caught him foxing her.

He hadn't heard his father come back, didn't know what time his mother had finally slept. Vinny now crept to the top of the stairs and cautiously opened her bedroom door. He put his finger to his lips, warning Patrick. The little boy, waiting at the bottom of the stairs, mimicked his eldest brother. He put a pudgy finger up to his own lips and said 'Sshh.'

Vinny took a last careful look at his mother to make sure she was fast asleep, that he had time to do what he had to do. She mustn't know; it had to be his secret. He closed the bedroom door quietly and made his way back downstairs, knowing that he would hear her if she got out of bed and turned the handle.

He lifted Patrick and kissed him on the top of his head.

'Good boy,' he said in his mother's tone. 'You're a good boy.'

He carried Patrick back to the end of the hall and sat him down on the floor.

'Stay here,' he whispered.

Vinny went into the kitchen and scooped up an armful of wooden alphabet bricks. They were old, their paint peeling so that the letters were barely recognisable. It didn't matter: Patrick wouldn't know the difference anyway. He put them down gently beside his little brother. Then he went back into the kitchen again and carried out the sturdiest of the four wooden stools.

Stepping onto it with ease, Vinny reached up to the lintel above the sitting-room door and felt along it for the key. He wasn't supposed to know it was there. Patrick was looking up at him, wide-eyed. Moving the stool out of the way now, Vinny put his finger to his lips again, and bent down to insert the key into the lock. He held his breath, willing it to turn silently.

Inside the sitting-room there were two worn armchairs, a heavy sideboard that used to belong to his Nana, a radio and the big clock on the mantelpiece. There was a picture of the Sacred Heart on the chimney breast, and a framed certificate signed by Pope Pius XII. It was a blessing for their marriage, she'd told him.

His mother used to polish the green speckled lino of this room every week, starting over at the fireplace. Down on her hands and knees, she would dip her duster into the tin of Mansion and rub vigorously, polishing in small circular movements. She would work her way backwards like this, until she reached the hall. Vinny loved the waxy feel of floor polish, the smell of the yellow dusters after she had finished. Although they rarely used the good room now, she insisted that everything be kept spotless. He'd noticed that she hadn't been doing much polishing for the past few weeks; maybe it was because her stomach had grown so huge.

The baby was late. She'd been glad that it hadn't been born on time, because that was the day Vinny had made his First Communion. But that was two weeks ago now, and lately she was always tired and complaining.

The big clock was not ticking this morning. Vinny knew he shouldn't, that if he was caught she'd probably be cross, but he couldn't help himself. He wanted to understand what he thought he'd heard last night, why she'd sounded so angry. He took off his shoes and stood on the hearth, the brown and beige mottled tiles cold under his thin socks. Gently, he eased the clock a little to the right, so that he could slide his hand in behind it.

The wooden back slid down with a clatter, and Vinny stayed still, suddenly terrified. But there was no movement from the room upstairs.

He felt around with his left hand, holding on to the clock with his right. His fingers sensed something. There was definitely something there. Slowly, he drew out a thin, whitish-coloured book. It had a harp on it and a number. 'Leabhar Coigiltis' was written in large letters across the front. He knew that *leabhar* meant book; he didn't think he had ever seen *coigiltis* before.

He opened it cautiously. Dates and figures were written in small, competent handwriting. Black, circular stampings overlapped. At the end of the third page there was the total amount saved: £6.14s.3d. The last date was February, three months ago. He fumbled again, this time putting his hand right inside the clock. His fingers grasped at something crisp and crumpled. He pulled out a ten-shilling note, like the one his Nana in Galway had sent him for his First Communion. There had been others too, he was sure of it, and half-crowns from some of the neighbours. His mother had taken it all to mind for him until he was older. He put the orange note back, replaced the *Leabhar Coigiltis*, and eased the back of the clock into place. There was a little brass finger which kept it closed. Almost at once, the comforting tick-tick began again.

Vinny knew he had seen something he shouldn't have. He began to understand something he shouldn't have known. Deep in the pit of his stomach, anger twisted and pulled, rising to fill his chest until he could hardly breathe.

He hated that voice in the night, threatening, bullying,

insisting that everything was *his*, taking whatever he wanted. He had no *right*.

Vinny lifted Patrick off the floor and brought him into the kitchen. He went out into the hall again and made sure the sitting-room door was locked. Then he returned the key to its hiding-place on the lintel. Once he'd put the stool back where he'd got it, he gathered up all the alphabet bricks. Only then did his heartbeat begin to return to normal.

Slowly, he put on the kettle and reached up for the tea caddy. When the water was hot enough, he heated the teapot carefully, just as she had shown him. He swirled the hot water round and round, watching as the dark brown inside of the teapot grew darker, releasing its bitter, comforting smell. By the time he had thrown the water down the drain, the kettle had boiled. He spooned the tea-leaves into the pot. The ritual was soothing. The tightness in his chest began to loosen.

The tea was already milked and sugared by the time he heard her door opening. He called out to her at once.

'Hang on, Ma, I'm comin' up.'

He turned to Patrick, playing silently on the floor beside him. Vinny had almost forgotten about him. He sprinkled sugar thickly on a slice of bread and butter, and quickly folded the slice in half.

'Here y'are. I'll be down in a minute.'

The little boy's eyes lit up, and he grabbed the bread with both hands. He grinned delightedly at his big brother.

Grasping the cup in one hand and a slice of bread and butter in the other, Vinny made his way up the stairs to his mother, wishing with all his heart that he could make it better, wishing with all his heart that he had never found out.

Now that he knew, he was going to have to *do* something, anything. He had to make sure that last night never happened again. He would have to be on the alert, prepared to do whatever it took to protect her. He had no idea what that could be.

★ ★ ★

Farrell thought about the woman in Reception all the next day, and the day after that. She swirled around him, a confusion of images. Her face danced before his eyes, her mouth blinded him. He remembered how the vividness of her blue suit, in some soft material, had matched the deep shade of her eyes. He tried to recall the tone of her voice, the exact colour of her hair. He could still see the way she'd smiled, the kindly amusement in her eyes as she'd looked up at him. The memory of her filled him with a mixture of longing and exhilaration, so that he could no longer concentrate on his work. For the first time in almost twenty years, he became careless. His chisel slipped and sliced the base of his left thumb. He cursed out loud and Christy came running.

'Jaysus, man, that's a bad gash. You'll need stitches.'

Farrell saw the white of knuckle, the red rush of blood. It didn't hurt, at first. Christy wrapped Farrell's white cotton cloth around the wound, told him to keep his hand up high. Then he said:

'You go on, I'll tell Browne. D'ye want anyone to go with you?'

Farrell shook his head, angry at his own stupidity. Women had always had that effect on him. They made him feel speechless, awkward; he tripped over steps and stumbled into doors, made clumsy by their presence. Now his hand began to throb.

14

'You'd better get a tetanus jab while you're at it. Let me know how long you'll be off.' Christy was looking uneasy. Farrell could tell what he was thinking. There goes my end-of-contract bonus.

'I'll be back tomorrow. It's only my left hand,' he said curtly.

Christy looked relieved, then ashamed. A glance from Farrell made him decide on silence.

On his way out, she was there. She smiled at him, and then she saw the clumsy, bloodstained bandage. Her face immediately showed concern.

'What's happened?'

Farrell's heart began to pound. An inept, common labourer. At his age.

'Nothing much. My wood-chisel slipped and I've cut my hand a bit. It's nothing.'

He kept his voice steady, smoothing over the rough edges of his accent. He wanted to be gone, didn't want her to see him like this.

'You're like a ghost. My car is out the back. Come on, I'll drive you to Casualty.'

She didn't wait for his reply. Farrell followed her down the long hallway, out the back door to the parking spaces. He began to feel light-headed and absurdly happy. He didn't care about the pain in his hand. This was fate.

She pushed open the passenger door.

'Can you manage?'

He could only nod, feeling his throat tighten as she leaned across him, tugging at his seat-belt.

'You keep your hand upright; I'll belt you in.'

He noticed that her hair was jet black, smooth against her pale face. She smelt of some delicious perfume. Farrell wanted to touch her so much it hurt.

'My name is Grace, by the way.'

Farrell's reply was caught somewhere at the base of his throat.

'Mine's Farrell,' he said.

Their journey was an almost silent one.

'Are you sure you're OK?' she asked him once.

He could only mumble in reply, raging inside once more at his silence, his uselessness. The words were drowning, trapped together somewhere underneath his voice; they refused to come to the surface. She didn't speak again until they drove into the hospital grounds and pulled up outside Casualty.

'You go on in. I'll find somewhere to park.'

'Thanks,' was all he could manage.

Casualty was quiet. Wednesday morning, not much in the way of street fights or domestics. Farrell made his way to the glass-fronted hatch and gave his name and details. He waited as the printer whined its way across the page. There he was; all summed up.

When he turned around, she was already there, waiting for him. He sat down, awkward on the small, grey, plastic chair. He felt too big for his surroundings. But at least the words were ready now; he knew what he was going to say to her.

'I'll be fine,' he said. 'There's no need for you to wait.'

His tone was polite, reassuring. He hoped he'd got it right. He was conscious of needing her to go, wanting her to stay.

'I'll just see how long it's going to take.'

He watched her as she walked away from him, her limbs loose and assured, her whole body confident of its place in the world. Jesus, if only he didn't feel so awkward. He was easily fifteen or sixteen years older than she was, but he felt like a little boy. He had never walked with such sureness, never really believed that he had a right to belong.

She came back with a nurse. He found the courage from somewhere.

'Please, don't feel you have to stay. I'm sure you have things to do.'

Her clear blue eyes held his for a moment.

'I'm going to ring my father and tell him where I am. Once your hand is stitched, I'm going to leave you home. It's not a problem.'

Again, she didn't wait for his reply. A pain grew deep in Farrell's chest as he watched her cross the room to the telephone. Black silk skirt, soft white blouse, round swaying hips. The nurse had to repeat herself, twice, before Farrell realised he was being spoken to.

'I'm sorry?'

The nurse was smiling broadly. Farrell felt the back of his neck beginning to get warm.

'I said the doctor is ready for you now.'

Without meeting her eyes, Farrell went with her. He walked with his head down, followed the soundless white shoes. He was glad to be in the cubicle, welcomed the sting of needles, stitches. It was easier to bear than being beside her and not even having a chance.

He wished he was wearing a suit, carrying a mobile phone. She was not for the likes of him, he knew that. She was miles away from north inner-city childhoods, where kids made swings on lamp-posts and scutted on the backs of lorries. No father had ever shouted drunken abuse at her. No mother had ever given up on her, quietly fading away, stealing off into a young death.

She, Grace, had had elegance, prosperity, silver spoons, all her life. It was written all over her. Her name said it all. He watched her again in his imagination as she crossed the room to the phone. Her smooth face, her glossy hair, her youthfulness. Farrell found it hard to breathe as he thought about her.

17

As the doctor rolled a bandage snugly over Farrell's thumb, it hit him. Her father. P.J. It had to be. He felt his insides turn to water. Well, that was definitely that.

She was still waiting for him, leafing through a magazine. She pushed her hair back from her forehead a couple of times, running her fingers absently along the crown of her head, allowing the thick, shining hair to fall back around her face again. Farrell could have watched her do that all day. He tried to ignore the great ball of misery gathering inside him.

She looked up and saw him standing there. She smiled at him warmly, putting the magazine down at once.

'Everything OK?'

He nodded numbly, not trusting himself to speak.

'You look really shook. Would you like a cup of coffee?'

'I think I'll just go home.' He spoke carefully. 'They said to lie down for a while.'

God, he hadn't even said *thanks*. And he could see the kindness in her eyes. He wished she wouldn't look at him like that. Kindness was not what he wanted to see there.

'Of course. Come on, I'll drive you home.'

How could he argue? It was another silent journey, except for his directions through Rathmines. He could see that she was puzzled. He caught her glancing at him a couple of times. Once, he thought she was about to speak. He could feel something between them, hanging there like a dull, heavy cloud. His thoughts were strangled, his mind incapable of any attempt at conversation. He grew more and more embarrassed. This awful, tense silence was his fault. He made a last, frantic effort to be pleasant.

'Just pull over here. You've been very kind. I really appreciate it.'

His words were slow, measured. Even to his own ears, he sounded stilted, overly polite.

Her blue gaze was steady.

'No problem. I told P.J. you probably needed a couple of days at least. Have you painkillers?'

Farrell almost laughed outright. Now what pain might she be talking about? His hand was nothing; that would get better, in time.

'Yeah. The doc gave me some for today. I've a prescription for more tomorrow, if I need them.'

She nodded.

'OK. Well, take it easy.'

'Yeah. Thanks for everything.'

Farrell stretched and opened the car door awkwardly with his right hand. Luckily, he got it first time. He turned to say goodbye and was filled with her perfume. She was watching him.

'See you,' he said.

' 'Bye – mind yourself.'

She waved and waited until he'd opened his front door. A casual glance behind her, a smooth changing of gears and the car slid away from the footpath.

Farrell let himself into his flat. He took two painkillers with a glass of water, and put on the kettle. He stood at the window, looking out at the yard full of rusting sinks and bits of old bicycles, as he waited for the kettle to boil. He warmed the teapot, taking two tea-bags out of the caddy. It was awkward, trying to do everything with one hand.

He sat down at the little table in the kitchen and replayed the scene over and over again. Sipping the hot tea made everything worse, not better. This was not something that could be comforted by the warmth of tea, the ritual of the familiar. He thought of all the ways he could have made it different. He could have joked about his clumsiness and made her laugh. He could have made the effort to hide his unease, chatting to her like a normal man. If he'd been friendly and funny, she mightn't even have noticed the occasional jarring of his accent. He could have tried to be anything other than what he was. The mass inside his chest grew bigger. He thought of crystal and lace, lamp-posts and lorries.

Then he folded his arms on the kitchen table, put his head down, and wept.

★ ★ ★

For a moment, Vinny couldn't figure out what had woken him so suddenly. There was a strange quietness in his bedroom. A quietness that held its breath, waiting for something to happen. Vinny felt his heart begin to speed up, his stomach begin to fall down, down. He listened.

There was a noise again downstairs. He could hear a murmur only, no words. It was the absence of doors slamming, raised voices, anger, that really frightened him. This was going to be one of the bad ones, he could feel it.

Vinny felt the familiar sensation of something warm and prickling across the back of his neck, down between his shoulder blades. He sat up, careful not to wake Patrick. Every muscle strained as all his energy went into listening. The silence was terrifying.

Suddenly, there was an explosion of sound, an unleashing of fury. Vinny heard the sounds of breaking glass, of something being dragged across the floor. Something that moved heavily. He waited, nausea prodding at the back of his throat.

Then he heard his mother. Not what she said; just the begging, pleading tone that made Vinny's vision go black.

Blindly, he leapt out of bed, slammed open the bedroom door and took the stairs three at a time. They were in the kitchen. Vinny pushed the door open with all his strength and it crashed against the wall with a satisfying splintering of wood.

His mother was on all fours, her head held low, her back to the fire. His father was bending down to her, holding her by a handful of long, greying hair. His face was very close to hers. In his other hand, he held a cigarette, almost casually. Vinny knew that he had been just in time.

In slow motion, Vinny's father looked up at him. His face was a strange colour. The boy counted the veins on his father's forehead that he had never seen before. He saw how much smaller he looked, bending down. Ridiculous, almost; great big belly, surprisingly small hands for such a large man. Vinny almost wanted to laugh.

'Leave her alone,' he said to the blue-blotched face.

Vinny's mother was trying to shake her head at him, waving her hand wildly at him to go away. But he wasn't going anywhere. He was very tall for nine; could nearly meet his father eye to eye.

Slowly, without taking his eyes off Vinny's face, his father almost gently let go of the handful of hair. Still his mother did not get up; she just kept shaking her head, begging Vinny wordlessly not to. Her face was dead white, the eyes blue-black, huge with fear, saying please, don't. They were locked on every movement her son made.

Vinny never even saw his father raise his hand, never knew where the blow came from. One minute, he had been standing in the kitchen. The next, he was on his back in the hall, scrabbling to right himself, like some helpless insect, arms and legs flailing. His mouth was full of something warm and coppery.

'Get the fuck back upstairs!'

His father was standing over him, ready to swing again. Before his jaw started to hurt, Vinny was glad that he had fooled him. His father rarely had enough anger for two. He was almost spent. He wouldn't go at her again.

Vinny pulled himself up off the floor, the lino suddenly cold under his bare feet. He turned towards the stairs. He had made no sound, he knew that. Looking down, he placed one foot in front of the other, deliberately, on each cold step of the stairs. He felt his father's eyes watch his progress. And he knew that he had won. He would leave her alone now. He'd shout for a while and then fall asleep in the chair by the fire, snoring and rumbling. He'd wake much later, stiff, and make his noisy, faltering way up to bed.

It was over.

Vinny went into the bathroom and spat into the sink. His whole head had begun to throb. He put his mouth to the tap and swirled the cold water round and round. It hurt. He spat again. The stain was getting pinkish, now. It'd stop bleeding soon.

He went back into the bedroom, quietly pushing the door to behind him. It took a minute or two for his eyes to become accustomed to the darkness. There was something white in the corner.

Vinny looked again. Eoin and Jody were sitting on the floor, Patrick in between them. They were trying to keep him quiet. They had wrapped him in the thin, scratchy blanket off their bed, each of them hugging him close.

Vinny went over to his little brother. He forced his own arms and legs to be still, to stop trembling.

'It's OK, Patrick. It's OK.'

He lifted the sobbing little boy up and held him close, pressing both their faces together to help stifle the crying. Soundlessly, Eoin and Jody climbed back into their own bed. Baby Jenny was still fast asleep in her cot, thumb lodged in her mouth.

Vinny's heart sank as he sat on the bed, Patrick on his knee. The sheet was soaking. The whole bed he shared with his youngest brother was soaking wet. Patrick had pissed himself again. His vest and knickers clung to him, coldly, stickily.

Vinny turned over the mattress, rolling the sheet into a ball and shoving it under the bed until morning. Then he pulled his school jumper over Patrick's head, telling him over and over again that it was OK, things were OK. It took a long time for the child's teeth to stop chattering.

That night, Vinny's mother did not come in.

Tomorrow, he would put the sheet and Patrick's under-wear into the bucket in the kitchen before he went to school. She would be there, buttering bread for their school lunches. For a day or two, she would avoid his eyes.

For a month or two, there would be only shouting at night.

Then, it would happen all over again.

Day by day, Vinny watched his mother shrinking. Her body was becoming smaller, thinner, frailer.

She was beginning to disappear.

★   ★   ★

Two days later, Farrell could stand it no longer. He rang Christy to say he'd be back on Monday. He knew by the sound of Christy's voice that Gerry wasn't working out.

He could take the pain in his hand. He could take anything except not seeing Grace. He was terrified that she would steal away from him.

All weekend in the empty flat he'd thought about her, dreamt of her. Driven to despair on Sunday afternoon, he walked all the way from Rathmines to Fairview Park, taking longer and faster strides until he was breathless. But nothing could dislodge her from his mind. Every dark-

23

haired woman on the street made his heart lurch. He imagined bumping into her, imagined what he would say, what she would answer. He could smell her perfume. He heard her speaking everywhere; in the park, even on the bus home. The sound of her voice surrounded him.

Maybe he would have a chance. He was only thirty-nine, still young enough. He was a good craftsman. Maybe he could even start his own business, wear a suit, carry a mobile phone. He had to show her that there was more to him than she had seen. More than the silent workman she had driven to Casualty and treated with kindness. Anything was possible if she wanted him; he could do anything. He had to have courage now; he had to find a way of holding onto her before she slipped away from him.

Farrell arrived at work at eight-twenty exactly on the following morning. He walked straight to the back of the building, towards the toilet. Once inside, he opened the window at the top and peered out. His mouth went dry. Her car was there.

He washed his hands, waiting for his nerves to calm. He walked purposefully towards Reception, practising his lines, making sure they would come when he summoned them. The painters had finished this room over the weekend; Grace and P.J. were already installed. Farrell was genuinely overwhelmed at the transformation. He imagined that he saw her hand everywhere. Dark green carpet, peach-coloured walls, Roman blinds in tones of peach, cream and green. Blinding white shutters; the fire-places revealed and filled with baskets of silk flowers.

'Well, do you like it?'

Farrell swung around to find her standing behind him. He hadn't heard her come in.

'It's really beautiful. You've done a great job.'

The enthusiasm in his voice was real. He was glad he

didn't have to pretend. And the words had come to him easily.

Her whole face lit up as she smiled.

'Thank you. I'm glad you like it. Sometimes it's hard to get the balance right – P.J.'s only interested in *function*. We have to compromise.' Suddenly, she said: 'How's the hand?'

'Fine. Just a bit stiff. It'll be grand once I get the stitches out.'

'Good. You're looking better than you did the other day. Have you the time to come with me for a moment, please?'

Farrell felt a small shock of pleasure. 'Yeah – of course.'

'I want you to show me everything that needs to be fixed or replaced. P.J. wants the complete picture by this afternoon.'

Farrell nodded.

'Sure, no problem.'

He felt the beginnings of an ease between them. It made him walk with a lighter step. He was proud to be asked.

They walked together throughout the whole building. He saw her take notes when he pointed out the damaged cornices, the occasional missing stair-rail. He explained how the marble fireplaces could be restored, the old skirtings replaced, the floors repaired and polished.

Under her encouragement, he suggested ways of draught-proofing the old wooden windows in the rest of the building. P.J. wanted to get rid of them and replace them with plastic-coated horrors, she said, but she was adamant.

She turned and looked directly at him when their tour was finished.

'You've given me more than enough ammunition to attack P.J. I've been trying to convince him for weeks, but he wants to rip out everything that causes trouble and replace it with aluminium or plastic. Can I call on you to back me up?'

Farrell suddenly remembered his place.

'Well, Christy is the foreman. You'd need to talk to him.'

Grace looked at him coolly.

'But I prefer your approach. Christy has no finesse – he's quite happy to row in with whatever P.J. wants. So is the architect. He's been told to save money. I don't want yes-men. I want someone who knows what he's at.'

It had been a long time since anybody had praised Farrell. He felt needed, acknowledged. It was a good feeling; he had almost forgotten it. He found the courage to look directly at her. For a fleeting second, he thought he caught something in her eyes that was not mere kindness. His chest expanded. He was filled with ridiculous hope.

'I'd be delighted to help, if I can,' he said.

'Good. I'll be calling on you.'

Before either of them could say anything else, P.J. blustered in, followed by a cloud of cigarette smoke.

Farrell made to leave, conscious that it was past starting-time. She walked out with him to the hall.

At the door, she put her hand gently on his arm. Farrell felt his heart quicken. It wasn't an accidental touch: she had reached out to him. He kept his hands firmly in his pockets, feeling the palms begin to prickle and sweat.

'What do I call you?' she asked. 'I don't know your first name.'

He shrugged.

'Everybody calls me Farrell.'

She smiled at him again, and he had to steady himself. He planted his feet more solidly on the floor. The tingling in his hands seemed to increase.

'OK, Farrell, I'll be talking to you soon.'

He floated down to the basement, filled with incredible possibilities.

★ ★ ★

Vinny and Eoin got the tea together that evening and lit the fire. Their mother smiled at them a lot, chatting easily in a way she hadn't done for a long time. In the firelight, she looked almost well. The flames had brought a deep pink flush to her cheeks, and her eyes were bright. Her hands rested quietly on the rug on her knees; tonight, she was no longer her brittle, restless self. Her only movement was to smooth the rug's worn surface, to settle it around herself more comfortably. She sipped at her tea and ate three slices of the bread Jody had toasted for her on the flames. The room was getting nice and warm. Patrick and Jenny were quiet, sleepy. Vinny felt almost happy.

Just as tea was over, there was a scraping sound at the front door. For once, Vinny froze. He was unable to reach out and stop Eoin from running into the hall. He watched, dreamlike, as Eoin answered the door, allowing his father in. It took a moment for the younger boy to realise what he had done. White-faced, freckles standing out like brown paint, he ran in fright to his eldest brother, half-hiding behind him.

Vinny watched his father's bulky progress up the short hall. He seemed to have grown even bigger and broader since the last time. His overcoat smelt darkly of rain; his hair was dripping, plastered onto his skull. Cigarette-smoke shrouded him, half-hiding his air of defiance. He was angry almost at once.

'What's the matter with you?'

He yanked Eoin by the arm, pulling him towards him. Vinny wasn't quick enough to stop him.

'Can't you say hello to your own *da*?'

Vinny hated the way he smelt. Smoke, dirty rain, the sweet-sour smell off his breath, and something else that Vinny couldn't name. All he knew was, it was there when his father was angry. And he was angry now.

Vinny stood in front of his father, eyes level. He had already made his decision.

'Leave him alone,' he said softly.

Something flitted across his father's face that Vinny had never seen there before. With a great surge of joy, he recognised it as fear. He stood up straighter. He had seen the same flicker of uncertainty on faces in the school playground, just before he went in for the kill. His whole body was suddenly sure that he could win.

'What did you say?'

The black face approached, menacing. But Vinny didn't waver. He stood, his feet planted firmly on the floor, right in front of his father. Let him do his worst. He no longer cared. He couldn't just do *nothing* any more.

'Vincent?'

His mother's voice, stronger than usual, broke the pull of anger between them. Reluctantly, drawing harshly on his cigarette, Vinny's father turned away from him and made his way into the kitchen. She was now plucking nervously at the blanket on her knees. Jody and Patrick were sitting quietly on the floor beside her. Jenny was on her lap.

Even from the back, Vinny could see how enraged his father became. His neck went red and seemed to swell. His shoulders stiffened. He placed his feet further apart, as though testing his balance. Silence was everywhere.

'Please, Vincent,' his mother whimpered.

Vinny was angry at her then. Why did she beg? He had

no right to make her beg, to make her feel grateful for not being dragged across the floor and thumped in the face. *He* would not beg.

Vinny grabbed his father's sleeve and pulled him roughly around to face him. The look of astonishment on his face almost made the boy laugh. Eyes round, mouth open, great big cheeks: his whole face was like one giant O.

'Why don't you leave us alone?'

He saw the blow coming this time, watched in fascination as it moved from his father's face, down his arm, flowing into the fist that finally smashed into Vinny's left cheek. Thrown against the back wall, the boy rebounded and came back at his father, both fists pounding on the livid, angry face.

He had the advantage of surprise. The older man was winded for a moment, and then came at his son again, roaring.

Vinny could sense, rather than hear, the cries from the kitchen. He had to get him away from there, away from picking on the others.

He made up his mind quickly.

'Fuck you!' He spat the words right into his father's face.

He had never felt such strength before. He was made of rock, of iron. This felt good. The pain in his head was nothing. He was winning.

Suddenly, everything slowed down. Vinny watched as his father deliberately took the belt off his trousers, staring all the time into his son's eyes. Vinny knew the moment had come. He kicked him, twice, on the shins. Taking advantage of the gasp of surprise, Vinny fled past him down the hall.

He knew he didn't have time to open the front door and escape. His father was already moving heavily after him. He ran up the stairs, two at a time, easily gaining now on the clumsy step behind him. Even as he ran, Vinny was aware of his father's strange, breathy silence.

He slammed the bathroom door to, and locked it. He opened the window, ready to go at any moment. One foot on the toilet bowl, one hand on the window-frame, he was coiled, ready to spring. O'Gorman's shed-roof waited. Safety.

And then, abruptly, everything went still. There was a wide, deep silence, except for the pounding in his head. Then he heard the front door slam. His heart lifted. Had he gone?

Suddenly weak, lights dancing in front of his eyes, Vinny sat down on the bathroom floor, bending his head to make the sickness go away. Still silence.

After a few minutes, he stood up, rinsed his mouth, and scrubbed at his T-shirt with toilet paper soaked in water. It left a crumbly white trail behind it.

After what seemed like a very long time, there was a tap at the door.

'He's gone, Vinny. Mam says you're to come downstairs.' Eoin's voice was shaky.

Vinny ran his hand through his hair, sloshed cold water on his eye.

'Coming,' he said, cheerfully.

He closed the bathroom window. He felt elated. Fight back. That was what you had to do. Don't let him know you're afraid. Stand up for yourself.

He would never let him win again.

Vinny opened the bathroom door, and grinned crook-edly at his brother.

'Come on,' he said, 'old fat-arse, shorty-legs is gone for another while. Next time, I'll kill him.'

And Vinny made his way downstairs to his family.

* * *

Grace did call on him again, very soon. She had discovered a huge Victorian dining-table in an antique shop in Francis Street. But it needed work. She had talked P.J. round to using it in the boardroom, she said, but it had to be finished well in advance of the official opening.

She was excited. Her eyes shone when she described it to Farrell. She could see its beauty, under all the damage.

'Will you come with me and see if it can be saved?'

'Now?'

Farrell's mind was racing. He could postpone having his stitches out, use the time to be with her instead.

'Well, yes, now if you like, but I thought perhaps Saturday? Then if it's no good, maybe we could look for something else?'

She was speaking quickly, nervously even. Farrell felt a small tug of hope. It wasn't just his imagination; she did want to be with him.

'I've told P.J. I want you to do the work. He'll pay cash,' she added, looking a little embarrassed.

'I don't care about the money,' Farrell said truthfully. 'I'd love to get my hands on a real job like that.'

'Then is Saturday OK?'

Farrell smiled at her, feeling suddenly, happily, at ease.

'Saturday's grand. We'll start early, give us plenty of time.'

We. Us. The words had come to him again without effort. Surely, everything would come more easily to him after this.

'Great. I'll pick you up at nine, if that's OK?'

He bent down slightly to brush the dust off his overalls, where he had been kneeling. He looked downwards for a fraction longer than was necessary, taking care to hide the little shock of delight that had made him pause.

'I have to pass your door anyway, to get into town,' she added, seeing that he hesitated.

'Sure. Nine's fine,' he agreed.

They both laughed at the sudden rhyme. When P.J. appeared, there was no more conversation. Farrell left the hallway at once and went back to work. He was filled with a sense of elation. He was glad, too, that she had understood the need for caution. He was now sure that there was something real between them, a delicate feeling as yet, something fragile and barely balanced. Any clumsiness on his part, any suspicion on P.J's, and it could topple, its shattered pieces revealing all the reasons she should have nothing to do with him. He would not allow that to happen.

He was glad to have work to do, silent, concentrated space where he could begin to absorb what was happening to him. The basement was finished, ready for plastering. He was now moving up, up to the ground level, nearer to Grace. He was working his way closer to her all the time.

He thought Saturday would never come.

Without telling her, he used his next two lunch-times to scour the dozens of antique shops in Francis Street. He found the table on the second day, and knew instantly that this was it. He recognised it as a Victorian telescopic table. He examined the four massive, turned legs for any damage. They seemed to have retained all their solidity, apart from a few gouges and scratches in the mahogany. Farrell began to get really excited. He wanted this; he wanted to make it perfect for her. He loved its solid ugliness. Without its extra leaves, it looked squat and badly-proportioned; with them, it looked long and untidy. Seeing these contradictions, Farrell nodded happily to himself; it was just right, just as it should be. He knew he could fix the problem of the split and broken leaves. There was evidence of old woodworm; he could fix that, too. He searched for new signs, getting more and more hopeful every minute. It was in bad enough nick, but he could do it. He could make it right again, bring it back to what it once was.

'How much?' he asked the man hovering in the background.

'Well, it's Victorian, about 1870, oak and mahogany. It's a good, solid piece. The damage is only superficial. You're looking at two grand, at least.'

Farrell didn't care about the money. It wasn't his to worry about.

'Can you hold this for me until Saturday? I think it'll suit, but I'll have to come back.'

The man looked doubtful.

'I don't know. There was a young lady here the other day who seemed very keen. She said she'd be back on Saturday, there was someone she wanted to look at it with her.'

Farrell smiled.

'That's all right, then. That's me. We'll be looking at it together. Can you do anything about the price?'

The man scratched the back of his neck and sucked his breath through his teeth. He put his head on one side, reminding Farrell of a serious little bird.

'Well, I don't know about that; I'd have to see.'

To be able to say he had beaten the man down, for her. That was all Farrell wanted.

'You think about it, then. If the price is right, I can guarantee you a sale.'

'If you do that, I can give you ten per cent for yourself, in cash.'

The man was looking directly at him now, keen, beady little eyes. For an instant, he reminded Farrell of Brother McCormack.

Farrell shook his head.

'No. Take it directly off the top, for her.'

'The girlfriend, is it?'

Farrell shook his head, embarrassed. 'No.'

Then the man leered at Farrell in a way that made him angry.

'Ah, it's like that, is it?' he asked, grinning.

Farrell simply looked into the greedy little eyes and the man took a step back, suddenly confused.

'Right, right, whatever way you want it.'

'Don't sell it before Saturday,' Farrell said coldly. 'I'll leave you a deposit.'

The man waved away Farrell's money. He wanted him gone.

'No need, no need at all,' he said quickly, with a false, brittle smile. 'I'll take your word for it. I can see you're serious.'

'Right,' said Farrell, and pushed his way, deliberately, past him and out into Francis Street. He was angry all the way back to Merrion Square. Dirty-minded little bastard. He would not allow her to be looked on like that.

Then Grace's luminous beauty swam before Farrell's eyes, and his anger subsided. Working silently all afternoon, he thought of nothing but Saturday. He had a strange sense of peace, a feeling that he might be coming home, that he might belong and have someone belonging to him. If he couldn't have Grace, then he didn't want anybody, anything. He had waited long enough for this. She was beginning to fill his whole life. He tried not to think of P.J., of all the differences between his, Farrell's, life and theirs.

He thought instead of how he could make her happy, how he would love her. He had a fleeting memory of another time, another woman. A mistake. Farrell realised with sadness that he had been too young, hadn't known what he was getting himself into. He wished that he hadn't had to cause such pain. But that was in the past; Martina had been nothing like this.

On Saturday morning, Grace was very punctual, arriving at nine on the dot. He was out instantly to meet her. He wasn't yet prepared to have her on his territory. Although the flat was meticulous, clean and bright, he was suddenly ashamed of the way he lived. It was not her way. His painted walls and cheap, flatland furniture seemed very mean to his eyes now. Grace needed, deserved better surroundings than these.

And he could provide them, would provide them, if there was even a chance of her loving him.

'OK?' she asked him, after his brief tussle with the seat-belt.

He was able to smile at her then, the knot in his stomach uncoiling.

'Yeah. Fine.'

The Saturday-morning traffic was light all the way into town. She was able to park almost outside the shop door. The owner was opening up as they arrived.

Farrell wanted to explain to her in detail the restoration work that was needed. He wanted her to understand everything he could do. They held the leaves against the edges of the table, and Farrell measured its length once it was fully extended. He was pleased. It would be a perfect fit for the first-floor boardroom.

'It's huge! I didn't realise it was this big.' Grace looked at him anxiously, wanting his advice. 'Will it suit the boardroom? Can the room take this, and the chairs, without looking cluttered?'

He smiled at her.

'It's just what we want. It'll suit the proportions of the room perfectly *and* it'll seat twelve or fourteen, no problem.'

He was walking around the table now, passing his hand over the damaged surfaces. He could feel how good the wood was, how rich it would look. It was hard to stifle his enthusiasm.

'The Victorians had big families, you know. They needed tables like this. They usually just attached the leaves for dinner-parties. You can do the same in the boardroom – just extend it when it's needed.'

He watched her face, wanting her to be convinced, to trust him.

'I'll make a place to store the leaves so they won't get damaged. Look at these.'

They bent down together, hunkered at one end of the table.

Farrell pointed to the enormous legs, whose mouldings he had once heard described in disgust as inverted cups and saucers.

'It'll be very comfortable to sit at. The legs are deliberately placed in the extreme corners where no one ever sat. I know they're heavy and ugly, but I like them. They belong to a certain style. And this is the genuine article. It's not pretending to be anything it's not.'

They measured it again, and Farrell sketched out what it would look like in the room in Merrion Square. He had even thought to bring graph paper with him. Grace looked and listened carefully, asking him questions from time to time. Farrell felt again with a great thump of joy that she valued his opinion. He felt himself grow, expand under her questions, questions that showed she had been really listening to him.

'So it can be done, then.'

It was more a statement than a question.

'Yes. It'll take time and patience, but when it's finished and French-polished, you won't recognise it. It'll be the business.'

She turned to Beady Eyes. He had hardly dared look at her since they had entered his shop. He was polite, respectful towards her. Farrell noticed his attitude with satisfaction.

'We'll take it. How much is it?'

The man averted his eyes from Farrell's, gestured towards him instead with a deferential spreading of his palm.

'This gentleman is obviously something of an expert; he beat me down to eighteen hundred.'

Grace turned to Farrell in surprise.

'You've been here before?'

He nodded.

'I wanted to see it for myself. If it was no good, I wanted to see what else was around. I didn't want you to be disappointed.'

There was something very gentle in Grace's eyes as she looked at him.

'Thank you,' she said simply.

'No problem.'

But there was a different tone to her voice. She was acknowledging his thoughtfulness, looking at him in a new way. He felt himself being transformed in her eyes. He was becoming something other than the awkward tradesman in blue overalls, whose accent slipped from time to time. *You're good, lad; a craftsman*, Mr Casey's voice reminded him softly. He felt himself rise in her estimation.

The way she smiled at him then made his stomach contract. He began to panic. It wasn't even ten o'clock yet. What would she do now? Go home and leave him? He tried desperately to think of a way of holding on to her, even for another hour.

She wrote a cheque for the table, and turned to Farrell.

'There's nothing else here of interest. Come and help me buy light-fittings and other bits and pieces for the boardroom.'

Farrell felt the frozen mass inside his chest begin to warm.

'I'd love to.'

The rest of that day was like moving underwater. Farrell found everything around him slow and dreamy. They wandered through Francis Street and the Coombe, in and out of cramped and crowded little antique shops.

When they went for lunch, Farrell drank coffee; Grace had a glass of wine. He didn't want anything to alter the way he felt. If this was all there was, then he wanted to remember it like this for ever.

Leaving the pub, crossing the road, Grace slipped her hand through his arm. It was a natural gesture, protecting herself from the now noisy traffic. Farrell was afraid to move, afraid to acknowledge the touch, in case she suddenly realised what she had done. Her hand filled his mind again with racing impossibilities. He wanted to shield her, to protect her from more than traffic.

Before Farrell knew it, it was nearly six o'clock. He began to feel sick. Now she really would go. How was he going to survive the rest of the day without her? The thought of losing her to P.J., to Saturday-night social life, to probable boyfriends, filled Farrell with an anxiety that felt almost like rage. Fear made him reckless.

'Are you in a hurry home?'

'No.' She was uncertain. 'Are you?'

'No. I'd like to buy you dinner to celebrate our beautiful table. I can't wait to get started on it.'

'I'd love to, but dinner's on me. You've already saved P.J. two hundred quid. Now let's enjoy spending some of it.'

He argued with her, and she argued back, good-naturedly. It diffused some of the tension between them. Farrell's senses were on edge, as though he were in the presence of electricity. Eventually, she won.

'Next time,' she said. 'It can be your treat next time.'

He almost wept with happiness. They settled on Chinese, another hopeful sign. Farrell loved Chinese food. Maybe he could cook it for her some day. He loved cooking, loved the ritual of shopping and elaborate preparation. He would make something special to show her how well he would care for her, if she would only give him the chance.

Inside the restaurant was cool and dimly-lit. Farrell had never been there before. He was a little nervous at first, afraid that he would knock something over with his elbow, or that he would suddenly lose the power of speech. But they were shown to their table without incident, and the atmosphere between them was not disturbed. Gradually, he began to relax and enjoy his surroundings. Everything on the table was gleaming. Stiff, white linen cloths, dark green napkins. Plates of food arrived and disappeared without fuss. Only the growing murmur of conversation indicated that the room was filling up. Grace's eyes were shining in the candlelight. The waiter had just brought hot, moist towels and they cleaned their fingers. She cupped her hands around her wineglass.

'Well, what's the verdict?'

Farrell made a circle with his thumb and forefinger.

'Great. I really enjoyed it.'

'Are you going to tell me why you don't use your first name?'

Whatever he had expected, it was not that. Farrell was at a loss for words. How to tell her without revealing too much of his life before her? He was suddenly frightened, a Rubicon to be crossed. But her expression was so kind that he knew he could not pull back, not now.

'My first name is Vincent. It was my father's name, and I didn't want to be called after him.'

Farrell had acknowledged that aloud only once before, many years before Grace. He felt a mixture of pain and relief, of opening up and salving old wounds at the same time.

'Why not?'

'Because he was a bully and a drunk. I always hated him. The life he led my mother killed her. I wanted nothing to do with him.'

'When did she die?'

'When I was ten. She was never strong. Five kids in nine years, a waster of a husband, no money to speak of. She had a dog's life.'

'So what happened to the family?'

'I grew up very quick. We all looked after one another; we had to. The day after my mother died, my father went missing for weeks. When he came home, he was broke and filthy. He couldn't even remember where he'd been. Then he went on one almighty bender that lasted on and off for five years.'

Farrell searched her face quickly for clues, for signs of disgust, contempt. But there were none. She was leaning closer to him, listening as she had listened in the shop.

'Go on,' she said softly.

'He died in December 1967, exactly five years to the day after her. Then the social workers came and the other kids were taken into care.'

'And what about you?'

'I was fifteen, nearly sixteen. I basically hid out with neighbours until they gave up looking for me. Our neighbour, Mr Casey, started taking me out on jobs with him. He was a cabinet-maker, a real old-fashioned craftsman. A hard taskmaster. He got his employers to take me on, me and a couple of other no-hopers. He made carpenters out of the lot of us.'

'Didn't you go to school?'

Farrell shook his head angrily.

'I hated school then. Brothers worrying about the

margins in your copies when you hadn't even had breakfast. Back in Primary, there was one, Brother McCormack, who tried to break me. He beat me until my hands blistered, but I wouldn't cry for him. After that, I never felt the same about it. I just couldn't see the point. But I went more or less regularly until my father died. Then I gave up.'

'What about your brothers and sisters?'

Farrell stopped for a moment and sipped at his wine. She had stirred emotions he had thought long dead. All the anger, all the guilt. The oldest, and not able to protect anybody.

'Three brothers, one sister. I went to see the youngest ones once, when I'd turned sixteen and the social workers couldn't get me. But I never went back. They had a new family, a real family, a new name. I didn't want to become an embarrassment to them. The youngest was only eight. She was better off forgetting.'

Farrell suddenly didn't want to say any more. *He* was better off forgetting. It was all history. He could see by Grace's expression that she sensed his mood. She finished the conversation for him.

'It's a sad story, but you've come through,' and she smiled at him.

Farrell noticed the way her face shone when she smiled. They were silent for a moment. It was getting easier each time to find the courage to speak.

'And what about you?'

He was hungry for detail, wanted to know everything about her. She shook her head, still smiling.

'I'll make a deal with you. You buy dinner next time, and you get my story too.'

Farrell could feel his face glow with happiness. He felt very comfortable with her now, the churning in his stomach was stilled. He could bear anything, now that she would see him again.

'You've got yourself a bargain. Next Saturday?'

'Next Saturday it is.'

It seemed natural to take her hand as they crossed the road. It was warm, reassuringly content in his. They walked back to her car. Before she opened the door, she turned to Farrell. She looked almost shy, like a little girl.

'I had a really lovely day.'

Her eyes told him it was time. He reached out for her and enfolded her in his arms. Her head barely reached his chest. In the darkening street, he held her close, held on for dear life. He tilted her face towards his. He was happy and terrified at the same time. It was too soon, he knew it was much too soon, but he could no longer stop himself.

'I love you, Grace.'

She kissed him then, holding him for a long time afterwards.

'I know,' she whispered. 'But I don't want to rush into anything. You'll have to give me time.'

She could have anything she wanted; he would give her anything.

'Take all the time you need. I won't change.'

He could have stood there for the rest of his life. Right in the middle of Francis Street. He could have loved her like that for ever.

When they reached his flat, he kissed her again. He would not ask her in; this must not be hurried. He would wait for her, as he had promised.

He was filled with the day. It was enough.

Chapter Two

Vinny's tenth birthday passed very quietly. There was a present of a new jumper from his mother; he had watched her knit it slowly all through the winter. Eoin, Jody and Patrick bought him some penny bags of sweets, and Mrs Casey baked him a cake. Mrs Casey was spending a lot of time in their house now, coming in every dinner-time to cook while Vinny's mother sat in her chair, the rug around her legs.

He knew that she was sick. Soon after Jenny was born, she had started to get thinner and thinner. Recently, she had suddenly lost all her energy. Under her eyes, the dark shadows grew deeper, making her face look hollow, haunted. She no longer polished the lino or washed the front step every day. Instead, she sat by the fireplace, staring into the flames if the fire was lit, and into the empty grate if it was not.

Vinny knew, in some way he did not yet understand, that she was moving away from them, beginning a journey of her own where no one could reach her. Gradually, he started to take over the jobs he had watched her do. Even baby Jenny came to him for comfort when she hurt herself, snuggling into his chest, sucking her thumb. She would watch him with wide, unblinking blue eyes.

His father hardly ever came home now. When he did, Vinny's heart would hammer as he heard the huge, lumbering figure stumble upstairs, roaring and rumbling at the world which had handed him a raw deal.

On those nights, Vinny bit deep into his knuckles, lying

rigid in his bed. He was afraid that if he moved, he would smash his fists into his father's face, hurtling him down the stairs to certain death. It was satisfying to imagine it. Then the pain of teeth on knuckles kept him conscious, allowed him to fight off the waves of rage which threatened to carry him blindly away.

Mrs Casey had tried to get him to go back to school, at least in the beginning. Now even she saw that it was hopeless. There was nobody else, only him. Nana in Galway had died shortly after Jenny was born, had never even seen her. The one day that Vinny had tried to get back to school, they had been waiting for him.

Like a stone from the sky, Brother McCormack fell upon him at the school gate, dragging him by the ear to his office. When he'd produced the strap, Vinny held out both his hands, and made himself a promise that he would not cry. The black arm had fallen heavily again and again, beads of sweat standing out on the brother's shiny forehead. Still Vinny would not cry. Holding his hands out from his sides when the brother had finished, Vinny had walked out the school gate, not even hearing the shouts of Brother McCormack ordering him to stop, to come back this minute. Line after line of boys watched him silently, a gangly figure in short, grey pants, walking away with his head up.

Just before Christmas, they'd taken his mother into hospital. Vinny knew that he would never see her home again. Her chair by the fire was frighteningly complete without her: he could no longer imagine her sitting there. Her place had changed, she now belonged somewhere else. Mrs Casey took him and Eoin in to see her a few days before she died. Her skin was transparent, stretched tight against her skull. She tried to touch their faces, but her hand was too heavy for her to lift. She picked at her blankets instead, her eyes hugely following them as the nurse whispered it was time to leave.

In a way, Vinny felt better after she died. It was as though a long period of waiting was over. Once she was gone, the neighbours quietly took over and eventually, reluctantly, Vinny got ready to go back to school.

Mrs Casey had come in to see him one morning in her coat and hat. He had been surprised to see her all dressed up. She'd stood in the hallway, her handbag held sternly in front of her.

'You're going back to school tomorrow. There'll be no more trouble. Brother McCormack will never touch you again.'

To Vinny's surprise, she was right.

Everybody left him alone. Mrs Casey told him to do his best. So he tried hard, but he knew that his real job was looking after his brothers and sister.

And so, for five years, under Mrs Casey's watchful eye, Vinny grew taller and taller and watched over his family. He watched with such a fierce, protective, loyal eye that Mrs Casey often feared for him.

* * *

By unspoken, mutual consent, Farrell and Grace were formal with each other all of the following week. Their conversations were brief, businesslike. Grace told P.J. the table would be delivered on Thursday. In Farrell's presence, they discussed where he should work on it. Grace had got P.J. to agree that the first-floor drawing-room, overlooking Merrion Square, would be the most appropriate place for the boardroom. It was already plastered, but not yet painted.

It was Farrell who'd suggested putting the table there straight away, and working on it *in situ*. Grace had agreed at once. Seeing it at home, as it were, would show her what other pieces of furniture were necessary to complete the room. She wanted a matching pedestal sideboard, and as many original chairs as possible, Farrell already knew that.

But P.J. had had the last word. On time and under budget, he'd demanded. All the other pieces were to be repro. He couldn't have people fiddling around for ever. He had a business to run.

When he turned his back, Grace grinned at Farrell. A broad, mischievous grin that transformed her pale face. Farrell felt his chest constrict as he thought of Saturday night. He prayed to an unseen, unfelt God that she would not change her mind.

He was impatient to start work on their table. Grace gave him keys to the office, showed him how to work the alarm. On Thursday night, barely giving himself time to eat, he cycled back to Merrion Square from Rathmines. He wanted to show her instant progress, to impress upon her his power to transform the ordinary, to make lovely the ugly.

He worked until eleven, undisturbed. He made notes of materials he needed, advice he would seek, opinions he would ask. He was sure the woodworm was not a problem, but he treated every inch of the table, just in case.

He was happy as he cycled home. He felt the more beautiful he made the table, the more Grace would trust him. It was a joint project. Old Casey's words filled his mind as he showered before bed. He *was* a craftsman; he *could* fashion a life for her, for both of them. And Mrs

Casey had been right. You didn't have to follow bad example.

On Friday evening, Grace came to him.

'I have to go now. Are we still on for tomorrow night?'

Farrell, conscious of Christy hovering in the background, was cautious. The memory of the man in the antique shop still darkened his memory. He made sure to face her fully, turning his back completely on Christy.

'Of course. About half eight?'

She nodded. Farrell was sure that Christy could not know what they were discussing.

She smiled in the way that Farrell was getting used to, feeling his heart turn over.

His back still to Christy, he said: 'I'm looking forward to it.'

Her face coloured a little.

'So am I,' and she was gone.

Farrell went shopping early on Saturday morning. He had decided to cook for her. He had never cooked for anyone so special before. Fresh asparagus soup, steak *au poivre*, Chinese-style mushrooms, stewed fresh tomatoes. Everything he bought was fresh, top quality. He might not be a great cook, but he was a good one, making up for any lack of flair with careful, painstaking preparation. He came close to delirium, shopping for her.

He spent the rest of the day getting everything ready. He was glad that October afternoons were dark. Artificial light made the flat look cosier, more welcoming. Even the curtains he'd bought in the summer sale, before Grace, looked vibrant, distinctive.

He drank a whiskey at eight, for courage.

She arrived exactly on time. He had a white apron on as he answered the door. He bowed, exaggeratedly, sweeping the tips of his fingers against the floor. He wanted to make her laugh.

She put her fingers to her mouth, eyes all blue amazement.

'Welcome, *Madame*. Your slave has cooked for you.'

She laughed outright at the absurdity of his pose. Then she kissed him. Farrell knew that he had never before, in his whole life, come this close to being happy.

His meal was a complete success. She was charmed by his thoughtfulness, his flat, his skill at cooking. Farrell wished she would never go home.

Over the second bottle of wine, he said: 'We have a deal. Tonight, I've earned your story.'

She sat back, put a cigarette between her lips, and Farrell leaned the candle closer to her.

'OK,' she agreed. 'Where do you want me to start?'

'Wherever your story starts,' he said quietly.

The atmosphere between them was suddenly stilled. Farrell felt that all the dark spaces in the room were filling up with ghosts.

She pulled deeply on her cigarette. She smiled at him.

'I'm sorry. I love smoking.'

He said nothing. He knew she was hedging.

'Well, I'm the youngest of three girls. No boys; a big disappointment to P.J.'

Farrell waited.

'Anna and Ruth are both married to boring old suits. They talk about cars all the time and think of nothing but making money. P.J. is thrilled with them; but that's not the kind of life I want.'

Farrell felt hope nudge again. Please, God.

'I got a place in art college, five years ago. I worked hard for it. I really wanted it.'

She drew deeply again on her cigarette.

'I've been making dolls ever since I was a child. Rag dolls, to start with. Dolls with painted faces, lacy bonnets, pretty dresses. I was always good at it and I loved doing it.

48

The year I left school, I took a stall in the Blackrock Market at the weekends and I made money. I said nothing at home, but I was doing really well. Mothers and little children loved the dolls: I got lots of orders. I thought P.J. would be proud; *I* was proud.'

Farrell sensed what was coming. He refilled her wineglass.

She sipped at it, abstractedly.

'When he found out, he was furious. He insisted I find a career, a real career. He wanted me to do business studies; he expected me to carry on the family business. No daughter of his was going to earn her living like a travelling salesman.'

'So what did you do?'

She raised both her shoulders and her eyes simultaneously.

'What could I do? I gave in. Himself and my mother never let up on me. I gave up my place in art college. I did a business studies degree and came to work for P.J.'

She tapped her ash into one of Farrell's saucers. He watched as her eyes filled with tears.

'He paid my fees, opened a bank account for me, even wanted to buy me a car. But I would take nothing from him. I remembered what he'd told me once, you see. He'd said that gifts to people were like investments in getting your own way. The more they accepted from you, the more they owed you; the more they owed you, the more they'd do what you wanted. He was talking about a business deal that was going right, he was delighted with himself. But I never forgot it. So I kept on making my dolls and kept myself in pocket money.'

Farrell wondered at how wrong he had been. Maybe their fathers hadn't been so different after all.

'If he knew what I was doing, he never said. We never mentioned dolls, or cars, or art college ever again. As long as I was doing what he wanted, he was kind, the perfect father. Two years ago, I couldn't take the pressure. I ended up in hospital for six weeks. I didn't even know my own name. Does that upset you?'

Farrell was crowded with memories of a time when he, too, had forgotten his own name. Darkened rooms, sudden noises, shouting, children hiding in corners, sheets drenched in urine.

'No,' he said softly. 'It doesn't upset me. I understand just what you mean.'

'I'm fine now.' Her tone was defiant. 'And P.J. and I made a deal.'

Farrell waited.

'I agreed to work for him for three years, to help manage the move to Merrion Square, to act as office manager and personal assistant. Then, if I still wanted, I could be free. My debt discharged. I can do whatever I want. I've two years to go.'

Farrell was watching her eyes. Pain flitted in and out as she lit another cigarette, watching him.

'And what do you want?'

'I want to make dolls. It sounds ridiculous, I know. But I don't want what Anna and Ruth have. I want my own life. I want to leave P.J. behind. I know he figures that in two years' time he'll have fixed me up the way he's organised Ruth and Anna's lives. But he won't do that to me.'

Her face suddenly changed, became closed to him. Farrell was too terrified to move.

'Grace. I can help you. There's nothing ridiculous about what you want. You can do anything, anything at all.'

He reached across the table, held her hand tightly, urgently.

He had wild visions of the two of them, together, making and crafting, transforming oak, teak, mahogany, into toys, dolls, cradles.

'Make your dolls. I can show you how to make cradles, prams, whatever you want. It's all possible, Grace. I can make it possible.'

She half gulped, laughing up at him.

He moved towards her, pushing his chair back, pulling her to him.

'Don't waste your life, Grace. Get free. I love you.'

He kept kissing her, pushing her hair back from her forehead, kissing her face.

'Wait!' she said, pulling his hands away gently. She reached for her handbag.

Farrell thought he had lost her, that she was about to go home. He heard the bathroom door close. When she came back, she held her arms out to him.

'Come here,' she said softly.

Farrell was almost sick with apprehension. He remembered Martina. He put his hands on Grace's shoulders, bending down until his eyes were level with hers. He couldn't speak, couldn't bring himself to ask her. But she understood. She stroked his face.

'It's all taken care of.'

'You're sure?'

'I'm sure,' and she reached up to kiss him.

Lying beside him, her head resting on his chest afterwards, Grace told Farrell he had given her hope.

'I think I can bear the next two years if you'll help me. Teach me what I need to know.'

He felt the sound of her voice echoing deep inside him. It was almost as though she were speaking through him. Peace filled him. He'd been awkward with her at first, and fumbling. It had been a very long time since he'd been with any woman he really cared for. He'd wanted so much to be tender, but his body had been clumsy. He was a confusion of angles: all elbows, shoulders, knees. He had been afraid of hurting her. But she had made him feel loved and wanted, and his jangling nerves had finally calmed. Now she was telling him how much she needed him. His happiness was complete.

'I'll teach you, Grace. I promise you.'

When she got up to leave later on, Farrell held her close.

'We'll have to be careful that P.J. doesn't find out about us,' Grace whispered. 'At least not until you've finished working in Merrion Square. He'd make your life hell. He's capable of making them fire you.'

Farrell didn't tell her that he couldn't care less. What he did care about was P.J. taking her back from him.

'We'll be very careful. You'll come here to me when it's safe. Otherwise, we'll keep our distance.'

Farrell sat on the sofa for a long time after she'd gone. He'd expected to feel completely happy. Instead, he was filled with a dread he couldn't name.

His sleep was filled by dozens of short-legged little men. They smoked incessantly as they approached, while row after row of severed heads made pathways for their feet. Their eyes mocked him as they held out formless gifts, wrapped in silver paper and green satin ribbons.

* * *

Vinny was upstairs in the bedroom he shared with his brothers when the doorbell rang. Instantly, he knew there was trouble. It was only half nine in the morning; a week to the day after his father's funeral. Mrs Casey had stayed late every night, cooking and cleaning and washing for them. She would tuck the younger ones into bed before she left, eyes red and brimming. Vinny took special care of Jenny; he was the only one who could get her to stop crying.

Now he waited until Mrs Casey opened the front door. He could make out nothing, voices were deliberately softened. He crept from the door across the room to the window, taking care to avoid the creaking floorboards. His blood began to pulse loudly in his ears. There was a squad car outside, with a uniformed Garda sitting in the driver's seat. The other doors had all been left open, just.

Vinny was filled with rage. He had seen this before, had heard women whisper about Places of Safety. He remembered the Byrnes, had seen the women try to give comfort to that family of small, bewildered orphans. A family like his.

Vinny decided that they would not take him. Voices were beginning to be raised downstairs. He could hear Jenny screaming. His heart stopped when he heard her cry: 'I want Vinny! I want Vinny to mind me!'

There were the sounds of scuffling. He heard Eoin shouting: 'He's not here! He ran away after the funeral!'

Vinny did not wait to hear any more. He had been given his cue. He crossed the tiny landing swiftly to the bathroom. He had made his exit like this many times before. He pushed open the small window, and, standing on the toilet bowl, he eased his long frame out onto the windowsill. It wasn't too long a drop to the roof of the O'Gormans' shed.

He had learned a long time ago how to fall, almost silently, onto this flat roof. Once he landed, he half-fell, half-rolled, arms locked around his knees, onto the grass beneath. He hoped Old O'Gorman wasn't looking. He got really pissed off if you landed in his vegetables.

Vinny took off down through the back gardens until he reached the corner, and safety. Peter Casey answered the door to him. He didn't need to speak. Everyone had seen the squad car, the men and women with briefcases. He pulled Vinny inside, and closed the front door.

'Quick!' he said. 'You can see from the bedroom!'

He shot up the stairs before Vinny. He was about the same age, but much smaller, more stocky.

Vinny followed, taking the stairs two at a time. What he saw never left him.

A woman in a long, dark overcoat was trying to peel Jenny away from Mrs Casey's legs. As soon as she freed one arm, the other, octopus-like, would snap back again and hold on for dear life. Mrs Casey was wiping her own face, and stroking Jenny's hair at the same time. Finally she bent down to say something to her. The woman in the overcoat eventually got Jenny to accept the doll that she was holding out to her. Then, together, they got into a second car. Almost at once, both cars pulled away from the kerb. Vinny was sure that he could see little faces turning around, straining to find him. Once they were out of sight, the street began to flood with people, gathering around Mrs Casey, talking in tight little knots. By then, he had seen enough. He had to get out of the house or he would smash something. He slammed back the bedroom door, and went crashing down the stairs.

'Wait!' floated a voice behind him.

'Wait!' floated a stronger voice, out in the street.

But Vinny was waiting for no one. He ran through all the streets that were familiar to him. There were faces that loomed at him from time to time, but he kept on running.

He was nearly knocked down as he crossed the street at the Five Lamps. It was a miracle he wasn't killed, the way he dared the morning buses to splatter him. He ran all the way to Fairview Park, then up and down the hill that he used to play on with his brothers and sister. Up and down. Up and down. Up and down until his legs would no longer do as he willed them. He made his way, blindly, towards the bandstand. Sick with exhaustion, he vomited until he was empty. He sat there for a long time, his head in his hands. Gradually, he began to hear sounds around him again. He began to focus on the flower-beds. The soil was still heavy, black.

He moved away from where he had been sick, and wiped his mouth on his sleeve. He sat where he was all day until the early afternoon darkness came, and the trembling had stopped. Then, unsteadily, he began to make his way towards home. He knew the Caseys would be waiting for him. And he was suddenly starving.

Vinny pushed away the images of that morning, as he crossed again at the Five Lamps. He tried to blank out the sounds that had come from downstairs. He was fifteen, nearly sixteen. There was no way they were going to get their hands on him. He approached the Caseys' house carefully, through the back gardens again. He was too quick for the barking dogs. He could see through the lighted kitchen window that there were just the six of them, sitting down at the table. Christmas decorations still hung over the kitchen door. Merry Christmas, said a red and white banner.

Vinny went up to the back door and knocked softly. It was opened at once.

'Vinny, love, come in.'

Then, the tears came. Vinny wept for all those who had been taken away from him. He wept for himself.

And then he made himself a promise.

Never, ever again would he hide, keeping himself safe, while someone else took away what was his.

After dinner, the children left the kitchen and Vinny was alone with Mr and Mrs Casey. He sat rigid at the table, a

cup of tea in front of him. He felt as though he was
balanced on a ledge somewhere, about to topple over into
darkness. Finally, Mrs Casey spoke.

'Vinny, love . . .'

He jumped up from the table, pushing his chair back
violently so that it fell over.

'That's not my name!' he shouted. 'I don't want to be
called after him!'

Mrs Casey put her hand on his arm. She did not raise
her voice. Mr Casey never even moved.

'That's fine. What would you like to be called?'

'Nothing!' he shouted. Then, in frustration, 'Farrell,
just Farrell!'

'OK, Farrell. Now sit down.'

Farrell couldn't decide whether to sit, dash the chair
against the floor, or run out the back door. He was so tired
of running; he wanted to be still.

He picked up his chair and sat down again. Furiously,
he beat the tears back. Mrs Casey continued talking as
though nothing had happened.

'Now that you've chosen your name, what sort of a life
are you going to choose for yourself?'

He looked at her stupidly. What was she talking about?

'Just because you have someone's name, doesn't mean
you have to follow their example. Nobody has to follow
bad example. Do you understand me?'

Farrell nodded. His anger began to seep away. She
seemed to be offering him something, holding out a
chance. He looked around him, avoiding her eyes. He had
always liked the Caseys' house. It was full of nice things,
bright, and there was a definite sense of order. Mrs Casey
had things under control. She was not going to steal away
anywhere. She would not abandon her children to the
worst.

'You should be in school, but . . .' Mrs Casey raised her

hand to quell his outburst. 'I know you won't go back for different reasons. Some good, some bad. You're nearly sixteen, aren't you?'

He nodded.

'We've talked about this, Vin . . . Farrell, and you can stay with us, on one condition.'

He looked at her. Suspicion lingered just below his hope.

'Joe's going to ask his firm to take you on. They'll train you, give you a trade. You'll probably have to go to school at night, but it'll be different. Are you interested?'

'Yes,' Farrell said at once.

He didn't know where the enormous feeling of relief was coming from. He didn't even know that he'd been terrified of what was going to happen to him. He had only thought as far as escaping, running off blindly and leaving it all behind. Doors everywhere had kept slamming in his face. Now he felt that a tiny chink had been left open for him.

Mr Casey was gruff.

'There'll be no hanging about street corners, no messing. You'll work hard, and it'll be only pocket money at first. And another thing, there's no smoking in this house.'

Farrell nodded. He had only just started, it shouldn't be too hard to stop. He felt that something was expected of him in reply.

'Thank you,' he said. 'I'll do my best.'

Mrs Casey smiled at him, and Mr Casey grunted. He stood up from the table.

'You'll pitch in here and do your bit.'

It was a statement, not a question.

'Yes, sir,' Farrell said.

He was suddenly, unbelievably, happy. A grown-up,

with a trade. He could make something of himself, get his family back. They could all be together again.

Peter opened the kitchen door.

'Vinny, come on, *Top of the Pops* is on.'

Mrs Casey smiled at him.

'Go on,' she said. 'Enjoy yourself. The hard work starts on Monday.'

★ ★ ★

Farrell was glad when the three months under P.J.'s roof were up. Everything was finished on time; he had seen to that. Without saying a word to Christy, he'd continued to go in at night, even after the table was finished. He'd made sure that he would not be one day longer in Merrion Square than he had to be.

When Christy came in, in the middle of the final week, he was surprised to find everything so complete.

'That's a full three days earlier than we'd reckoned,' he said, looking at Farrell. Farrell did not encourage the implicit question. He merely shrugged and bent down to put his hammer in his toolbox.

'Just making up for the time I lost with my thumb. I don't like loose ends.'

Christy was grateful, eager to reward him. He couldn't hide the enthusiasm in his voice.

'Our bonus is safe as houses, then. There'll be something extra in it for you, for making it happen.'

Farrell nodded, glad to be out of it.

'Thanks, Christy. Is the hotel job still on for next week?'

'Absolutely. Now we have a head start on it. Would you

go over to the site tomorrow to have a look? Maybe we can start before Monday, now.'

'Sure thing.'

Farrell continued to put his tools away carefully. He spoke without looking at Christy, keeping his voice deliberately casual. 'Are you goin' to see old Browne, then?'

He closed his toolbox finally, tucking the leather strap away neatly. He was grateful for the aura of busyness these tasks created, glad he didn't have to meet the other man eye to eye.

'Yeah. I'll do that now. He said to let him know the minute we were done. Now he has a few extra days to organise his official opening.'

Farrell waited for a few minutes until he judged Christy was safely in P.J.'s office. Then he made his way quietly to Reception.

Grace was already in the hall, waiting for him.

'I believe you're all finished?'

He nodded. She was paler than usual.

'I'm going to miss you here during the day.'

He squeezed her hand, keeping an eye on the door behind her.

'Tonight?'

She nodded.

'Around nine.'

He kissed her briefly and stepped out into the December evening.

He was worried about Grace. She was tired, working flat out for P.J.'s reception in ten days' time. She was constantly on the phone, to florists, caterers, wine merchants. P.J. kept hovering around her, checking up on every detail. Farrell thought that the man's edginess was caused by something more than the tension around the official opening. It was as though he were willing Grace to fail, wanting to catch her out. There was something going on, something not quite reaching the man's abrasive surface. Once, as Farrell climbed the stairs from the basement, he thought he'd heard P.J. shouting at her.

She'd begun to look brittle, the skin stretched tight across her cheekbones. Farrell knew she wouldn't make it through another two years. He had a plan, which he'd been working on for almost two months now. Early mornings, weekends, late evenings when he was on his own: he'd used his time well. He'd said nothing to her. Tonight was the night.

She arrived, breathless, at half-past nine. He'd been beginning to get worried; she had never been late before. Any small change in her behaviour, any slight misunderstanding, any alteration in her expression filled him with terror. He pulled the door open before she rang.

She walked straight into his arms. He had to half-carry her to his door as she sobbed uncontrollably, fighting for breath.

'I can't bear it, Farrell. I just can't do it any longer. He's screaming about details, pushing me harder and harder all the time. I'm afraid I'm going to crack. I don't know whether he suspects anything about us, but he's punishing me for something.'

He held her until the last waves of sobbing had ebbed. He kissed her forehead and pushed her hair away from her face. He felt almost sore inside as he looked at her. He knew that his timing had been just right; now he had to make things better.

'Come with me.'

He took a key off the mantelpiece and held out his hand to her. She came with him obediently. They walked up a flight of stairs to the first half-landing. Farrell opened the door and reached in to switch on the lights.

'Is this your flat, too?'

Grace's tone was puzzled, uncertain.

'Yes. I sublet it over two months ago from a student who's away in France until March. Come on in.'

Her face was tight, strain etched in the skin right down to the base of her throat.

'Come and have a look.'

Farrell watched as the tension drained and her eyes lit up like a child's. Arrayed all over the room were old-fashioned wooden spinning-tops, trains, toy soldiers, a doll's cradle, toys of all different shapes and sizes. Each one was shining with varnish or brightly-coloured paint. One touch of Grace's finger sent the cradle rocking gently. She ran her hand over the spinning-tops, made the wheels of the trains turn, held the painted soldiers to her cheek. She moved from one to the other, silent, in a world of her own. She seemed almost to have forgotten Farrell. Then, quite suddenly, she turned back to face him.

'Where did you get all of these?' she asked.

Her eyes were huge, purple-black.

'I made them for you. To show you what can be done. I can't make the dolls, but I can show you how to do all of these. I've made templates for most of them. Look.'

Farrell brought a large cardboard box from the corner of the room. Piece by piece, he handed her the templates he had worked on for nearly two months. He felt suddenly nervous. There was a lot of himself invested in each smoothly-crafted piece of wood.

'This is a really simple one, look.'

He held a completed toy out to her, a shiny Noah's ark, painted in bright blues and yellows. She turned it over and upside down, taking in its simple shape, its symmetrical parts. Her eyes were wide, amazed, as she looked up at him.

'It's lovely! It's the colours and the little windows that make it so special.'

He could sense her growing excitement. He plunged ahead.

'And look at these. You can buy these ready made; all you have to do is paint them, or leave them plain for kids to paint themselves.'

Farrell laid the animals out, two by two.

'The ark is an exact replica of the one I saw in Malahide Castle. It's a Victorian toy; the kids were allowed to play with it on Sundays. It was used to teach them Bible stories.'

'What a lovely bit of history!'

She was smiling at him, her grief forgotten for now. Then her brow furrowed in the way that Farrell loved.

'But do you think I'll ever learn how to make these on my own?'

'I'll show you how to use all the tools you'll need. Once you have the templates, it's really straightforward. We can use this room until March, then we can look for some-where else for you to work from. With these and the Victorian dolls you'll have a high-quality product not matched by anyone else. I've checked.'

He stopped, realising how quickly he'd been speaking. He felt he'd said enough. It was a long speech, for him.

Grace got up unsteadily from the floor where she'd been kneeling. Slowly, she raised her eyes to his face.

'You did all this for me?'

Her eyes searched his. He remembered what she'd said about gifts. He was careful to measure his words, to answer her properly.

'Yes. If you like, they're mine. I made them only to show you what's possible.'

Her arms reached up and her hands met, with difficulty, around his neck. Farrell leaned towards her, bending his head to make it easier for her.

'I love you,' she said simply.

Farrell's head filled with a strange noise, his ears buzzed.

For a moment, he had difficulty concentrating on what she was saying.

She was watching his face.

'I don't believe you heard me. I'll say it again. I love you.'

He lifted her right up off the floor then, crushing her to him. For a moment he was afraid that this was gratitude, not love the way he loved her. Then he didn't care. Whatever way she chose to love him was good enough for him. He could conquer the world now. He couldn't hold her close enough; he wanted no barriers between them. He wanted to melt and flow into her.

They stood like that for a long time. She kissed his face, his mouth, whispering over and over again that she loved him. Finally, he released her. Her face was glowing. She touched each of the toys once more before they left, as though to reassure herself that they were real. She was reluctant to leave them behind. Farrell was almost ill with happiness. He wanted to go out and shout from the rooftops.

She stayed with him until late that night. He watched her from the bed as she dressed. She had become suddenly very quiet. He knew that there was something coming.

'I'll stay with P.J. until after the official opening. Then I'm going to tell him about us. He can find someone else to manage his office.'

Farrell's head began to feel light again, dizzy with relief. She sat down on the side of the bed, slipping her feet into her shoes.

'All hell will break loose,' he said quietly.

She nodded. 'I know. As long as I have someone to escape to . . .'

Farrell knew the answer before he asked. He reached for her hand. Steady, steady. The noise inside his head almost drowned his words.

'Will you marry me, Grace?'

She looked at him for what seemed like a very long time. Farrell wondered what she was thinking. Where he came from, his age, the job he did, even the way he spoke. It all made a difference; he knew that.

'It won't be easy, you know,' she said softly.

'I didn't ask for it to be easy. I asked, will you marry me?'

He had difficulty in keeping his voice from wavering.

'Yes,' she said as she smiled at him. 'I most certainly will marry you.'

They sat still and silent for a long time, their arms wound tightly around one another. Contentment filled the room. There were no longer any dark ghosts hiding in shadowy places. Farrell felt that some god somewhere was rewarding him for all his hard work, for all his patience. The world was a benign place after all. Finally, Grace whispered that she really had to go. He allowed himself to look forward to the time when she would not have to leave him, not ever. He pulled on his jeans and a jumper and stuck his feet into his working shoes. He held her coat for her and wrapped her scarf warmly around her neck. Holding her to him, he walked a little unsteadily down the steps towards her car. It was shortly after midnight and the streets were still busy.

'Drive safely,' he reminded her. 'The pubs have only just closed.'

She smiled at him as she tugged at her seat-belt.

'Don't fuss,' she said. 'You're worse than P.J.,' and she blew him a kiss as she drove off. It was meant as a joke, Farrell knew that. Nevertheless, he didn't like it. He shook the feeling off with a quick shrug of his shoulders. He noticed how cold it was. He watched as Grace's car turned the corner, and then went back into the flat. Even in the heat, he couldn't stop shivering. It took him a long time to get warm.

Farrell was glad to be out of Merrion Square. He had walked by the office on the night of P.J.'s official opening. The windows had blazed, chandeliers glittered. He'd had a brief glimpse of Grace, dressed in black. White-coated waiters had carried trays of champagne; waitresses offered canapés. All the windows had been closed against the December chill, but Farrell had imagined he could still hear the roar of conversation. He had been afraid to hang around for too long, in case someone got the wrong idea. What if one of the security men stopped him? He'd walked briskly around the square twice, but caught sight of Grace just the once.

For the next three days, he'd waited anxiously to hear from her. Having seen her in black, diamonds at her throat, Farrell did not underestimate the power of P.J. to keep her for himself. By the third evening, he was almost sick with fear, a fear that turned to rage when he imagined fat hands, waistcoats, cigars.

Finally, the telephone rang.

'Can I come round?'

Her voice sent needles of fear all over his skin. What was waiting for him?

When he opened the door to her he had the impression that she had grown smaller. Her eyes were red and her hair unbrushed. He had never known her not to take care of herself. His mouth suddenly went dry and he had the sensation of his blood going chill, his body slowing down.

He took her coat, sat her down, brought her an ashtray. While she lit a cigarette, Farrell put on the kettle. It was something to do while he waited. He stayed standing, leaning against the draining-board, watching her. He kept his hands safely in his pockets.

'I've told him,' said Grace finally.

She tapped her cigarette nervously against the new ashtray.

'And?'

'As you predicted. All hell broke loose. David Sim-
monds, the architect, was sitting outside in Reception. I
didn't even know anyone had come in. So I suppose
I chose my moment badly.'

David. Dark suit. Door slamming. 'Night, Gracie.

Farrell felt the dark stir of jealousy. With difficulty, he
kept himself still. He stood, resting all his weight on one
leg, hoping the pressure against the floor would make him
feel more grounded. His other foot he kept crossed, with
apparent casualness, the toe of his boot resting gently on
the varnished wood. He waited for Grace to continue.

'As it happens, it's probably just as well he was there. P.J.
exploded when I told him about us.'

Her tone became more matter-of-fact. She inhaled
deeply.

'He opened the door of his office and literally threw me
out. He was shouting. "Go ahead, waste your life on a
nobody! Don't come crying to me when it doesn't work
out!" His face was purple. I thought he was going to hit
me. Then I saw David, so I ran to him for cover.'

Farrell had to stand up straight now, to move about in
an effort to stem the racing flood inside him. His head felt
suddenly hot, his hands weak and incapable. He took them
out of his pockets, then put them back in again.

'He caught hold of P.J., and stood between the two of
us. Eventually, he got P.J. to go back into his office. He sent
me off to make myself coffee. He was very calm. It
stopped me from having hysterics.'

Farrell had a vivid image of Gardaí and women with
briefcases; a memory of low voices, pretending to be kind.
While he hid. And now, years later, still not able to protect
those he loved.

'I went home then to pack my things. He followed me
almost immediately. He was still furious, but controlling

himself. He said I needn't work in the office any more, not if it made me so unhappy. He hadn't realised how strongly I felt.'

Grace stopped. She stubbed out her cigarette on the ashtray in front of her. Farrell concentrated on the little grinding sound it made. She lit another one almost at once.

'He made me promise not to do anything for a couple of weeks until we'd talked everything through. He apologised for getting so angry; said it was only because he loved me so much.'

Farrell could see the strategy. P.J. had given her the gift of her freedom. Now he would make her pay by giving up Farrell. Two years, two weeks, what was the difference. Farrell was very afraid that Grace was not strong enough to fight him.

'And did you promise?'

'I said I'd think about it. That I'd had enough grief for one day, and would he please leave me alone.'

'What did he say?'

'Nothing. He just left the room very quietly and closed the door. I slipped out soon afterwards and came straight to you.'

She smiled at him, her eyes beginning to fill again.

'We'll be all right, Farrell, won't we?'

He knelt down beside her. He put his hands on her arms, anchoring them firmly.

'You're not going back there, Grace. Your home is with me. We'll go and see him together, when you're ready. You'll never have to go through that again.'

She began to cry. Farrell stroked her hair. But there was a sense of something coming to an end; her weeping was not so anguished.

'Look. I've got something for you.'

She looked up, curious. She took the heavy books Farrell handed her and opened the first one carefully.

'*Dolls of the World*,' she said aloud, slowly.

He watched as her expression changed.

'Where did you get them?' Her voice was full of wonder. She reached for another.

'*Miniature Toys and Dolls*.'

It was as though something was beginning to come alive inside her again.

He was careful to keep his voice neutral. This balance must not be disturbed. He would not push her; she would come back to him in her own time.

'They're from all over the place. ILAC Library, mostly; some are inter-library loans; the others I bought. I asked Fred Hanna's to track them down for you.'

He sat beside her as she turned the pages. Georgian toys, Victorian toys, traditional Russian dolls, Dutch dolls, American dolls. They were all there.

'*The Book of Toy Making*.'

She was laughing delightedly now.

'They'll help you think up new designs. Get your ideas flowing again.'

'Farrell, they're wonderful. I haven't made anything in so long that I've been afraid to try. You make me feel I really can do it again.'

The dullness had gone out of her eyes. She was beginning to return to herself.

'You can, and you will. We still have the flat upstairs, and in the New Year, you and I are going to do some serious house-hunting. You need a proper home of your own, with enough room for everything.'

She put the books aside and sat on his knee. He loved the way she twined her arms around his neck.

'I love you, Farrell.' Her eyes were shining now. She was light-hearted. 'What would I ever do without you?'

For the first time, she stayed the whole night. She did not get up at midnight to get dressed and go home. Farrell had feared she would change her mind, now that he had given her strength.

'Wherever you are is my home now,' she whispered in the darkness. 'I'll never leave you again.'

Farrell held her until she fell asleep. He planned his visit to P.J., practised everything he wanted to say. The vision of the little man hiding behind his huge desk filled Farrell with anger. He would not tell her until it was all over.

This time, he would not fail. This time, he would protect her.

* * *

Mrs Casey had tracked down Patrick and Jenny in the middle of June. She had arranged for Farrell to visit them; she knew how he missed them. Now they were waiting for him.

Farrell went to the library at Charleville Mall in the morning, for something to do. He liked the quietness there, and the librarian was friendly. She always found him as many books as he wanted; he loved the ones on furniture-making. He liked showing Mr Casey that he was a good pupil. Sometimes, over a game of chess in the evenings, Mr Casey would quiz him on what he had learned. He always felt proud, showing off his new knowledge.

He spent the hours there quietly, that Saturday morning, absorbed. He owed it to the Caseys to make something of himself. Mrs Casey had been right; night school was different.

He ate the sandwiches that she'd made for him, although he was too nervous now to feel hungry. Every time he thought of Jenny and Patrick, his insides filled with vague, fluttery sensations which took the place of real feelings. Killing time, he sat by the dirty little Royal Canal in the warm midday sun. He watched as the colours drifted over the muddy water, followed the lazy progress of crisp packets and bits of sticks until they finally got trapped, swirling at the lock gates. He liked the lock-keeper's cottage, the bright white painted walls and rows of orderly flowers.

Shortly after one o'clock, he made his way back to the main road and stuck his hand out for the 31 bus. As it slowed, he grabbed onto the steel pole, swinging himself on board. He stayed downstairs. He wanted to make sure he didn't miss the stop.

He took the bit of paper Mrs Casey had given him out of his pocket. He knew it by heart already; he was just checking. They were expecting him at two o'clock. He wondered how much Patrick and Jenny remembered. Only seven months had passed since the day they went away, but it all felt like a very long time ago. It was as though the years before that belonged to someone else, in another lifetime. But the memory of how he'd let them down still cut deep. He was the eldest; he should have held onto them for dear life, he shouldn't have let them be taken away from him. A family should stay together.

Farrell got off the bus in Raheny village, opposite the Green Dolphin pub. He followed Mrs Casey's directions to a quiet cul-de-sac. There were children everywhere. Farrell's heart began to thump in his ears as he searched all the freckled faces. Mrs Casey had told him it would be hard. He was to think only of what was best for them, she had said, not of himself. That way, she'd promised, he'd be able to bear it.

They weren't out on the street.

Number thirty-four was the last before the high wall of the cul-de-sac. The garden was neat, the grass edges trim and straight, the flower-beds full of roses and wallflowers. Farrell didn't know why, but seeing the flowers and the bright yellow front door only made the pain worse. He fought the sudden, violent instinct to run, not to go in at all. Why had he said he'd go?

The door was opened before he'd even knocked.

A woman in her mid-thirties smiled up at Farrell. She was wearing a dark skirt and pink cardigan, with little flowers embroidered across the front. He felt suddenly awkward, conscious again of his height. He only forgot about it when he knew people well. He never minded the Caseys teasing him about his feet dangling over the end of the new single bed. But this was different. Here, in front of a stranger, he felt uncomfortable. His body was too big for him.

'You must be Vincent.'

The woman was holding out her hand to him.

Farrell couldn't reply. He shook her hand, looking at the squared patterns on the lino. How could he say No, I'm not Vincent. That's not my name. So he said nothing. Her smile faded. He looked past her into the kitchen. The back door to the garden was open; he could hear childish shrieks. He was mortified that he could think of nothing to say. He knew he must appear rude.

Like a gurrier, Mrs Casey's voice said sternly to the inside of his head, Where's your manners?

He could sense the woman's disappointment. She had probably been prepared to like him.

'Paddy and Jenny are in the garden. Would you like to go out to them?'

She spoke very quietly. She had a nice voice.

Farrell nodded. He took his hands back out of his jacket

71

pockets. They were in his way; he didn't know what to do with them.

He really tried to make a good impression. He had to have something good to tell Mrs Casey. But he was beginning to get angry. He didn't like her familiarity. He didn't like the way she had shortened Patrick's name. His real mother never called him Paddy or Pat. She didn't like any of the short versions. Paddy is an insult, she used to say, and Pat is only for girls. The child had a right to his proper name.

Jenny came running up the path the minute she spotted him.

'Vinny!'

She threw herself into his arms.

Then he felt hot tears nudging. He lifted her up to him, hiding his face in his sister's long, dark hair. He hugged her for a long time. Patrick walked towards him slowly, warily. Farrell was astonished to see how fat he had become. He obviously wasn't missing any meals here. He kissed Jenny's forehead again and set her back down on the grass. He stroked her soft hair. He nodded to his brother.

'Hiya Patrick.'

'Hiya Vinny.'

He handed them the packets of sweets he had brought. Jenny was still holding onto his hand, swinging out of him. She kept smiling up at him, the sun in her eyes as she swung round and round, pulling out of his right hand, circling behind him, then taking hold of his left hand again as she returned to face him. She never stopped looking up at him, holding one hand to her forehead to shade her eyes. She never stopped smiling at him. She obviously didn't blame him.

Mrs Casey had sent her a doll, a soft, floppy one with a smiley face and a bendy hat. She'd sent Patrick a *Beezer* annual and some *Hotspur* comics. Both of their faces lit up, but Mrs Casey seemed a long-ago memory to both of them, especially to Jenny.

'How are ya gettin' on?'

'Fine,' Jenny said, cradling her doll. 'Would you like to see my bedroom?'

Before he could reply, Farrell's gaze was drawn towards Patrick. He couldn't shake off the old memory of the small, skinny ghost in a wet vest and sticky knickers that now stood beside his little brother in the July sunlight. Patrick was opening his sweets, pushing three, four, even five into his mouth all at once. Farrell thought he would cry, watching his baby brother stuff his face like that. For some reason, it made him feel terribly sad.

This was a mistake. He should not have come.

The woman came out into the garden with a tray full of glasses, a big bottle of Bulmer's Cidona and a plate of biscuits.

'Sit down, Vincent, please.'

She indicated the two striped deck-chairs, placed in the sunshine, sheltered by the coal-shed. Bright orange, dark brown, narrow stripe of beige. Hard to get out of. Farrell's mind was desperately locking onto all the details, trying to avoid looking at the brother and sister who were no longer familiar to him. His eyes were drawn again to Patrick as the younger boy's eyes gleamed at the sight of the biscuits. His little brother's greed hurt him.

They were both well-dressed, well-fed, well-looked after. But they weren't home. Farrell's anger bubbled that his mother had given up on them all so soon. His chest filled again with all the old feelings. He wanted his father to be alive right now, to stab him, to smash him to death for letting this happen, for letting them be taken away from him.

He took the glass of Bulmer's the woman handed him, glad to be able to say something.

'Thank you.'

But he couldn't eat. The biscuit shattered into separate crumbs in his mouth, each one tasting like your hand smelt after holding onto pennies for a long time. He focused on the bottle of Cidona, willing the tears to stay away. He heard again the scrape of the stone stopper against glass, usually a glad sound.

The woman was talking to him, offering more Cidona.

' . . . And they're both doing very well at school. Jenny won a prize for handwriting; her copies are always so neat. And Paddy will be going into sixth class in September, won't you Paddy?'

Patrick nodded, his mouth stuffed to overflowing, his eyes small in his full-moon face.

Farrell didn't want to see or hear any more. This was more than he could bear.

'I have to go now.'

He spoke abruptly, pushing himself up out of the deck-chair.

Jenny was playing with her doll, Patrick was eating the last of the biscuits. They didn't need him. Nobody needed him.

The woman looked hurt, puzzled.

'You're welcome any time.'

'Thank you. I have to go now.'

Sudden inspiration.

'I have to work this afternoon.'

The woman looked relieved. Her face cleared. Farrell was glad. It wasn't her fault, he knew that. But still.

On his way out, he noticed how clean the house was. The lino was gleaming, the kitchen was tidy. The red tiles on the front step were polished to a high gloss. A riot of chrysanthemums and bright green ferns stood in a glass vase in the hall.

Farrell wanted to be gone.

He remembered his manners. He wasn't a gurrier.

'Goodbye and thank you.'

He shook hands gravely with the woman. What *was* her name? Mrs Casey had told him, but he couldn't remember. Patrick and Jenny waved at him from the front step. As he turned the corner, Farrell looked back. He saw Jenny hold her doll up to the woman. Patrick had already gone back inside.

Farrell wished he had never gone. He wished it had never happened. He'd have been better off leaving them alone, better off not knowing that they'd never be home again. He could have kept on living in hope.

He walked all the way back into town. He battled against the rabble of feelings surging upwards, cramming against the top of his head. Feelings he'd thought were almost buried. He couldn't name them, couldn't separate one stabbing pain from the other.

That night was the first time he'd ever got drunk. He met Jimmy and Mick by chance, fell in with them, grateful for their noisy sanity. He got sick outside the pub. Jimmy's voice boomed inside his head from a long way away.

They brought him back to the Caseys. Mrs Casey was waiting up for him. Farrell cried a lot. Snatches of how they'd looked, what they'd said, kept coming back to him. Mrs Casey made him tea, gave him Aspro and sent him to bed.

Neither of them ever again mentioned that night, nor that day.

★ ★ ★

Farrell got up very early the next morning. He had slept

75

little, conscious of Grace's uneven breathing beside him. His mind raced ahead, trying out vivid, livid scenarios with P.J.

Grace barely stirred as he was leaving. He kissed her forehead and whispered that he'd be back very soon. Even in sleep, her face was trusting. His heart gave a great lurch as he looked at her. He would *not* let her down. As he waited for the bus, he stamped his feet on the pavement, blowing into his hands. Jesus, it was cold. His breath smoked out in front of him. All the way into town, he rehearsed what he had learned off by heart the night before. It was good practice; he could feel rage glowing coldly inside him. Farrell had only felt strongly about a few things in his life. His family, the Caseys, and now Grace. For her, he reserved intense, concentrated determination. He would have her. P.J. would not take her back from him. She was now his.

By the time he reached Merrion Square, Farrell was beyond anger. He had reached a place where his mind was totally clear, focused like a narrow, powerful beam on the object of his loathing. He lifted the heavy brass knocker and rapped twice. He hoped that the sound was authoritative. He knew that at least four of P.J.'s employees had moved from the old offices at around the time of the official opening. With a bit of luck, one of them would open the door. They wouldn't know anything about him.

A man of about Farrell's age was looking at him questioningly.

'Can I help you?'

The tone was a little puzzled, not quite dismissive. The tone of a busy man, with important things to do. Farrell didn't miss a beat.

'Good morning; I have an appointment with P.J. Browne at nine. Don't worry, I know my way.'

He stepped quickly into the hallway, taking advantage

of the other man's moment of confusion. He took off his coat as he spoke, revealing the dark suit and silk tie he had dressed in while Grace slept. Farrell ignored the man's uncertain 'Excuse me . . . sir—' and made his way straight to P.J.'s office. He was too quick for them. He could give all of them the slip.

He had timed it well; there was no one else in the office. P.J.'s face blackened as Farrell closed the door quietly behind him. He placed his coat carefully on a chair and stood in front of P.J.'s huge desk. It helped to remember the man's little short legs, to imagine them dangling, not quite reaching the floor. Farrell stood up very straight, his hands loosely clasped in front of him, his feet solidly planted under him. P.J. was already reaching for the telephone.

'You can just leave that alone and listen to me for five minutes, if you care about your daughter.'

Farrell's voice was flat, controlled. His tone conveyed authority, the tone of a man who would not be messed with. P.J. looked surprised. Good. Farrell knew well, from his other life, the advantage of a surprise attack. Like the time he'd kicked his father on the shins. He could still hear the gasp of amazement. Farrell remembered how that sound had opened up a little space for him, a place where he could be the winner. He plunged headlong into that same place now, while he was still in control.

'Grace is with me, staying in my home. She is safe and, when I left her this morning, happy. I know what happened yesterday, and what you think of me. I came here to tell you that it really doesn't matter. Grace and I are going to be married.'

He paused for a moment. The conflicting emotions on P.J.'s face renewed his courage.

'I love Grace,' he said quietly, 'and I intend to give her a good life. I intend to continue to make her happy.'

77

He laid just enough emphasis on *continue* to make the other man's eyelids flicker. Farrell saw something in the eyes of the enemy. It was not respect, more a glimmer of recognition. He took strength from it and continued speaking.

'You and the rest of your family are going to have to accept that. As far as I'm concerned, you can like it or lump it. For Grace's sake, I suggest you pretend to like it.'

Here, Farrell's prepared speech ended.

He picked up his coat, and remembered one more thing.

'Don't attempt to put pressure on her. She's stressed enough already. In future, you will see her with me, or not at all.'

At that, P.J. began to stir. Farrell thought his face had begun to sag. For a moment, he could share the other man's pain. He felt almost sorry for him. He knew how he would feel if he were ever to lose Grace.

'Does my daughter know you're here?'

My daughter.

Farrell looked him straight in the eye.

'Absolutely,' he lied. 'I am here at her request.'

Farrell smoothed his coat over his left arm. He turned his back squarely on P.J. and opened the door which led to Reception. It was strange to see her desk. P.J.'s assistant was sitting there, and Farrell noticed with satisfaction that he was now looking distinctly nervous. Grace's presence was still everywhere. Farrell could taste P.J.'s emptiness. He closed the hall door behind him very carefully, and walked out into the street. He sensed, rather than saw, the other man's eyes on him from the ground-floor window. Farrell walked straight and loose, head up, legs confident. Liar. He walked all the way home in the watery sunlight. He processed what had happened, decided what to tell Grace.

The confrontation had filled him with an elation he had known only dimly once before. *Fight back.*

He felt as though the best of his life was just beginning.

Farrell pushes the sleeping image of Grace out of his mind. He fills his whiskey glass again and tops it up with water. He closes the curtains at both ends of the long room, noting as he does so that the street is empty. Saturday night on the southside. Everything as normal.

He goes through the swing doors into the kitchen. Grace had hung them, years ago, under his direction. She'd been proud that they never squeaked, that they closed easily and smoothly.

He opens the fridge and pulls out all the bags he'd put there – was it really only this morning?

Farrell has always loved cooking. He loves the sense it gives him of providing for others, of pleasing and caring for them. Grace has often sat here at this kitchen table, smoking a cigarette and chatting while Farrell happily made the dinner.

Tonight he is preparing duck. Not boring old duck à l'orange, but duck with pomegranate juice. It has been a hard slog, finding all the right ingredients.

He begins chopping enthusiastically, filled with excitement at the elegance he is creating for her, for Grace.

This meal must be perfect. After all, it is her birthday. Or it will be, when everything is cooked.

He browns eight portions of duck in his favourite cast-iron saucepan. He sautés the onion carefully, making sure to stop when it is golden, not brown. Then he adds the chopped, fresh walnuts and seasonings. Finally, he pours over the strained, blood-red pomegranate juice and it is ready.

The Persian herbed rice is already prepared. And here's one I made earlier. Farrell laughs out loud. A *Blue Peter* badge for the cook.

He stops laughing abruptly. He is going to need a steady hand. No more whiskey.

He adds more butter to the rice dish and places it on the bottom shelf of the oven. He's tried it before. He knows it will be done at exactly the same time as the duck.

Twenty-four hours from now they will come. He'll be ready for them.

Farrell makes himself some strong coffee and loads the dishwasher.

He rummages in the dresser drawer for the instruction booklet for the oven; he's never set the timer this far in advance before. Then he checks the back door, and goes into the dining-room.

Now the answering-machine must be set up, the wine chosen, the table set. There is no room for mistakes.

This has to be a birthday party that no one will ever forget.

Chapter Three

After his visit to P.J., Farrell was filled with confidence. He took two weeks off coming up to Christmas; he wanted it to be a special time for himself and Grace.

On his first day off, they had gone together to Grace's old home, to pick up her clothes and the bits and pieces she missed. The atmosphere had been formal, polite. Farrell had not left Grace's side for a moment. As they were leaving, P.J. had put a hand on Grace's arm. The grasping fat fingers had left Farrell almost breathless with anger. I am not letting you go, they said; you are still mine.

'Your mother and I just want you to be happy, you know,' he'd said quietly.

With a strength that had surprised Farrell, Grace said: 'I *am* happy; very happy. I've never been happier. Farrell and I are going to be married as soon as we can . . .'

'We just don't want you rushing into anything.' P.J.'s tone was curt.

Grace continued as though she hadn't heard the interruption.

'I'd love both of you to be there, but it's up to you.'

Farrell had seen the shock in P.J.'s eyes. Her conviction, her passion were not part of the daughter he knew. Farrell had felt himself grow taller. He'd been filled with pride. She *had* chosen him.

Mrs Browne, Maura, had said nothing at all. Farrell wondered what sort of a mother she was. She hadn't even tried to be kind to Grace. Her eyes had been fixed only on her husband. And she'd barely acknowledged Farrell.

Once in the taxi, Grace had begun to tremble. Farrell had hugged her.

'You were wonderful,' he whispered.

By the time they'd reached the flat, the trembling had almost stopped. Farrell took a deep breath. Now, finally, she was home. Half-laughing, half-crying, she hung her clothes in the wardrobe, placed her things on the shelves Farrell had cleared for her. She was restless, fragile, spent after her show of strength.

'Are you ready?'

He wanted to take her out, to allow the room to settle in their absence, to lose its strangeness.

'For what?'

He loved the blue-black of her eyes when she was surprised.

'To buy our first Christmas tree.'

She clapped her hands together.

'Oh, *yes!*'

That night, for the first time in his life, Farrell allowed himself to believe that it was finally going to happen. At last he would be able to walk down Grafton Street on a Saturday with his arm around a woman's shoulders, stopping to look in shop windows, taking time for the occasional pint, going to the cinema as though it was the most natural thing in the world. He wouldn't have to look at other couples any more, wondering what edge on happiness they had been given. He was an insider now. He knew the secret.

He hadn't a clue about Christmas, how to manage it. For years he had spent it alone, crowded with bitter memories. Now Grace was planning it, taking it over with a zest that thrilled him. They lugged their tree home through Rathmines, getting wetter and wetter as the fine, freezing rain fell relentlessly. They laughed helplessly as they tried to carry the tree up the steps, laughed at stupid knock-knock jokes until they were breathless. There was a feeling of release, of cleansing after the visit to P.J., and both were a little hysterical.

Farrell made them hot whiskeys while Grace towelled her hair. He placed the tree in its stand, and it suddenly didn't look so huge any more. It filled one entire corner of the room, but comfortably. Grace liked its full shape, its roundedness.

Now it was her turn.

'Right, are you ready?'

'For what?'

He had just sat down, nursing his glass. She pulled him to his feet, laughing as he unfolded his long body from the chair.

'We can't leave it like that! It's bare! We've got to go and buy decorations – now!'

He'd have done anything to see her that happy, always. She was the only one who mattered. He made a pretence of groaning. She ran over to where his coat was hanging on the back of a chair.

'Come on! Things to do! Places to go!'

She helped him struggle into the heavy overcoat.

'It's still wet,' he grumbled. But he knew that she knew he was only teasing.

'Come on – don't be such an old fogey!'

They stayed up until three o'clock, tying on the old-fashioned decorations which Grace had fallen in love with. Tinsel and fresh holly hung everywhere. Farrell did as he was told and, under her direction, the room was transformed. A last testing of the bulbs, and Grace turned off the main light. They switched on the tree lights together, on her count of three.

Then they sat together in the big armchair, sipping hot whiskey, admiring their creation.

'It's magic, isn't it?' she asked him, her eyes shining in the soft light.

Farrell kissed her in reply.

The fire, the Christmas tree, Grace. This was the way home should be. He had a moment when fear sliced through him.

This was a bubble, fragile, fantastical.

Its fragility made Farrell want to work his hardest to prove to Grace that she had, without any doubt, made the right choice. He watched as, day by day, she grew stronger. She even started to buy materials for her dolls. She was happy.

He would make it last as long as he could.

Exactly a week before Christmas, Farrell left Grace sleeping one morning and walked into Grafton Street. He was walking everywhere these days; they both were. He had grown to like the exhilaration of cold morning air, fast footsteps. It gave him time to think, to plan.

He knew that P.J. had suffered only a temporary setback; he had not yet been defeated. Farrell was nervous, wondering about the man's next move. King's Bishop to Queen Bishop's fourth. He worried about his ability to fight P.J.'s strategy. Farrell did not doubt Grace's love for him. Nor did he doubt her father's ruthlessness.

Sometimes, the silence, the non-communication with the enemy filled Farrell with dread. He had had the same uneasy dream for two nights running. He would return to the flat, from somewhere nameless, and find Grace gone. He knew it was their flat, because so many things were familiar, in their right place. But the dream flat was strange and unfamiliar, too. The rooms closed in on him as he entered them; they shifted and fell away into nothingness when he opened the doors. He would search for her everywhere, but every trace was missing. Not even cigarette butts remained in the kitchen bin. He woke up each time with the message ringing in his mind: she is not yours, she never has been.

He was worried about leaving her alone this morning. But this time, she could not come with him.

Farrell joined the long shoppers' queue in the TSB. It was moving quickly. Tellers and customers were in Christmas good humour. Even at this early hour, Grafton Street was already crowded. Farrell didn't care. He knew exactly where he was going.

He withdrew fifteen hundred pounds from his savings. He hadn't touched the money in nearly twenty years; he had never wanted anything much. He'd been waiting. A little something for a rainy day, Mrs Casey used to encourage him. Another reason to be grateful to the Caseys. It wasn't their fault that he could never feel really part of their family. But if they could not give him a sense of belonging, they had given him so many other things. Farrell knew now that all the work, all the training, all the skills had been leading him to this time, to Grace. He was glad he had never spent much on himself, glad that all that money was there to create his first real home.

He pushed his way through the crowds in the Powerscourt Centre, and went upstairs to the little antique shops he and Grace had browsed through together. He had found out her ring size by subterfuge; now he was collecting her Christmas present. An antique gold engagement ring, simple and elegant, like Grace herself. A small, brilliant diamond, twisted together with a deep, blue sapphire, her birthstone.

They were not a modern couple, he had decided. He wanted everything to have roots, to be solidly planted in times less shifting and uncertain than each of their lives had been over the last few years. This ring spoke to him of endurance, stability. He wondered what its history was, whether the woman who had worn it had been happy. He hoped there was no sinister reason for its ending up like this, in a shop, rather than passed on to daughters, cousins, nieces.

His doubts vanished when the assistant showed him the ring, adjusted to fit Grace's small finger. Newly polished, its stones were even brighter than Farrell remembered. It was placed carefully in a dark wine-coloured velvet box. Farrell chose the wrapping with care from the sheets the assistant offered him. Silver, with a dark green satin ribbon. The contrast pleased him.

All the way home, he tried to imagine her face. He bought her roses, something to give her while he created the moment for her gift. Grace created beauty so effortlessly; he wanted to make sure that this moment would be special for her. He patted his coat pocket, checking that the little box was still there. His heart was thumping as he put his key in the lock.

The flat was oddly quiet. The tree lights were off, the kitchen looked as though it had been abandoned, mid-breakfast.

And there was no sign of Grace.

Farrell immediately felt the blades of panic twist inside his chest. He smelt P.J.'s hand in this. No, no – maybe she had just gone upstairs to work. All the conflicting explanations passed through Farrell's mind in a flash. He crashed out through the still-open door of the flat, upstairs to the sublet. He tried to keep his voice calm, in case she really was in there.

He knocked.

'Grace?'

No answer.

Farrell put his key in the lock with a shaking hand. Nothing. The room was undisturbed, the same as they had left it the last time they'd worked there together.

He ran down to his own flat again. Mouth dry, chest hollow, he went back into the kitchen, to look for clues. Toast half-eaten, coffee poured. Had he kidnapped her? What had he done? Waited outside all this time until he saw Farrell leave on his own, and then pounced on her?

She had left him. He was on his own again, after all that.

All the past defeats, all the fears of another failure built up inside Farrell, tearing through him like a hurricane.

He upended the kitchen table, sending cups, sugar-bowl, coffee-pot flying. They smashed to the ground with satisfying fury. He wanted to break everything, smash everything they had ever used together.

The tree. Blindly, Farrell made his way towards the tree in the sitting-room, wanting to wrench all the decorations from its limbs, tear it branch from branch.

Suddenly, he stopped. There was the sound of the hall door opening.

Was it *him*, coming to tell Farrell he had won? Or had she come back?

Then he heard Grace's voice, normal, cheerful, greeting someone on their way out. An extraordinary stillness came over him. He felt paralysed, almost dreamlike. But the pounding in his head and heart did not go away.

Grace came in and saw him standing by the tree. She was startled.

'Farrell! What's the matter? Are you all right?'

He couldn't speak.

She had a litre of milk in her hand.

'Farrell? What is it?'

Her voice was cautious and afraid, expecting bad news. Farrell sat down heavily on the armchair, and stared at the grey embers from last night. Grace took off her coat quickly and dropped it on the floor. She left the keys and the carton of milk beside it. She knelt in front of Farrell, and took his hand.

'Farrell? Please, what's the matter? Are you sick?'

His face was a ghastly colour. He was trembling and he seemed to have lost the power of speech.

'Wait, I'll get you a drop of whiskey.'

She ran to the kitchen, and as though from a great distance, Farrell heard her exclamation of surprise. She was back instantly with a little whiskey in a tumbler.

'Here, drink this.'

She pressed the glass to his lips. She took one of his hands and placed her own over it, so that they both held the glass as he sipped. The sounds he began to make were like whimpers. Something in his face made Grace begin to understand. She stroked his hair gently with her free hand.

'My poor love. You came back early and thought I'd gone.'

Farrell's face began to regain its normal shape. The formlessness of anger and desolation began to disappear. His eyes finally focused on her, and he looked at her with enormous gratitude. Still unable to speak, he just nodded. A tidal-wave of shame began to grow inside him for having doubted her. She was now the strong one, he realised; he had helped make her like that.

'Listen to me, Farrell,' Grace said, taking the glass away from him, making him look straight at her. 'Are you OK now?'

'Yes, I think so.' His reply was faint, but audible.

She knelt on the floor in front of him, resting her elbows on his knees.

'I love you, Farrell. We're together now, and I'm not going anywhere,' and here she smiled at him. 'Except to go out to get milk. I don't like black coffee.'

Farrell felt tears nudging. A couple escaped, and Grace wiped them away with the tips of her fingers. It was as though the madness had finally been released. All the crazy energy was gone. He felt spent, at peace.

'I'm sorry, Grace. I'm really sorry.'

'It's OK,' she said softly. 'It's OK. Now we know what we need to talk about.'

She stood up and took him by the hand.

'Come on – you look exhausted. We can talk again later.'

She led him to the bedroom. He barely made it to the bed before his head started to spin. His last half-thought, before the flashing lights behind his eyes ceased, was that he would prefer never to let her out of his sight.

Then, he could be sure of her.

Grace bent down and picked up the roses. Most of them were still intact. The headless ones she crushed into the bin. She took the scissors out of the kitchen drawer and cut their long stems at an angle. She arranged them in the simple vase she had brought from her father's house and placed them on the table in the sitting-room. But there was still a greyness to the room which disturbed her.

She wanted to create cheer, brightness, comfort. She wanted Farrell to understand that everything was back to normal now, that no damage had been done. She glanced nervously at the Christmas tree; she could still see his face as he'd stared, haunted, at its branches. Brushing away the image with a physical effort, Grace moved towards the corner and switched on the lights. They worked. She felt a huge sense of relief. Their multicoloured glitter reassured her; she had been afraid that they would, somehow, have ceased to shine.

Full of purpose now, she pulled out newspapers from

the shelf under the stereo. She cleaned out the fire quickly, getting rid of the dead ashes. She stuffed them into the bin immediately, glad to be rid of them. Then she went down to the basement and put the bin-bag outside the back door, out of her sight. She piled sticks, small bits of coal, almost a full packet of fire-lighters on top of each other in the dusty grate. She placed a centre sheet of newspaper across the opening, creating a draught. Flames roared up the chimney. She let the paper go and it was sucked away from her with a violence that took her by surprise.

A few minutes later, she went into the kitchen to clean up the rest of Farrell's mess.

It was eight o'clock that evening when Farrell woke.

He felt absolutely calm, his head very clear. He was also starving. In the sitting-room, the fire was burning, and the tree-lights were switched on. The little table was set, and there were two candles lit. There was a delicious smell of food coming from the kitchen. Farrell was puzzled; Grace did not like to cook.

He looked around the door, cautiously. His sense of great shame had abated; now he felt back to normal, just embarrassed at his over-reaction. Grace was taking something out of the oven. The kitchen was clean, not a trace of his crazy morning remained. There was a new coffee-maker, sugar-bowl, mugs. She must have gone out again.

And she had come back.

Farrell felt warmed all over. Grace turned to find him smiling at her. Her face was flushed.

'You're just in time,' she said. 'I was about to call you, once everything was hot. I don't know how you manage this cooking lark at all, I really don't.'

There was a landslide of foil containers from the Indian

take-away. The fridge was open, there were some bottles of beer on the shelves, others on the floor waiting their turn to be chilled.

Farrell moved in beside her.

'Here, let me help.'

Swiftly, he bagged the empty containers, and brought the bowls of food to the table. He took the heated plates out of the oven, closed the fridge door, and opened two bottles of beer. He did it all in what seemed like one clean sweep.

Grace laughed and threw her tea-towel on the draining-board.

'To hell with this, I'm going to sit down. You can take over!'

Farrell decided that now, tonight, he could make his moment. When he had let it slip from his grasp earlier, he had wondered if he would ever again find the right time. He switched off the main light, and they sat, in the rosy glow of fire, candles and Christmas-tree lights. Farrell had a moment of pure terror when he thought of just how close he had brought himself to losing her. He would have had nobody to blame but himself.

He waited until the meal was finished, just before Grace reached for her cigarettes.

'This is why I went out so early today,' and he placed the little silver parcel on her table-mat.

'My Christmas present?'

Her eyes were large, dark, shining in surprise. She was smiling at him.

'Let's say your pre-Christmas present. This is something I want you to have now.'

'We're even beginning to think alike.'

Grace reached down beside her and he saw that she had a flat, rectangular box in her hand. She placed it on the table in front of him.

'Happy Christmas. You go first,' she said softly.

Farrell felt the lump grow in his throat as he opened the slim, black box which revealed an old-fashioned watch and fob, the kind gentlemen used to wear attached to their waistcoats. He flipped open the cover. The face was delicate, gold Roman numerals on a dark background. The engraving said: 'To Farrell. For ever. Love, Grace.'

He leaned across the table to her, holding both her hands in his. She kissed his face tenderly. Finally, he was able to speak.

'It's perfect. Thank you.'

He gestured to the little parcel.

'Come on,' he said. 'It's your turn now.'

He watched every movement of her face as she carefully undid the green satin bow. She smoothed the silver paper gently. She saved all sorts of wrapping paper, always.

She gasped when she saw the ring.

'Oh, it's beautiful!'

He took the ring out of its box and slipped it onto her finger.

'This time next year,' he promised, 'Christmas in our own home, as husband and wife.'

She held her hand out in front of her, admiring the flash and twinkle of the stones in the candlelight. Then she stood up.

'Come here to me!'

They were both laughing now, waltzing wildly around the room, almost knocking over the Christmas tree in their crazy dance.

Suddenly, Grace exclaimed: 'I want to go out. I want to walk down Grafton Street and see Switzer's window. I want to see all the kids' faces!'

They ran down the steps to the street and arrived at the bus stop at the same time as the bus. Grace shoved him on in front of her. He stumbled, surprised at her strength.

Then she jumped on board and he pulled her down beside him on the long back seat. She suddenly started to giggle, seeing the amused stares of the other passengers.

'They think we're drunk,' Grace whispered to him.

'We are. With happiness.'

Grace held his arm tighter. Farrell thought he would explode.

By the time they reached the city centre, Farrell had planned and mapped and fashioned the rest of their lives.

* * *

Farrell was feeling very proud. It was the best night of his life. He was no longer an apprentice. At nineteen years of age, he was ready to take his place in the world. He felt grown up, finally in charge of himself.

He, Jimmy and Mick had decided to celebrate their success together. Quietly, saying nothing to the Caseys, Farrell had booked a room in Gaffney's pub for Monday night. Then he invited them to join him for a drink. His quiet insistence had eventually worn Mrs Casey down.

'I'm not one for public houses, as you well know. But I'll join you this once, in honour of the occasion. Your mother would have been proud of you.'

And she had reached up to Farrell, pulling his face down to hers, kissing him on the cheek.

When they arrived at the pub, Jimmy and Mick were already there with their families and friends. A great roar greeted Mr Casey's entrance. His mouth actually fell open in surprise and he turned to Farrell at once.

'You lanky bastard!' was all he said.

But Farrell could tell he was delighted. He sat with the Caseys all evening. He was conscious of wanting to say thanks. He waited for a quiet moment, and leaned over towards Mrs Casey. His tongue a little loosened by Guinness, he felt able to say what he wanted to say.

'Thanks for everything. For taking me in, for setting me up. I'll never forget it.'

Mrs Casey smiled at him.

'We've loved you like one of our own. And we're proud of you.' She squeezed his hand gently. 'I know it's not the same, but we're family as long as you want us.'

He felt strangled then. Love, gratitude, pride all seemed to gather together at the base of his throat, like hard little pebbles. They were difficult to breathe through. He knew that now was the time for him to move out. He already had a job lined up for Thursday, he had money in his pocket, he was content. She was a wise woman, Mrs Casey. She was letting him go; she was telling him it was OK. She wasn't looking for any reply.

Farrell leaned over and kissed her on the cheek. She pushed him away, laughing.

'Go on out of that!'

Mr Casey growled at him.

'Tide's out!'

Farrell grinned at him and went back up to the bar. A few minutes later, Jimmy and Mick called him over to their table. They were ready. All three left the bar quietly.

To a hushed and expectant room, the three of them returned ten minutes later, dressed in spotless blue overalls. Each of them was holding a sweeping-brush firmly in front of him. Farrell stood in the middle, ludicrously taller than Jimmy and Mick. They waited solemnly until the giggles had subsided. Then to the tune of 'Dicey Reilly' they sang a song about Mr Casey and his sweeping-brush.

Poor aul' Mr Casey he has taken to the brush . . .
Poor aul' Mr Casey he will never give it up . . .

Everyone became helpless with laughter. Mr Casey tried, without success, not to smile. A great roar of approval went up as Farrell presented him with a giant-sized yard-brush, wrapped in multicoloured layers of crêpe paper, swathed in ribbons and streamers.

'*And guess where he can put it!*' Loudly, from Jimmy and Mick, bowing from the waist as they sang the finale.

Mr Casey shook his fist at them and refused to make a speech. Instead, he raised his pint-glass to the three of them, and lowered its contents in one long swallow. Loud whistles and fists banging on tables cheered him on and everyone clapped, even Mrs Casey.

When they had all stopped looking in his direction, Mr Casey suddenly leaned over towards Farrell.

'You're a good lad,' he said, wiping the moustache of Guinness from his upper lip. 'A craftsman, much more than a tradesman. Remember I said that.'

'I will,' Farrell promised.

Farrell met Martina at the bar. Jimmy's sister, he had seen her around for years. Nineteen, same age as himself, long dark hair swinging, laughter always bubbling. But now she was angry because the barman was ignoring her.

'He's just served three men in front of me' she fumed. 'I was here before any of them!'

'Tell me what you want,' Farrell said.

Towering above the others, he gave her order as well as his own. It was no effort for him to catch the barman's eye. Height had its advantages, after all. Before handing over the ten-pound note, he raised his voice, just a little.

'Make sure you serve the lady the next time,' was all he said.

The clamour at the bar was suddenly stilled, one of those strange moments of absolute silence before uproar takes over once again.

Something in his face made the barman nod acknowledgement, and avert his eyes from Farrell's. Martina's response surprised him. He had hoped for gratitude, maybe even a little admiration. If anything, she was even angrier. But her anger was not directed at him.

'That fucker!' she spat. 'He asked me out and I refused him. He's been doing this to me ever since!'

But her anger was short-lived, and she stayed at the bar, chatting easily to Farrell. He was pleased that she seemed in no hurry to leave; he felt comfortable in her presence. He was torn between wanting to stay with her, and remembering his duty to the Caseys. Regretfully, he went back to their table. He owed them his presence tonight.

Before he left the pub, Farrell went looking for her again. He had summoned just enough courage to ask her out. Terrified that she'd refuse, he pretended unconcern. He'd been silently practising what to say, just in case.

'I promise not to ignore you if you turn me down.'

She grinned at him, tossing her long hair over her shoulders.

'I'm not going to turn you down.'

He enjoyed her energy, her irreverence. She often made him laugh. She was his first real girlfriend. Proudly, he grew in his own mind to be one of the lads. He was conscious of developing a new status.

Friends; new job; new flat with Jimmy and Mick. And now Martina. It was a kind of belonging.

★ ★ ★

'Grace, what do you want to do about seeing your family? We should be able to work something out . . .'

Grace looked up suddenly from the material in front of her. Abruptly, she stopped what she was doing, tailor's chalk in her right hand. The suddenness of her reaction stopped Farrell in mid-sentence.

'I don't want to see any of them. For the moment. I've had them all up to here.'

She placed her left hand under her chin. Farrell was struck again at how well the ring suited her small hand. Her nails were painted, her hair was glossy. She always looked groomed, unruffled. He was proud of her.

'I don't want them to think I'm stopping you,' he said.

'I don't care what they think. None of them made any effort to contact me, although I'm sure P.J. knows exactly where I am. I want some space. I might feel differently at some stage in the future. Then we'll see.'

He nodded. He liked the implication of the long future together, of the 'we'. He was reassured by that. But still, he'd needed to ask. He knew that her family was not going to go away. He felt it was safer to acknowledge their presence, rather than feel their absence grow silently between them, choking like a weed.

He watched as Grace's scissors followed the chalk-lines on the folded fabric. Not for the first time, he admired her deftness.

'I feel very strong, Farrell, and I'm happy. I just want to enjoy the feeling. Getting in touch with my family would mean not enjoying it. Do you understand?'

She placed the pieces of fabric on the growing pile to her left, smoothing them into place.

He did understand. He knew exactly what P.J.'s pressure had done to Grace before. Before he'd met her. But he still feared the pull that P.J. could exercise, even at this distance, if he put his mind to it. The silence was unnerving.

They did not speak of it again for some months.

Grace had begun to work seriously on her dolls again. When Farrell went back to work early in the New Year, she took her radio upstairs to the sublet, and worked there until Farrell came home. The room was filled with catalogues, samples of material, naked doll bodies. Sometimes, the sight of so much naked pink baby flesh disturbed Farrell. But he admired the delicacy of her touch, the attention to detail which transformed a child's toy into a work of beauty and precision.

Things had been quiet in the building trade since Christmas. Farrell had had the time to go looking for more and more restoration work, making himself known in the antique shops, promoting his work by his portfolio of before-and-after photographs. Gradually, he built up an impressive album. All that spring he was kept busy from street to street in Ranelagh, as the houses gradually changed their status from bedsits to family homes.

Farrell approved of this change, and not just because of the work it brought him. Things should always stay as they were meant to be, he thought. He liked seeing kids playing on the street, kicking football, roller-skating. He even found himself searching the little faces for something he could recognise, some dim memory of his brothers and sister. But it never worked. Being with Grace made it hurt that little bit less.

He became known up and down the streets for the rightness of his taste, his painstaking attention to detail, his neatness. He still went wherever Christy sent him, but more and more he began to believe that there was a living to be made from what had once been only an interest.

Walking to work each day from the flat in Rathmines, he kept an eye out for the For Sale signs which seemed to grow everywhere, shooting up in gardens overnight, like stiff, gaudy trees. He kept his ear to the ground, waited patiently for news. He had decided that he wanted one of these Victorian homes for himself and Grace; he wanted something with a past. Modern houses insisted that you brought your own past with you. He didn't want that. He wanted to transform something damaged and neglected into something perfect, something that was theirs. The worse the condition, the better for him.

One Saturday morning at the end of April, he struck gold.

Drinking tea in the antique pine kitchen he had just finished, Farrell fell into conversation with the owners.

'There could well be more work for you on this street,' John remarked as he refilled their cups. 'I believe number fourteen is coming up for sale. The tenants have just been given a month's notice. The fella who owned it died recently, and the son wants the cash. Apparently, his business is in danger of going belly-up.'

'Oh, really? Who is the owner, then?'

Farrell tried to keep his voice steady, politely interested.

'A fella called Duggan, Peter Duggan, I think.'

'Peadar Duggan,' Christine corrected from the doorway. 'He lives in Templeogue somewhere. Don't worry. When we see him, we'll give you our highest recommendation!'

She was running her hands over the smooth surface of the table Farrell had crafted.

'This is just lovely,' she smiled at him. 'Thank you so much for all the care you took.'

Farrell accepted what he believed to be a signal to go. He drained his cup, and stood up, putting his money carefully into his inside pocket.

'You're welcome. Thanks for the tea.'

He wiped his hands on his white cotton cloth, and strapped up his toolbox. He left and went straight to the phone box on the main road. Duggan. Not too common a surname, he should be easy enough to find. Farrell hoped he wasn't ex-directory. If only he knew what business the man was in . . .

The entry leapt out at him. The only Peadar he could see, in bold type, living in Templeogue. Farrell copied the address down on the back of the envelope he'd been given his money in. This was not something to do by phone.

He caught the first bus to Templeogue. His stomach was sick with excitement. There hadn't been any estate agent's sign outside, *maybe* that meant that this Duggan hadn't signed up with anyone yet.

Farrell had never gone looking for his own home before. He'd always felt his life to be temporary, like walking on shifting sand; a house was such a for ever thing. Now, he knew that he wanted this, almost as badly as he had wanted Grace.

He found the house easily enough. There was a brand-new Hiace van outside, with 'Peadar Duggan Plant and Tool Hire' painted on it, in large red letters. Farrell rang the doorbell. A boy of about sixteen answered.

Farrell stood up to his full height.

'Good afternoon. I'm looking for Peadar Duggan.'

He caught the boy's slight hesitation.

'He'll want to see me.' Farrell added, 'I'm buying, not selling.'

The boy opened the door wide, and Farrell stepped inside.

'I'll get him for you now.'

Farrell looked around the hall quickly. Everything was just that little bit faded. There was an air that he recognised at once. It was tension.

A man of about fifty came out of what Farrell presumed was the kitchen, and closed the door behind him. He was unshaven, wearing a T-shirt and jeans.

'Afternoon, Mr Duggan,' Farrell said before the other man could speak. 'My name is Farrell.'

He held out his hand. The other man shook it tentatively.

'How can I help you?'

He was already opening the door into the front room, and he gestured for Farrell to come inside.

Farrell decided to waste no time.

'I believe you have a house for sale in Ranelagh, number fourteen Meadowbrook Grove.'

He stood up straight, looking down at the other man. He had his arms casually folded in front of him. It got his hands out of the way.

Duggan's eyes suddenly widened, and his mouth fell open.

'How in the name of God do you know that?'

Before the man had time to get angry, Farrell shook his head, allowing himself to smile a little. He raised one hand, waving the question away. He was in control, master of the surprise attack. He continued quickly.

'That doesn't matter. What does matter is that I'm prepared to make you an offer now, which will save you agents' fees and advertising. I'm also prepared to offer you a ten-thousand-pound deposit, in cash – immediately – once you agree to sell to me.'

Farrell waited for his opening offer to sink in before he continued.

'I know all those houses well. I also know the market value of the ones in bad condition. I'm prepared to offer you eighty thousand, with a cash deposit, straight away. I have no house to sell, I'm ready to move now.'

The man looked suspiciously at Farrell.

'How do you know what condition it's in?'

Farrell was ready for him.

'Because I've worked on the roof next door, and I've seen that yours needs to be re-tiled. All the sash windows need to be replaced. I also know that there's no central heating. Ten years of student lodgers leads me to believe that there may be considerable internal work to be done as well. My offer's a fair price, and you won't have to wait months for your money. Nor do you have to pay any estate agent's commission.'

Farrell stopped. He had said enough. That was all he had practised on the bus. He hoped he'd got the tone right, formal, businesslike, a little offhand, as though he did this every day. Peadar Duggan was clearly taken aback at his forthrightness. Farrell was pleased with himself.

'I'll have to discuss this with my wife.'

Farrell nodded. Already, he could see the man's thoughts. A bird in the hand.

'Of course.'

Duggan left the room, closing the door very quietly behind him. Farrell had begun to sweat. If his opening offer was even being considered, then he had a chance. He unfolded his arms, and put his shaking hands into his jacket pockets.

Duggan returned after about ten minutes. Farrell could see that he was hooked.

'I'm interested, Mr Farrell, but your offer is too low. I'd be prepared to accept eighty-three, with a bigger deposit up front. That way, we both win. Your estimate of eighty is much lower than any of the others I've got.'

Farrell knew it was all over bar the haggling.

A few minutes later, both men shook hands. Farrell asked for two pieces of paper, and dated them. He knew by heart all the elements of a contract. Years of working in other people's houses had taught him a lot. He wrote that Duggan had agreed to sell to him, at the price stated, with a twelve-thousand-pound deposit payable immediately. Both men signed both copies, and Farrell put one in his pocket.

'Show that to your solicitor on Monday morning. I'll

get the cash for you straight away. Here's my address and phone number.'

Farrell himself was suddenly terrified. Now, he'd have to move mountains to get a mortgage. Building Society managers, he'd been told, tended to be very suspicious of men who made their living with their hands. But he was determined. He would prove that he could pay it back. His savings book was evidence enough for anybody.

He could do all the work himself. When the house was finished, it would be worth far more than he had borrowed. He was not prepared to take no for an answer.

Farrell noticed that the other man looked as though a physical burden had been lifted from his shoulders. Even the lines on his face were easing out. Farrell felt sorry for him.

'I'll be in touch,' he said, shaking hands again. 'Do I have your permission to see inside?'

The other man shrugged.

'Sure, as long as the tenants don't decide to be difficult.'

Farrell wondered how long it would take for his purchase to sink in. He floated towards the bus stop; he'd have burst into song if he'd known how. He couldn't wait to go and tell Grace he had just bought their first home.

She was sitting by the fire, reading the paper. She had Mendelssohn playing softly in the background. Although officially nearly summer, the afternoon was still freezing. Her face lit up with pleasure as Farrell walked in. No matter how often he saw her, or how familiar her face became, Farrell found something new to admire, something different to love, every time he came home to her.

But now his throat was dry. His palms were sweaty. He needed a pint.

He hoped she would trust him in this, that she would

believe he knew how to make the best choices for both of them.

He pulled her to her feet.

'Come on, we're going for a walk.'

'But you're only just in!'

'Yes – but I've got something special to show you!'

Appealing to her curiosity always won.

'Is it a surprise?'

He nodded.

'Oh, good!' She stood on tiptoe and kissed the bottom of his chin.

Holding hands, they walked towards Ranelagh, branching off to the right and right again, and finally left until they reached the quiet cul-de-sac called Meadowbrook Grove.

'This is where I've been working. Over there, number sixteen,' Farrell pointed it out to her.

'They're lovely houses,' she said wistfully. 'Are they very expensive?'

'Depends,' said Farrell cautiously. 'If they're in poor condition, you can still pick up good value.'

'Is there one coming up for sale? Is that the surprise?'

He put both hands on her shoulders and looked down at her.

'Not quite. Do you see number fourteen?'

Grace looked over.

'That's the one tucked into the corner there, with the yellow door?'

'Yes.'

'What about it?'

Farrell tilted her face towards him.

'It's yours,' he said and smiled broadly.

She didn't believe him, couldn't take in what he was saying.

'Farrell! What are you talking about?'

'It's true. I've just bought it for us.'

He lifted her up and swung her round and round until she was breathless.

'What happened? Tell me!'

Briefly, he told her the story. Her eyes grew rounder, bluer.

'And you haven't even seen inside?'

'I don't need to; I *know* it's in bits!'

He was holding on to her shoulders more tightly. He was bending down so that his eyes were level with hers. They were both laughing.

'But just think, Grace, what you and I can make of it! We'll work on it together, restore it to what it should be! Even if we don't want to live there, we can always sell it, move on somewhere else. We can *do* this, Grace, we can even make our living at it!'

She nodded slowly.

'Yes,' she said, searching his face. 'You're right. You're absolutely right.'

'I've even thought of a name for the company we'd form. We'd call it . . .' Here Farrell stopped, spreading his right hand in an arc across the sky, conjuring up imaginary lights.

'We'd call it "Amazing Grace"!'

She burst out laughing.

'God, you're a hopeless romantic! I should be *furious* that you bought it without telling me first! But I'm not!'

Still laughing, Farrell so relieved he was light-headed, they made their way nearer to the garden gate.

Grace tugged at his sleeve.

'Do we dare?'

'What?'

'Say we're the new owners, and can we have a look around?'

'Why not?'

Farrell was immensely grateful to her for her enthusiasm. He'd been so worried that she would see this as him taking over, organising her life without her permission.

The door was opened by a young man whose flaming red hair cascaded down well past his waist. There was the booming of music in the background.

'Hi. I'm Grace Browne. We'll be doing the renovations here once the house is sold. We have Mr Duggan's permission to come in and look around, as long as it's all right with you?'

Grace's tone was friendly, persuasive. Farrell admired her skill with people, her ability to inspire confidence, to get what she wanted. He watched as the hostility on the young man's face waned visibly. He shrugged at both of them.

' 'Spose so.'

He stood back barely enough to let them in. Then he disappeared.

Ten minutes in the house was long enough to confirm Farrell's worst estimate. But he was utterly happy; it was a good buy, and they would make it special. Grace was standing in the middle of the kitchen, which consisted of a very stained stainless-steel sink and an ancient gas cooker.

'It's in bits!' she said. 'Even the floor is rotten – look over there.'

But her eyes were shining. She had seen enough. She knew he could work wonders. She knew he could make up for all the years of neglect.

On the way out, she said: 'I suppose we should go home and discuss where we're going to get the money for all of this – a mere detail?'

'Let me buy you a drink and I'll tell you all about it.'

Farrell took her hand and tucked it into the crook of his

arm. Then he walked her towards McSorley's pub and felt, again, that he was the luckiest man alive.

★ ★ ★

After they had been together for six months, Martina came to see him early one morning. He was just about to leave the flat. Jimmy and Mick had already gone. He liked to stay behind for a while to clean up; she knew that.

He was surprised to see her at the door, shocked at her white face.

'What's the matter?'

'I'm late, Farrell.'

He looked at her stupidly. He didn't take it in, didn't know what she was talking about.

'I'm late; I've had no period. That means I'm pregnant.'

Her voice was brittle, angry.

Farrell felt the ground shift beneath his feet.

'Are you sure?' was all he could manage.

'Yeah, I'm sure. We have to talk about it. Will you meet me tonight?'

'Yeah, of course.'

Farrell cursed his awkwardness. He didn't know what to say.

'Right, then.' Abruptly, she was gone.

Farrell was clumsy all day. His hands felt stiff, awkward, no longer part of him. They refused to behave with their accustomed ease. Even the wood felt cold and harsh. The chisel almost slipped, once. He ended up with his hand full of splinters.

He had no idea how to manage all of – this. At first, the thought of a child gave him a great surge of happiness. A baby. A little baby of his own. He could love it and look after it. Farrell imagined being a dad, holding his little girl's hand, protecting her from bullies, from traffic, from danger. The more he thought about it, the more the idea filled him with joy. His own family at last. But there was something wrong with the picture. He was in it, his little girl was in it, but there was no place for Martina.

There was a cold truth behind all of this.

He did not want Martina. He did not love her like that, enough to want to spend the rest of his life with her. He felt as though someone had just woken him roughly from sleep. Now what was he going to tell her?

They met at eight and walked to Fairview Park. They sat together on one of the benches near the bandstand.

'I know I'm pregnant, Farrell. I was sick again this morning. The thing is, I can go through with this if you love me, if we can be together.'

Farrell was silenced by the pain of having to tell her. He just sat there, looking down at his hands, unable to form the words. Then she did it for him.

'*Do* you love me, Farrell?' she asked eventually.

'Not like that, Martina. No. I'm sorry.' He forced his eyes up to her face. 'I'm really sorry. What can I do to help?'

She was harsh.

'You can pay for the clinic. I'm taking the boat.'

He nodded.

'How much do you need?'

'I'll tell you as soon as I find out.'

'Do you want me to come with you?'

She stood up and was moving away from the bandstand, leaving him behind.

'No,' she said over her shoulder. 'I don't want you to come anywhere with me.'

Farrell watched her go, head bent, long hair flowing.

For a long time after that, his mother's face, Jenny's face, Martina's face swam before his eyes in the moments before sleep. He swore he would never touch another woman again, believing that all he brought was destruction. And he had kept his word to himself.

Until Grace.

Chapter Four

They had enough cash to do most of the renovations immediately. Farrell still couldn't believe that the loan had gone through without any problems. But most of all, he couldn't believe that Grace was still, happily, sleeping at his side.

During the day, she spent hours at her sewing-machine, surrounded by large sheets of drawing paper and swatches of material. She had been given an order for six rag dolls from a toyshop in Stillorgan. This was pure luck, she told him. This was her chance to prove herself. She first sketched each doll several times, specifying sizes and measurements in her swift, copperplate handwriting. Then she hand-dyed dozens of pieces of flannel, cotton and lace to achieve dazzling arrays of shade and colour. She was busy. He knew she was happy. So they kept on the flat in Rathmines, and spent every spare minute, after dinner and at weekends, in Meadowbrook Grove, number fourteen. The evenings were long and warm.

But Farrell was waiting. He knew the enemy would make his move, choosing his moment well.

It was a hot July Saturday. Gerry and Christy were giving him a hand with the roof. Farrell had climbed down the ladder with an empty 7Up bottle, in search of more cold water. He called out to Grace who was in the front room, tearing up the floor-covering. She came out into the garden with him, fixing the band around her pony-tail. Her face was flushed.

'That old lino stinks!' she said, laughing up at him, wrinkling her nose.

He bent to kiss her cheek.

'You're doing a great job – you'd think you were born to it.'

Grace went suddenly very quiet. Farrell was surprised. He'd said things like that a lot lately. It was a standing joke between them; their way of mentioning the unmentionable, of making light of the distances between their former lives.

But she wasn't looking at him. Instead, her eyes were held by a sleek, silver-green Mercedes creeping silently down the cul-de-sac. Farrell followed her eyes. What he saw drained his chest of happiness. She was rooted to the spot, her eyes riveted.

'Go, Farrell,' she commanded.

With legs that had difficulty obeying him, Farrell climbed the ladder to where Gerry and Christy were waiting. His face had gone grey. He felt that something inside him had been killed.

'What's up, man?' asked Gerry, taking the bottle Farrell handed to him.

'It's her old man,' Farrell replied, with a curtness he didn't mean, not for Gerry. By way of explanation and apology, he added:

'He threw her out when we got together.'

There was no more conversation. Farrell sat miserably, his back to the others, looking out over the tidy back gardens below him.

He was reminded of other back gardens, all those years ago. He'd thought, with Grace, that he had finally stopped running. Now, he had a mad instinct to leap from the roof, to charge insanely through fences and hedges, to proclaim defeat before it was announced. He wrapped his arms around his knees to stop them trembling, the same way he had curled himself before leaping onto O'Gorman's shed roof, such a long time ago. Goofy Gorman and his vegetables. The more things changed, the more they stayed the same.

Farrell began to get angry. What had it all been for? All the work, all the years of solitude, all the training and all the saving if Grace were to be taken from him? A coldness started somewhere in the pit of his stomach. He began to fear it, remembering the morning of the Christmas tree. He had to stay and face this, whatever it was.

Gerry was suddenly beside him. He held out a cigarette to Farrell, held it delicately between black and smeared thumb and forefinger. Farrell knew that Gerry knew he didn't smoke. He took the gesture for what it was, a silent invitation to conversation.

'No, thanks, Gerry,' he said, trying to keep his voice normal.

But the gesture had calmed the cold boiling in his stomach. He was grateful for Gerry's ordinariness.

They talked about the work left to do on the roof. Christy joined them and they discussed how to attack the next part of the job. They sat companionably, Farrell calmed by their presence and the silent, blue-drifting smoke.

Suddenly, he heard his name being shouted.

'Time for me to go, lads,' he commented as he responded to Grace's summons.

Her voice still sounded the same, not shrill or tearful.

He came down the ladder slowly, breathing deeply. She was waiting for him at the bottom.

'Come on in. P.J. wants to talk to us.'

Us? Farrell was damned sure that that was one thing P.J.

didn't want to do. He followed Grace into the kitchen, nodded to P.J. and washed his hands at the sink.

There was an uncomfortable silence. P.J. was the first to break it.

'Fine house,' he said.

'We like it,' Farrell replied softly.

He couldn't help the slight insolence, the slight emphasis on 'we'. It was the same tone he had used in Merrion Square, nearly a year ago, when he'd told P.J. he knew where the basement was.

Grace was not looking at him. Farrell suddenly felt ashamed of himself, on her behalf. He was playing right into P.J.'s court, acting like an ignoramus.

'We were very lucky to get it at the price we did,' he continued.

His voice was now friendly, courteous. He could see a flash of confusion on P.J.'s face; the man's discomfiture pleased him deeply. Farrell pulled up a chair beside P.J., leaving Grace on his left. He would not put her in the middle.

'Tea, Farrell?' she asked him.

'Yes, please,' he answered, smiling up at her.

Her answering glance was grateful. There was a paleness, a tightness again around her face and throat that Farrell remembered from the night she had come to him. He had not seen it since then.

P.J. was sitting easily now. Farrell guessed that this visit was, on the surface at least, conciliatory. He was not going to rock Grace's boat.

'P.J. came to discuss something with us,' Grace said, returning with his tea. Farrell arranged his face in what he hoped was a suitable expression, and turned again to the enemy.

P.J. uncrossed and crossed his legs again. Farrell remembered how short they were. In a way, that gave him courage. He waited for the other man to speak.

'I know we've had our differences in the past, but . . . well, there's been a lot of water under the bridge since then, and I hope we can learn to let bygones be bygones.'

Farrell said nothing. He was waiting for whatever was coming next. The man hadn't yet said one thing that was real, from the heart.

'I can see that Grace is very happy. This is a fine house; I can see that I underestimated you. I owe you an apology.'

Bollocks, thought Farrell. If you don't get what you want one way, you'll get it another.

Aloud, he said: 'No problem.'

The joy on Grace's face was physically painful for him to see. He wished that this wasn't happening, that they could have gone on as they were for ever. All the strings he imagined to this reconciliation depressed him. He knew he did not want to share her with P.J.

'Grace tells me you'll be getting married soon.'

Farrell's heart stirred with sudden hope. Was he really going to leave them alone?

'Yes, we hope sometime towards the end of September, all going well here. We've decided on something very small and quiet.'

He could feel Grace shifting on the seat beside him. What the hell. Might as well be hung for a sheep as a lamb. He thought he knew what was coming next. He was going to get his spoke in first.

'We'd be very happy if you could join us.'

Grace reached over and took his hand. She squeezed it hard. He looked directly at her.

'My parents want to make us a gift of the wedding reception.'

Farrell went cold.

Did she not remember, she of all people, who had told

him what her father meant by a gift? Of their wedding, of all things? He could see the hope in Grace's eyes, could read the longing to behave as though everything was normal. At the first real test, her strength was nothing more than an illusion. He knew he could not refuse her. With Mrs Casey's firm hand on his arm, and her voice in his ears, he said quietly:

'That is extremely generous of you, and I can think of nothing that would make Grace happier.'

'Good, good! That's settled then! You two decide what you'd like and we'll all meet again next week to work out the details.'

He stood up and offered his hand to Farrell. Farrell shook it automatically.

'Congratulations once again on your fine house. I wish you both health and happiness to enjoy it.'

He was jovial again, rubbing his fat little hands together. The gesture made Farrell suddenly shudder. He thought that he had never hated anyone more in his life.

Arms around one another, Grace and Farrell walked him to his car.

Farrell knew that it must all look so *ordinary*. As P.J. turned the car and crept away, Grace looked up at him.

'Thank you, Farrell.'

Her eyes were full of tears.

For a moment, Farrell thought it might almost have been worth it. Only for a moment. Then he thought of how well-chosen today had been, how skilfully he had been outmanoeuvred. Loving Grace, he could not refuse to have her among the others she loved on her wedding day.

Thus had the enemy calculated, and thus had the enemy won. He'd known all the right moves to make. He'd known how to get what he wanted.

Farrell knew that for the next time, he was going to have to be three moves ahead.

★ ★ ★

There was room for him in the very front pew of the church, but Farrell hesitated. He genuflected and moved in behind the family. He touched Peter on the shoulder. The young man turned, eyes reddened. His face broke into a smile of genuine pleasure when he saw who it was.

'Farrell! Come in here, with us.'

He began to move over, still holding onto Farrell's outstretched hand. He sensed the other man's reluctance.

'She'd have wanted you here, Farrell. You were like a son to her. And a brother to all of us. Come on.'

Numbly, Farrell stepped in beside Peter. He shook hands with them all, mumbling, 'Sorry for your trouble.'

'I'm really glad you're here. Christy said you were on a site in Drogheda. He didn't know how long it'd take him to get you.'

'I got his message just after lunch. I got the next train down.'

Peter blew his nose violently.

'She never felt a thing. The doc said it was a massive heart-attack. She can't have felt any pain at all.'

Farrell felt a great ball of misery begin to grow and swell inside his chest. As usual, it suffocated him, making speech difficult.

'I'm glad she didn't suffer,' was all he could manage.

'Angela called yesterday morning with the baby. Mam had been really looking forward to seeing little Joe. She

117

said he was the image of his granda. When Angela got no answer, she went round the back and let herself in.'

Farrell wanted him to stop. He didn't want to hear any more. He didn't want to see Mrs Casey disappear before his eyes.

'She was lying on the bed. She told Angela her stomach didn't feel well, she was going to stay lying down for a little while. Angela said she'd put on the kettle. When she got back upstairs, Mam was gone. She can't have felt anything.'

As he said this, Peter's eyes filled and he looked up at Farrell pleadingly.

'I'm sure she didn't.'

Farrell was saved from having to say any more by the arrival of the priest on the altar. The church was packed. Only when the prayers began did Farrell become conscious of his position at the edge of the pew. Kneeling down, his shoulder was just level with the coffin. He had a tremendous urge to touch it, to run his hand over its glossy surface. He had a sudden, painful memory of kissing Mrs Casey's cheek that night in Gaffney's pub, of her hand on his arm, offering him a family.

He felt suddenly loose, cut adrift from his moorings. He had no one now. He felt his own eyes fill, and he fought back the tears. He was not her son, he had no right to sob while her children stood, shocked and silent. She was not his mother. He had no right to feel stranded.

He was glad when the removal prayers were over. He wanted to go, immediately, felt it was not his place to shake the hands of all those people who filed past the coffin, offering their awkward sympathy to the family. But there was no escape. He stayed, recognising the faces of so many neighbours from his past. Mr O'Gorman offered his hand. The fingers were hooked, arthritic.

'Sorry for your trouble, lad.'

As he shuffled on to Peter, Farrell wondered did he still

grow his own vegetables. The ugliness of the old man's hands had shocked him, saddened him. The neighbours kept on coming, quietly queuing in a line that seemed to have no end. Farrell was surprised at how little most of them had changed; their faces all looked surprisingly the same, only older.

Outside, the men stood in little knots, smoking. The women dabbed at their eyes with handkerchiefs.

Angela's hand was suddenly on his arm.

'Come on back to the house, Farrell.'

He nodded, wanting to run away.

'Thanks, I'd like that.'

The house he knew so well was full of women making tea and sandwiches. He was reminded of another time, years ago, when this room had been full of children, sprawled all over the floor. Everyone hushed, excited, waiting to see the modern miracle of television. He pushed the image away. He didn't want to remember that night.

In the front room, Peter handed him a whiskey, taking the glass out of the sideboard. Farrell's insides lurched. He remembered her pleasure the first time she had seen it. He had made that sideboard, taking on the promise old Casey had made to her just before he died. Using the old man's specifications, Farrell had designed a modern, but substantial, sideboard for Mrs Casey's front room. Three sturdy drawers in the centre, flanked by sleek, plain doors. No hard edges; everything moulded. Only the best of wood. Farrell had aimed for clean lines, no clutter. He'd been proud of the finished product; its simplicity and solidity had pleased him. John had got his mother out of the house one evening just before Christmas, and Peter and Joe had helped Farrell to carry the sideboard in, lifting and pushing and manoeuvring it with difficulty in the narrow hall.

Five years ago. Farrell had bought a big fresh flower

arrangement to display on the sideboard's polished surface. The blooms had been bright, big, a complicated arrangement of dense foliage and stems reaching skywards. He had thought it a lovely contrast to the sideboard's simplicity. Angela had brought a delicate, white, lacy centrepiece. And Peter had carried in the chessboard from the kitchen, its pieces just as his father had left them. Farrell remembered how right it had all looked.

Five years. There seemed to be no time at all between the arrival of the sideboard and the departure of the coffin. Farrell imagined the same difficulties, the same lifting and pushing in the narrow hallway. He wondered where his life was going.

They had all sat down together to wait for Mrs Casey's return. Farrell now passed his hand over the smooth wood, remembering her joy. She had hugged him, hugged them all. And she had cried, just a little.

He could sense her presence everywhere. He could smell her soap, see her warm smile. The memory was overpowering. She was everywhere.

He drank his whiskey quickly and went out into the kitchen, offering to carry in trays of cups and saucers, plates of thickly-cut sandwiches. He had to force himself to quell the instinct to run. He had to stick it out. The lump in his throat just wouldn't go away. Farrell didn't know what he was going to do without her, without both of them. Years of empty Sunday evenings stretched in front of him. He knew that his visits would probably continue for a while, but all the Caseys were grown up now, had their own lives. For the last few years, he had really only come to see her.

At ten o'clock, he felt it was all right to go. People were gradually filtering home. The Caseys looked exhausted.

Farrell left on his own, taking the long way out of the

housing scheme. He didn't want to pass by his old house again. That was best forgotten.

The flat in Whitworth Road was cold when he got home. The storage heaters were on the blink as usual. Farrell made himself tea in the poky kitchen. He stood for a long time at the small sink, swirling hot water round and round the teapot, warming his hands on its sides. After the Caseys' house, his flat looked suddenly ugly, unwelcoming. On the spur of the moment, Farrell decided he would move again, go somewhere better.

He pulled the *Evening Press* towards him and tried to spread it out on the tiny table. He rested one knee on the kitchen chair, bending down low over the accommodation ads. One side of the newspaper hung down low over the edges of the table, like a dirty tablecloth. He stood reading for a long time, sipping tea. He was glad to have something to do.

At least it meant he didn't have to think about the evening he had just spent, or the funeral morning that lay ahead of him, silent, waiting.

* * *

Farrell was waiting for Grace to arrive.

Behind him, he could hear the whispers and rustles of the wedding guests. Beside him, Grace's brothers-in-law sat, silent. He was surrounded on all sides. He felt ridiculous, uncomfortable in his fancy clothes. He tried not to care; it would soon be over.

Suddenly, the church organ swelled and flooded all the crowded spaces around him. That was his cue to stand up. He had practised this moment, obediently, many times.

When he turned, he saw no one, only her. She seemed to float towards him, a small vision in satin and lace. Someone murmured at his shoulder and he stepped out into the aisle, his heartbeat loud in his ears. She was at his side now, smiling up at him.

He listened intently to the priest, wanting to make no mistakes, wanting to get everything right. He had been terrified that he would drop the ring, make a fool of himself. He was conscious of Ruth and Anna, of everyone, watching him, waiting. His hand was shaking as he placed the wedding-band on Grace's finger. He repeated all the words he had been taught. Her hand was warm. Her touch flooded him with happiness. He was only dimly aware of the rows of smiling people as they walked back down the aisle together.

Showers of confetti; shouts of laughter; hugs and kisses for the bride, Grace's arm in his.

His wife. It was over.

★　★　★

Farrell's feet didn't touch the ground for the next fourteen days. Amsterdam was a different world from the ones he knew. The city had the feel of having been just washed; water gleamed everywhere around them. They celebrated the first anniversary of their meeting, sitting outside in mid-September sunshine, sipping beer at a pavement café. Farrell had a comforting sense of distance from everything they had left behind in Dublin. He even began to believe that, now, maybe P.J. would let her go.

She couldn't wait to get back, to put the finishing touches to their home. Farrell had worked like a madman before the wedding, some part of him believing that the harder he worked on this house, the more perfect he made it for her, the more worthy of her he would become.

They had transformed the large attic into her studio, and Farrell had watched as she'd made it into a fairy palace, full of light and colour. She was eager now to get back to her dolls, proud that her old customers remembered her, anxious to please her new ones. Her six rag dolls had created quite a stir, displayed in the shop-window in Stillorgan. Farrell glowed with pride as Grace told him how she had grown to believe in herself again, how he had made this the best year of her life. She had him, her own home, her own work. He had given her a new sense of security. And for the first winter in all his forty years, Farrell was conscious of being happy, of knowing he was contented.

Ever since their return from Amsterdam, home had begun to *feel* like home. It was real: a safe, comforting place, a place where he could finally begin to grow roots. His sense of not belonging was slowly ebbing, too, and he began to draw strength from Grace.

Even the house appeared more solid to Farrell, now that all the work of restoration was over. He had left nothing unfinished. He couldn't rest until he had completed the last detail, lovingly replacing the missing tiles from the cast-iron fireplace in their bedroom. Then, he could stop. He began to feel properly grown up, in control of his and Grace's life. He felt that what he now had would not slip from his grasp any more. It was all in his hands. He could see their future together with a clarity which he had never experienced before. Grace was his new reality.

One evening towards the end of October, almost a month after their return, Farrell arrived home to find Grace in a state of high excitement. Her naturally pale face was glowing, making a stark contrast with the dark sheen of her hair. Farrell had the strong impression of a doll's face, freshly painted.

He lifted her up to him and she wrapped her legs around his waist, holding on tight to his neck.

'I've got great news!'

His heart skipped a beat. He hoped it was nothing to do with P.J., nothing to do with another gift.

'I've got an order for two dozen rag dolls, six Noah's arks *and* they want me to send them a prototype of the Victorian doll's cradle you made last Christmas!'

'Hold on, hold on, *who* wants all of this?'

'The new toyshop in Blackrock! I brought my portfolio into them the week before we got married, and they held on to it. They promised they'd be in touch, and they rang me today! I can manage the arks myself, but you have to help me make the cradle! Teach me how to do it!'

She could hardly contain her excitement. Farrell had never seen her so animated.

'Well, I don't know,' he said slowly.

He watched as her smile began to fade, a flicker of disbelief and uncertainty around her mouth. God, how he loved that face.

'After all, it's an original design of mine, so the lessons are going to cost you a fortune . . .'

He couldn't help the broad grin that began to spread across his face. He watched with delight as her eyes lit up again and her mouth curved into a smile.

'Farrell! Stop teasing me!'

He danced her the length of the room. Then he set her down on the floor and cupped her face in his hands.

'It's brilliant news; I'm very proud of you,' he said softly. 'I told you you could do it.'

She was tugging him by the hand.

'Let's make a start *now*,' she demanded. 'Never mind about dinner, we'll get a take-away or something later. Come on, I just can't wait any longer!'

Farrell was starving. He held up his hand to still her.

'Let me grab a sandwich – you go ahead and start taking measurements so you understand the dimensions of each piece. Then we can decide whether to make the cradle bigger or smaller – you can always offer them different sizes.'

She was already opening his toolbox, searching for his rule. She grabbed a notebook and pencil off the papier mâché table in the hall. Then she was gone, taking the stairs two at a time.

'Don't be long! Bring your sandwich up with you!'

Warmth spread through Farrell's whole body. He made sandwiches for both of them, and pots of tea and coffee. He took her cigarettes and lighter off the kitchen table. Then, with a light heart, he followed his wife upstairs. He loved her need of him.

He was careful not to spill anything.

He had a feeling it was going to be a long night.

He was amazed at how quickly Grace learned. She said he was a good teacher. But the truth was that her small hands were swift and certain, her eye unerringly accurate. She grasped everything he taught her, frowning with concentration while he explained and demonstrated. There was now a permanent little furrow between her eyebrows. Farrell loved looking at it, loved the earnestness which produced it.

He could feel her hands almost itching to try everything he showed her. But she was also remarkably patient when her turn came. She measured over and over again, cutting only when she was satisfied, and then with a precision which Farrell had seen only a few times in his career. He was filled with pride, teaching her.

For six weeks, every evening and all through the weekends, they worked together to meet Grace's Christmas deadlines. Farrell loved the silences that grew between them, the certainty of each other's presence. But sometimes, during these evenings, he experienced an inexplicable sense of loss, a sorrow that sliced deep into his core. It puzzled him.

Then, suddenly, he started to dream.

For nights on end, he had vivid, technicolour nightmares of running through Fairview, dodging morning buses. Cats fighting outside in the night became Jenny's howl as she clutched her doll, stretching her arms out to her eldest brother. He woke up sweating, the images staying with him into the early hours, so that he was afraid to fall asleep again.

The pain was at its strongest one evening as he watched Grace put the finishing touches to the last of her three cradles. She had smoothed the oak all over with three coats of beeswax; the cradle gleamed with a dull, soft sheen. He watched as she laid the satin quilt she had made in the base of the cradle, and tucked the doll in with a lace-edged cotton sheet. She passed her hand over the doll's forehead, straightening the filmy bonnet.

The old, old gesture made Farrell's heart turn over.

That night, he was restless as image after image took possession of the screen inside his brain. He saw his mother during her last illness, her wasted hands plucking restlessly at the covers of her hospital bed. A rosy, bright-eyed girl sat beside him on a bench near a bandstand, her dark hair framing her face.

Sleep would not come. He got up, afraid of disturbing Grace.

He made tea in the silent kitchen, swirling the hot water

round and round inside the teapot. It was the familiar ritual that finally did it. As though someone had just thrown a switch, great, gulping sobs started somewhere under Farrell's heart. He allowed the images to flood him, releasing them in huge, splashing tears, the like of which he had never seen before. His mother's hand gentling a sleeping forehead; two children playing in a sunny July garden; the bleak lowering of Mrs Casey's coffin. And himself; a restless ghost moving from flat to flat, looking for what he had lost. Even in his grief, he watched with a sense of amazed detachment as a grown man, apparently himself, heaved and wept at a kitchen table on a dark, normal, December morning.

When he had finished, Farrell felt the beginnings of a sense of peace, and the shaping of a new, urgent need.

Children. He wanted children. He wanted to correct all the old mistakes, to give his name to a child who would be proud to carry it. In that way, he could sever all the old links with the past. He could look forward to the future, to a family shaped by himself.

He must choose his time to tell Grace. He must let her enjoy her new sense of achievement in her dolls and toys. Then they must move on, when she was ready.

Farrell threw the dregs of his tea down the sink. He stood at the window as a dirty orange glow began in the sky to the east.

He had a new and powerful sense of himself, an understanding of the life that had brought him to where he was, to Grace. None of what he wanted was possible without her. The strength of his love for her frightened him as he stood there, watching the watery sunrise. He must be careful; he must not rush her.

He made Grace a cup of coffee. A good drop of milk, half a spoon of sugar. He'd make breakfast for her later. He went upstairs to call her and have a shower. He was filled with a strong sense of something within him moving forward, and of another, richer part of his life just beginning.

He was always on the alert for the enemy. He knew that P.J. would attack where and when he least expected it. He had waited for trouble at Christmas, but none had come. They had met Grace's family early on Christmas Eve, exchanged polite presents, had polite conversation, and then run away together like giggling children. They had done their last-minute shopping in Grafton Street on the way home. It was just after six when they got back. They locked their front door, made hot whiskeys and sat by the fire, music playing softly in the background. The room was filled with another huge tree, more decorations, acres of tinsel and lights. Grace had had a field day. Farrell felt as though the rest of the world had gone away, that he and she were alone in a safe, loving universe.

It seemed that nothing could go wrong. Grace had received an amazing amount of money for her dolls and cradles, so much that Farrell had joked about becoming her business partner. She had teased him, the pupil out-doing the master. They worked well together, in every sense. They were content.

Farrell kept her close to him, choosing his moment with great care.

'Grace, I need to talk to you.'

He told her about all the memories that had invaded him since their marriage. He loved the way she listened to him, the little furrow between her eyes growing deeper. He told her about the Caseys, about his First Communion money hidden in the clock, about his mother's death. He did not tell her about Martina, did not even remember Martina as he spoke to Grace. Nor did he tell her much about his father. He felt that they both understood the other's father, that there was a tacit agreement not to say any more.

Grace was sipping her whiskey thoughtfully. She ran one hand through her hair.

'What is all this saying to you, Farrell? About us?'

He swallowed, and took a deep breath.

'I know it's very soon, Grace, but I'd love us to have a child.'

Only then did the dream Martina flash in front of his eyes again. Nineteen, dark-haired, bright-eyed. The vision still hurt him. He wondered what she looked like now, more than twenty years later. He hoped she was happy.

There was a long silence. Grace reached for her cigarettes and lighter. Farrell cursed himself and his clumsiness. Too soon! Too soon!

She drew deeply on her cigarette, looking into the fire. Farrell saw the shadowy flames flicker over her pale face. Still she said nothing.

Then she held her cigarette up to him.

'I'd better get rid of these then. I believe they're not very good for babies.'

She drew her hand back and fired her cigarette deliberately into the middle of the flames. He was still unsure, afraid that he had pushed her.

'I want both of us to be ready.'

Her eyes mocked him.

'Have *you* a problem, then? I've felt ready for months. It must have been your cradle that did it.'

She rocked him gently, stroking his hair back from his forehead.

'If we have a boy, we're going to call him Vincent. That way, all the bad things will be forgotten. He'll have a name and a father he can be proud of. If it's a little girl, we'll call her Grace, for the same reason.'

She kissed the top of his head, and he could have wept with joy.

Farrell could never bear to think of that night afterwards. If he had known how much pain it would cause, he would have cut his own tongue out, like a biblical martyr. But he didn't know that then. He believed himself to be, once more, the happiest and the luckiest man in the whole world.

Shortly after New Year, Farrell went back to work. Christy still called on him, and was happy that Farrell always obliged him. In return, he recommended him for the tricky restoration jobs that were mushrooming all over town. Christy himself was a Formica and beauty-board man at heart, and looked on with a jaundiced eye at the Victorian and Georgian madness sweeping his native city. Nothing but a fad, he would sniff. Nevertheless, he knew there was money in it, and he recognised Farrell's ability to get everything just right. It was a comfortable arrangement.

Meanwhile, Grace's business was growing with almost alarming speed. The response to her Christmas toys had been overwhelming. By mid-January, she was already hard at work on new designs for the summer tourist season. Her studio was filled with bolts of beautiful cotton, hand-made lace, and delicately painted dolls' faces. Farrell marvelled at how she created a different expression for each doll, with just a flick of the paintbrush, or the angle of a hat. Each doll was unique. She never duplicated a design. She kept detailed records of size, shape, colour and materials. She used everything in a glorious medley – silk, lace, linen, cheesecloth, ribbons. And each doll had a name, embroidered into the hem of her dress.

Sometimes, Grace was reluctant to let her 'little ladies'

go. She formed an attachment to each of them, making them into individuals, each one with a distinct personality.

One afternoon, late in March, when Farrell came home early, he was surprised to find Grace's studio empty. The murmur of the radio was the only sound in the still house. He had to concentrate on fighting the creeping panic in his chest. He knew it was ridiculous, knew there was a simple explanation.

He went downstairs again, his senses sharpened. There were signs of her in the kitchen. But he saw *two* cups, two saucers.

Her handbag was there, right in the middle of the table.

He began to breathe again.

Although they had never discussed it, Grace had begun leaving him signs if she had to go out when he was not with her. Ever since *that* morning, well over a year ago, when she had found him standing, silent, by the Christmas tree. The handbag reassured him now. It said: See? I have not gone far. I have no money, no belongings. Wait, and I will be back soon.

Farrell put on the kettle, for something to do. The water was still hot. He began to relax. There was no sense of P.J. having been in the kitchen. The man had a very distinctive smell: a mixture of aftershave and stale tobacco. Farrell would have recognised it anywhere. There was a faint perfume from Grace's handbag, and from the silk scarf tied to it. But that was all. He began to feel less threatened.

By the time the kettle had boiled, she was back. Relief flooded him as he heard her key in the lock. He was casually pouring himself a mug of tea as she walked into the kitchen.

'Hello, love.'

'Hi, Farrell. You're back early.'

She walked over to him and lifted her face to be kissed.

There was something wrong. He stroked her pale face

and was content to wait. She took her coat off and hung it under the stairs. She took a sip of tea from Farrell's mug. But she didn't sit down. She was restless.

'Come upstairs with me. I want to pack the dolls. I've had enough for today. Will you give me a hand to finish?'

'Sure.'

Farrell followed her quietly, giving her space. He knew she would tell him eventually. She always did.

She started packing immediately. She wrapped each doll in tissue paper, separating each of the layers with sheets of fine plywood. Farrell noticed how she handled the dolls with tenderness.

'Isn't it awful to have to let them go? I get so fond of them. I had another order today, from a small craft co-op in Wicklow.'

She smoothed the last layer of dolls into place, sealing the box with big printed labels marked 'Bábóg'. She had designed the printed script to look like childish hand-writing. It was another touch that Farrell admired.

'The woman was lovely, I had a long chat with her on the phone. She said they have mailing lists for all over the States. They think that some of my stuff would do really well as mail-order.'

Farrell helped her carry the box to the corner of the studio. She looked tired, the beginnings of dark circles under her eyes. He stroked her hair. He decided to give her an opening.

'I hope you're not working too hard. Maybe you should think of getting somebody in to help you.'

Her eyes brightened.

'You're a mind-reader. I was thinking exactly the same thing myself,' and she smiled up at him.

They finished packing the last box and Farrell carried them all downstairs, ready for collection the following morning. Grace had fallen silent again.

'Come on,' he took her by the hand and went into the kitchen to make dinner.

She sat at the kitchen table while he worked, and lit a cigarette.

'First today,' she smiled at him, holding up the full packet.

The eyes were a dead give-away. She was unhappy about something. Farrell began to feel afraid again. She rarely made him wait as long as this.

He had his back to her, while he rinsed rice at the sink. Shaking the sieve vigorously, he asked casually:

'Anyone call?'

There was a second's hesitation. When she spoke, her voice was too bright.

'Yes. Anna dropped in. She left her car in for a service in Costello's, so she walked up. We had lunch together.'

'How is she?'

Not even a phone call since the wedding. A polite smile at Christmas. So what did she want? Whose messages was she bringing? Farrell felt the cold shadow of the enemy.

'She's pregnant.'

There was a break in Grace's voice and Farrell swung round to look at her. Her hands were over her face and she was sobbing. His astonishment changed to an unreasoning anger at Anna. He could read all of Grace's thoughts.

He pulled a chair up beside her, and took her hands gently away from her face. He wiped her eyes with a tissue.

'Grace, it's only been three months. We have to give it time.'

He tried not to let her see his distress. He wondered for a second if he was being punished.

'I know, I know, it's just that I was so sure this morning. I didn't tell you that I was late. I was so excited I wanted to surprise you. Then, ten minutes before Anna came, I knew there was no baby. I know it's very selfish of me, but it was hard to sit here and listen to her being so happy.'

Grace's tears started again. He couldn't bear to hear and see her anguish.

'I'm sorry, Farrell, it's just that I've felt all afternoon that there must be something wrong with me.'

He squeezed her hand.

'There's nothing wrong with you, Grace, nothing at all. Anna's been married for nearly four years. It doesn't happen all at once. We'll have to learn to be patient.'

He kissed her forehead tenderly, an old ache growing deep again inside his chest.

She nodded.

'I know. I know. I'll be fine. I'm OK, now, honestly.' She blew her nose. 'It's just a dose of the blues.'

Farrell saw that for now, she didn't want to talk about it any more. He became busy instead, pulling bags and containers out of the fridge.

'I think we deserve one of my Chinese specials. You sit there and tell me how we can lessen your workload, and I'll make you the best meal you've ever eaten.'

She smiled at him gratefully.

'I love you, Farrell.'

'I love you too,' and with a lighter heart, Farrell began chopping and slicing, nodding encouragement as Grace told him her plans for expanding, perhaps even renting a shop. She'd easily have work for one other person, maybe even two part-timers.

Farrell heard everything she said, listened hard for the things she didn't say. He was satisfied, for now. But wary. He knew that Anna hadn't come on her own. He knew that she had brought memories and the pull of home. That, as much as the news about the baby, had pushed Grace off centre. Now he had been warned. He had to be prepared, vigilant, ready to protect her from the enemy.

Three moves ahead.
As he cooked, Farrell planned what he had to do next.

From that day in March, when Grace first talked about looking for premises, Farrell had swung into action.

He'd said nothing to her. He had six months to find somewhere perfect. He wanted to surprise her in September. It was a special month, their month. The day they'd met, their wedding anniversary, Grace's birthday all fell in September. He wanted to make it into something wonderful this year. It gave him a great rush of pleasure to plan for her.

He chose two estate agents in the Blackrock area, and visited each of them in turn on Mondays. Every Monday afternoon, from the beginning of March until the beginning of September, Farrell took the bus to Blackrock. He had two standing appointments – one at three o'clock, one at four. He was very persistent. He got to know the staff in each office well, explained to them how important it was that this be done swiftly, quietly. It was for his wife; she was not to know. They were not to write to him or telephone him.

He called in person each Monday, every week; he telephoned every Thursday.

He would keep doing this until they found him something.

All that summer, Grace was very busy. Orders for her dolls were coming from all over the place. Farrell was glad that she was so occupied.

At first, he hadn't been happy with Anna helping out. She had given up her job in May. She wanted to enjoy preparing for motherhood. For Grace, the timing had seemed perfect. The craft shops, three new hotel gift-shops, the US mail-order business – everyone wanted Grace's dolls. In the evenings, Farrell worked with her, taking over the making of cradles and Noah's arks.

Anna was good with her hands. She did not have Grace's imagination; she was unable to grow a doll from an idea to a finished product, but she sewed quickly and neatly. At first, she'd just wanted something to do. But very soon, she became absorbed, even taking work home to finish at night. She was pleasant to Farrell from the start, sometimes even friendly. He began to believe that he might have misjudged her. Maybe she was the best of them.

No one ever mentioned P.J.

For weeks, Farrell worried that Grace would find it difficult, watching Anna's pregnancy grow. Instead, Anna became his unexpected ally.

One evening, after Anna left, Grace came downstairs to the kitchen where Farrell was preparing food.

Summer-evening sunshine was flooding the garden.

'I thought we'd eat outside,' he said to her. 'I've lit the barbecue.'

Grace came up behind him and slid her arms around him, pressing her face into his back.

'You're a little treasure, you know that?'

He could hear her smiling.

'Of course,' he said lightly, 'isn't that why you married me?'

He turned around to hold her. He pushed her hair back from her forehead, smoothing the little furrow there. She looked relaxed, her face less pale, coloured a little by the sun.

He kissed her.

'I see you two've been slacking. Lunch on the patio again?'

Grace stretched luxuriously. Her T-shirt and shorts made her look much younger.

'With weather like this, it's a shame to be inside. Anyway, I'm well up-to-date with the orders, thanks to you and Anna.'

She picked slivers of carrot out of the salad.

'I had a long chat with Anna this afternoon.'

Farrell waited, snipping chives into the bowl.

'You were right, you know. It took her well over a year to become pregnant.'

Farrell felt his chest loosen.

'She said all I need to do is relax, let it happen. I'm sorry if I've made things difficult for you, Farrell.'

He put down his scissors and took her in his arms. He hugged her close, silently, for a long time.

'You've always made me very happy, Grace. My only problem has been seeing you worry. I'm really glad you got to talk to Anna. Everything will be OK, I promise you.'

She stroked his cheek.

'Thank you for making Anna welcome. I know you didn't like the idea, but it's really been for the best.'

Farrell was glad that he had been able to hide the depth of his suspicions about Anna and his fears of all that she brought with her.

'We've got really close, Farrell. She wants me to be the baby's godmother.'

Disappointment, like a sharp, sad shock, ran through Farrell's body. He saw what that would mean. A christening. A family party. Polite conversation. P.J. He could see Grace being pulled away from him again, back to her roots. He tried to shake off the image. After all, Anna had been good for Grace. He had to find a way of accepting contact with her family, without this cold, creeping terror

137

in his chest. He knew he had to overcome this dread of losing her. He had to trust her.

'Do you feel OK about that?' he asked instead.

She nodded, smiling.

'Yes, I'm really looking forward to being an auntie. She thinks it's going to be a girl.'

Farrell made a supreme effort.

'We'll have to make something very special for the baby. I've got just the thing. Come with me.'

Grace's smile was the one he remembered, as bright as when he'd loved her first.

He brought her upstairs to the bookshelves on the landing. He searched the top shelf rapidly, knew exactly what he was looking for.

'Here it is.'

Farrell showed her the picture of a Victorian child's bed, made out of solid oak. It was built to expand as the child grew, changing from cot to bed with an elegance and a simplicity that had long ago caught Farrell's imagination. He had hoped to make it for his own.

She clapped her hands in delight.

'It's just perfect! Will we be able to get it done in time?'

'We've six weeks, haven't we?'

She nodded, eyes bright.

'Then we'll do it. We'll have to work at night, when Anna's not here. We'll leave it in the box-room during the day. Make sure you keep the door locked.'

She nodded eagerly.

'I'll get the wood in the morning and we'll start tomorrow night,' Farrell said, replacing the book on the top shelf. 'Now come on before this barbecue turns to ashes.'

Farrell was content to watch his happy wife all evening. He began to believe that she had turned a corner. He began to hope that now that she was relieved and joyful,

138

maybe the baby would happen for them after all. He pushed away the nagging feeling that P.J. was drawing nearer. They would handle that when it happened.

He could handle anything as long as Grace was happy, by his side.

Farrell had to learn to be patient. Business in Blackrock was booming. There was a queue of people waiting for premises; and nobody was selling up or moving out. Farrell particularly wanted Grace to have the shop in Blackrock, rather than anywhere else. He wanted it to be opposite the market. He wanted to thumb his nose at P.J., to say 'See how far she's come with me?'

But week after week, there was nothing. By the middle of August, Farrell was beginning to get desperate. There'd been hints and whispers of early September, but nothing definite. The lack of certainty had irritated him. He wanted to know that this was going to work out. He needed to be sure he would not disappoint her.

He could feel the band of steel across his chest that tightened with every new fear of failure. Sometimes, he'd scolded himself for giving into this terror, told himself to lighten up. Other times, more recently, he'd felt that there was something darker lurking just below it, not quite breaking its surface. On those occasions, he'd deliberately pushed the feeling down, drowning it in his conviction that everything was normal, just as it should be. This was a simple anxiety, nothing more, nothing less. It was a natural instinct, born out of love: a desire to please the woman he adored.

On the second Monday in September, Farrell missed his appointments with the estate agents for the first time since March.

Anna's husband, Peter, telephoned very early in the

morning, startling them both. Farrell struggled into half-wakefulness at first. He stretched out his arm and fumbled for the alarm-clock, uselessly. But the ringing was insistent. Then he heard Grace speaking and became instantly alert.

'When?'

His heart began to pound. He knew it was the baby.

'A little girl? Oh, Peter that's wonderful! Congratulations!'

Farrell kept silent as Grace listened. Her back was turned to him, she was cradling the telephone on her shoulder.

'But that's nearly nine pounds!'

Farrell waited, expecting her tears, fearing the worst.

'Of course, we'll be in later. Love to all of you!'

Grace replaced the receiver very gently.

Farrell thought what a crowded month September was. Maybe it was a good thing. When Grace turned to look at him, she was smiling. He searched her face.

'You heard?'

He nodded.

'Farrell, isn't it wonderful! I can hardly believe it! I can't wait to see her!'

'Let's take today off,' Farrell suggested. He reached out for her hand. 'We can go to the hospital first and have our lunch out. Let's make a day of it.'

Grace stroked his face with her free hand.

'I'm all right, Farrell, really,' she said. 'Stop worrying.'

She was smiling at him. Her eyes were bright. She looked happy.

But still. All that day, Farrell knew that he had to take great care of her. He was surprised and proud of how strong she was. They both fell in love with baby Eleanor the minute they saw her. Anna was sitting up in her hospital bed, radiant, waiting for them. She hugged Farrell as he bent to kiss her cheek.

Grace took the tiny bundle from her Perspex cradle and

held her close. The baby's eyes opened for a couple of seconds and stared straight up at her.

'Hello, Eleanor,' she said softly.

The eyes were two deep, milky-blue pools. Farrell slipped his finger into the baby's hand and she grasped it firmly. He laughed out loud in delight. He sat like that for a long time, terrified that someone would urge him to hold her. He couldn't do that; not yet. He kept watching Grace like a hawk, afraid that the strength was only a mask that might slip, but she seemed happy for her sister. Lately, she had been more serene, no longer gripped by either sadness or anger.

They left the Coombe Hospital late that morning, well in advance of P.J.'s arrival. Farrell didn't think he could bear meeting the proud grandfather. He was also determined that P.J. would have no chance to say anything to upset Grace.

All day Farrell remembered the first morning they'd spent together. They visited the same little antique shops again, had their lunch in the same pub, even bought a little Victorian occasional table which Farrell suddenly, urgently, wanted to own and restore. He remembered how, on that first day, he had tried to stop her from going home, from leaving him. He realised, with a little shock of sadness, that today he was still trying to do the same thing.

Later that night, back in the Chinese restaurant where they'd had their first dinner together, Farrell was tempted to tell Grace about his search for her shop. But he decided against it. He would be successful soon, he was sure of it. Grace seemed to be really happy; she didn't need any extra distractions. He would save it for another time when she might need it more.

Early on Saturday morning, a few days after Eleanor's

birth, P.J. called to the house. It was only the second time he had ever been across their threshold. Farrell saw his bulky frame through the stained-glass panels of the hall door. The sight made him angry.

P.J. was dressed smartly, his almost-bald head gleaming. He brought a trail of fresh aftershave, stale tobacco. His round face was all smiles. Farrell thought there was a smell of victory in the air. He felt numbness begin to crawl into his chest. He could sense the other man's excitement.

'Is Grace awake?'

'Yeah. I'll get her now. Come in.'

Farrell had difficulty with the invitation. He did not want the enemy under his roof. It was much too dangerous. He came back out into the hall and took the stairs two at a time. Grace was already half-dressed, having heard P.J.'s voice. Her face was pale.

'Is everything all right? What's he doing here?'

Farrell shrugged.

'I don't know . . . I think so. Whatever it is, it seems to be good news.'

Grace's face relaxed.

They went downstairs together. P.J. was pacing, looking pleased with himself. Farrell hated him thoroughly. He knew that the man's smug strut would be burned for ever into his memory.

''Morning, pet.'

He kissed her on the cheek. Farrell moved away from them, over to the sink to put on the kettle.

'I must say, you've made a lovely job of this house.'

He was looking all around him, creating his moment.

'Thank you,' Grace answered, waiting.

Something hung in the air. Farrell was angrier than ever, now that P.J. had both of them waiting, curious for his next words. He swirled the hot water in the teapot, and waited.

P.J. chose his moment with precision. Just as Grace was about to speak, her father held out his arms to her.

'A little birthday present for my lovely daughter.'

He took his hands from behind his back and dangled a set of keys in front of Grace's eyes.

'What is it?'

Farrell's chest hurt. He didn't want her to have any of P.J.'s gifts. He knew what they were. A long-term investment in her loyalty. A gift to his daughter in return for her self.

'Come with me and I'll show you.'

Farrell wanted to smash his fist into the fat, self-satisfied face. When Grace went upstairs to get her handbag, Farrell saw triumph on the face of the enemy. He excused himself and went to get his jacket. He was damned if he'd offer him tea.

In the back of P.J.'s Mercedes, Farrell felt that his whole body was gradually becoming paralysed. Even his feet felt weighted; to move his hands was a huge effort. He felt helpless, impotent. His mind became inert, his thoughts woolly and unformed.

P.J. refused to give anything away. Farrell remained silent; Grace tried to guess what the surprise was. Farrell listened to the banter between them; P.J. was enjoying himself hugely. Farrell couldn't blame Grace for her excitement. She loved surprises. And she was happy to be on such good terms with Anna, happy to be a godmother, happy to be back in the family fold again. She was ready to forgive and forget.

P.J. pulled up in the main street in Blackrock. Farrell spotted the shop at once. His stomach felt sick; there was a taste of tannin in his mouth. He saw that there was white polish on the windows, that the paint-work was jet black. It was exactly what he had been looking for, exactly what he would have chosen. It was perfect. Opposite the

Blackrock Market, tucked in between antique shops, a perfect location for shoppers with money to spare. Grace turned around to her father, her face bright with excitement, and she clutched at his arm wordlessly.

P.J. handed her the keys.

'It's yours. The lease is paid for a year. Happy birthday.'

He leaned over and kissed his daughter on the cheek. Grace finally exploded into speech.

'Oh, Farrell, look! It's perfect!'

Farrell's vision clouded as she hugged her father, her voice eager, full of love.

'It's wonderful! How did you know? It's just what I had in mind! Thank you!'

Farrell said what was expected, forced his legs to take him out of the car and across the road. It *was* perfect. It was just what he had hoped for. It couldn't have been better. If P.J. hadn't found it.

His words felt like stones in his mouth. He had to try, to pretend to be pleased. It wasn't her fault. He insisted on a celebration drink after they had examined the shop, inside and out, from all angles. He knew he could make it right for her, but there was no joy in that knowledge. He had been outmanoeuvred.

In the pub, he went into the Gents and leaned his sweating forehead against the white tiles. He ran cold water across his wrists, hoping to still the frantic beating of his heart. He washed his face. Back at the table, he responded to Grace's enthusiasm, wondering how she could have forgotten P.J.'s philosophy of giving. Perhaps she thought that all that was behind her now. Farrell knew better.

On Monday morning, he went back to Blackrock to visit the estate agents to smash somebody's face to a pulp.

'There must be some mistake,' the man said.

He was pale, feeling the quiet burn of Farrell's anger.

'Mr Browne was here on Friday. He gave me to understand that he was acting on your behalf.'

Farrell's ears began to buzz. Instantly, he realised how stupid he must look.

'The previous client pulled out at the last minute, Mr Farrell. Up until Thursday night, there was nothing available. We acted in good faith; everything was completed quickly and without fuss, as you requested.'

The estate agent, plainly unnerved by what he must have seen in Farrell's face, took refuge in formality, hiding his fear behind stilted language.

'Everything has been drawn up in the name of Grace Farrell. I understood that this was the name of your party, sir.'

Farrell knew that he had to control himself. He could imagine P.J., laughing at him still.

It wasn't this man's fault. He, Farrell, had wanted all this to be kept a secret. Even if the man had wanted to check with him, he couldn't have. He was following orders; Farrell's orders.

It was nobody's fault except his own.

Coldly, politely, Farrell took his leave. He went for a long walk along the sea-front. He walked fast, pushing the rage and humiliation away, breathing in the salt sea air.

Farrell knew that he had never been less than three moves *behind*. The enemy had won. And anyway, what could he have said to Grace? This was *my* idea; your father stole *my* idea? This was *my* surprise for you? How could he say that? She would despise him, and rightly so. He hadn't been clever enough. He had to swallow his pride, his pure hatred, as the enemy made Grace a gift of her very first shop. Even her rent was paid up for a year, to help her on her way. There was nothing left for him. P.J. had taken it all, made it all his. He'd even made a joke about how far she had travelled from her stall in the Blackrock Market. Striding along the sea-front, Farrell was blinded by the memory of P.J. hugging his daughter as he handed her the keys. All the past is forgiven, he said with that hug. You are mine again now. Over her shoulder, he had looked straight at Farrell, small eyes gleaming, mocking him.

Once more, Farrell had known the bitter taste of defeat. Checkmate.

He had never once thought of there being a spy in the camp, innocent though she was. He couldn't be angry with Anna. P.J. was only too capable of making the most of an innocent remark, of grasping what was in it for him. It wasn't her fault. He, Farrell, shouldn't have told her about his search. There was nothing more to be said. He was to blame, simply, totally.

Three moves ahead, my arse.

They delivered the gift, without fuss, the night before Eleanor's christening. Peter opened the door to them, putting his finger to his lips for silence. Anna suddenly appeared in the hall behind him.

'Oh, Peter! Don't be so silly! Voices won't waken her!'

She leaned past her husband to catch Grace's hand.

'Come on in, both of you.'

She kissed each of them, leading them into the sitting-room.

'Farrell, what would you like to drink?'

Peter followed them, a glass in his hand. Farrell felt a flash of irritation. Every time he had seen the man in the past six weeks he'd had a glass in his hand. He talked too much, couldn't hold his drink. Farrell thought him stupid; recently, he'd begun to feel contempt for him. So this was the type that P.J. had wanted for his youngest daughter. It helped Farrell to think like that tonight. He needed to be ready for tomorrow.

'Beer, please, Anna,' he said, smiling at her.

Grace had gone straight over to the Moses basket.

'She's got huge! She's grown so much in the last week!'

Anna went to Grace's side and rested her arm on her sister's shoulder. Farrell liked it that she was so gentle with her. Together, the two women leaned over the sleeping baby.

'Cheers, Farrell.'

He turned to see that Peter had refilled his own glass. He raised it to Farrell's in a toast, his face mock-solemn.

'Here's to your first.'

The words were slurred.

For a moment, Farrell didn't know what he meant. First drink? Then he saw Grace's shoulders stiffen. She had been doing so well. Farrell wanted to smash his fist into the man's stupid, grinning mouth. He wanted to feel the solid contact of knuckle on teeth.

But it was Grace who answered him. She walked away from the Moses basket, smiling as she reached her brother-in-law's side.

'Poor Peter!' she said softly, mockingly. 'You look whacked. I think you're having a lot of trouble keeping up with two women!'

The insult registered at once. Farrell didn't like the angry expression that crossed Peter's face. But he enjoyed seeing it there. He felt proud of Grace.

At that moment, the telephone rang and Eleanor woke. Peter disappeared into the kitchen and Anna followed. Grace lifted the baby, snuggling her against her shoulder, patting her back gently.

Farrell seized his moment.

'You stay here; I'll get the cot.'

Grace smiled at him over the baby's head. The yellow Babygro stood out vividly against her dark hair.

He needed to get outside. The emotions were almost too strong to handle. How was he going to get through the christening tomorrow? Peter, James, P.J. All of them so full of shit. And the hurt for Grace, deep inside Farrell's chest, that after eleven months, nothing.

Anna had given her hope. She was still patient and serene, waiting for it to happen. But Farrell was worried. Watching her with Eleanor, a dread had begun to fester. At times, he had had sudden flashes of insight, a sixth sense, warning him that this was not for her. He was no longer able to *imagine* Grace with his baby in her arms. The picture wouldn't come together. Its absence frightened him.

Eleanor was put lying in her new cot as soon as everyone came back from the church. Grace was glowing. Farrell had watched her face throughout the ceremony. He knew exactly what she was thinking. She stood beside Derek, the godfather, Peter's brother. She looked beautiful, and Farrell felt a stab of sadness as he watched her. Derek was elegantly dressed, sun-tanned, handsome. They made an attractive couple. Farrell felt awkward and jealous beside them, as though he was back in his old blue overalls again.

At the house afterwards, Anna was kind. She introduced him to dozens of people, made his gift a conversation piece. But Farrell was tongue-tied. He didn't fit in. These people made him uncomfortable. P.J. made him uncomfortable. He almost needed to put his hands in his pockets, out of his way. He would never forgive P.J. for Blackrock. He wanted to scoop Grace up and run off home.

Suddenly, she was there beside him. She slipped her hand through his arm.

'You're miles away. Isn't it a lovely day?'

He smiled down at her.

'Absolutely. And you look really beautiful,' he said softly.

Grace reached up and touched his face. She smiled back at him.

'We're going to serve the food now. Will you come and help pour the wine?'

Farrell went with her gratefully to the kitchen. P.J. was in the middle of telling a loud and jovial story against himself. Nevertheless, he was still managing to boast, to cast himself in the light of a clever, tolerant businessman. His audience was enthralled. They surrounded him while he stood, backside to the fireplace, rocking gently on his heels. He puffed occasionally on a massive cigar, blowing smoke straight upwards, contemplating the ceiling. Occasionally, his eyes caught Farrell's. They were amused, mocking.

Farrell had a swift, vivid image of slitting the man's throat as he spoke. He saw the blood surge downwards, soaking the front of his bright, white shirt. But more than anything, he saw the surprise on P.J.'s face as he gurgled, trying to form sentences, unwilling to let his audience go.

Farrell felt the satisfaction of having had the last word.

'Mind, Farrell, that's enough!'

Grace's voice brought him back to reality.

'Sorry,' he mumbled. 'I wasn't paying attention.'

She came closer.

'Are you all right?'

He nodded, smiled, cursing himself, his clumsiness.

'I'm fine, love. I just got distracted, that's all. Wasn't Eleanor perfect at the ceremony?'

Farrell's forehead felt damp. He had to get a grip.

Grace nodded eagerly.

'Yes, she's such a sweetheart. And talk about the proud grandparents! She's going to be spoiled rotten.'

Farrell's moment of panic passed. He'd be able to get through the rest of this nightmare, as long as nobody else nudged and winked about it being his turn next. Farrell filled and refilled glasses, avoiding P.J.'s eyes. He made polite conversation, ate a small salad and watched the clock until it was time to go home.

Farrell pulls out both leaves of the mahogany gate-legged table. A wedding-present from P.J. and Maura, Farrell has always hated it. He has always known the message it was meant to convey. A deliberate insult to a craftsman, who wanted to make his own. See, it says, I can buy what I want. I don't need to make. I don't need to wait.

Farrell had to accept it, as he had to accept many things. To make his own table after that would have seemed an act of unspeakable churlishness. An act to give rise to the question he has imagined P.J. asking so many times: What else would you expect? And he has imagined Maura's reply. She would sit there, agreeing with everything he said, nodding her head like a little mandarin at her husband's wisdom.

It is particularly pleasing that this is the table he is setting tonight. They have invaded his home, his love: the damask linen tablecloth is theirs, the Waterford crystal is theirs, the silver candlesticks are theirs. All gifts; all investments with a properly calculated rate of return.

Farrell sets the table the way Grace likes it. He polishes the elegant bone-handled cutlery, the glasses, the silver napkin rings. White plates with gold rims; dark green napkins. Her favourite colour.

Farrell melts some wax into the cups of the candlesticks and carefully positions the beeswax candles which Grace likes so much. They are bendy, irregular shapes, but she loves their imperfections.

He has a moment of intense regret that they will not be lit. Beeswax, after all, is fitting.

Finally, Farrell digs deep into the mahogany sideboard which he made to match P.J.'s table. It is one of the few articulate responses he'd ever managed. He pulls out a small parcel wrapped in stiff silver paper, finished off with a green satin bow.

He places it carefully where Grace usually sits. He adjusts the lighting and switches on the tuner, pre-set to her favourite classical station.

He keeps the volume low. No need to disturb anyone.

Then he closes the door and turns his attention to the answering-machine.

Chapter Five

Grace pushed her way along Talbot Street, through the surging crowds of Christmas shoppers. The rain was fine, freezing. It reminded her of her first Christmas with Farrell, lugging the huge tree up the steps to the flat. She remembered how happy she'd felt. And the next Christmas, in their own home. It was all a distant memory. This would be their fifth Christmas together. They were about to begin their fourth year trying. And still no baby.

Today, she had an important list to get through. Eleanor, the twins Fiona and Claire, and Ruth's two children, James and baby Zoe. Grace liked to put a lot of thought into her Christmas presents. This year, she was finding it difficult.

For the last couple of months, ever since their third wedding anniversary, Grace had begun to feel herself slipping. From time to time, she would hear someone speak to her, murmuring cruel things behind her back. She would swing around, startled, only to find that there was nobody there. She would try to calm herself. She knew that these sly voices were not real. She understood that it was her mind playing tricks. She accepted, on one level, that these voices, outside her head, were her own thoughts; distress made them *seem* real. The doctors had taught her all of that, a long time ago. She *knew* all of that. But still. It felt real every time it happened.

Recently, she had begun to take it out on Farrell, too. The row last night had been the worst in a long time.

He was concerned, worried about her. With reason. She knew that they were drifting apart.

When she'd come home yesterday evening from the shop, he'd had a Chinese meal all ready for her. The table was set in the sitting-room, her favourite wine was already open, the beeswax candles lit. But Grace had not felt hungry. She remembered again how Farrell's face had fallen.

His disappointment had made her angry.

'Grace, please have something,' he'd said, pleading. 'You've got so thin.'

'Just leave me *alone!*'

She had got thin. It was true. Just like before. She could feel her *self* slipping away from her. She knew that day by day, this grief was making her diminish. She could see it herself in the mirror each morning. But at least her reflection had not disappeared. Not yet.

The sight of his unhappy eyes had angered her even more. She'd wanted to hurt, to spread it around.

'How can I eat, how can I do anything! You can do nothing to make this better! You can't change it that I'm *barren!*'

His shocked face had given her satisfaction. Let him feel it, too.

'Grace, please . . .'

As suddenly as her anger had ignited, it burned itself out. Farrell was holding out his arms to her. She was shocked at how vicious she had felt, towards him, towards everything.

She had started to cry then, pressing her face into his chest. His warmth, the solid strength of his arms, began to make her feel grounded again.

'Oh, Farrell,' she had whispered. 'What am I being punished for?'

She had felt him stiffen. For the first time, she saw that this was hurting him, too; not just because she was suffering, but some deep, dark pain of his own.

She had reached up to touch his face.

'I'm sorry. I just don't know what to do.'

She had clung to him then and they had comforted each other. For the rest of the night they had drawn close, each being gentle with the other. But Grace could see that she had disturbed something in Farrell. He kept reassuring her that he was fine, but she was not convinced. Now, this morning, she knew that something had to give, something had to change. They could not go on like this.

Grace stopped at the lights and waited for the pedestrian signal. All around her were women with buggies. To her right and left, behind her, in front of her. She began to feel that she would suffocate.

Those women who were not pushing prams and buggies were pregnant, holding their huge bellies out in front of them, resting one hand comfortingly on the baby inside them. Their own baby. For a few minutes, Grace found it difficult to move. Right beside her, a very young girl was pushing a new baby in a brand-new pram. She couldn't have been more than sixteen. Her dyed blonde hair was a mass of tight, permed curls. She was smoking.

Grace was ashamed of her thoughts as she took in the girl's coarse features, the nicotine-stained fingers, the cheap tracksuit. *That baby would be better off with me.* She struggled to be fair. Who was she to judge? The baby was snug, well dressed, from what Grace could see, well cared for. But how long before this child got tired of her own child? For now, this baby was no more than a little live doll. It fed and cried, yes, and needed things done to it all the time; it gave itself up totally to its mother's loving control. And when it started to answer back, to be independent, to need more, more than a sixteen-year-old could give, then what?

Farrell kept telling her to stop torturing herself; he kept telling her how much he loved her, needed her. But it wasn't *enough*. Every month another little bit of her died. Soon, there would be none of her left.

She was afraid of that other time happening again. As Grace crossed O'Connell Street and made her way towards Henry Street, she was assaulted by a memory of doctors, hospital night-dresses and locked wards opening to admit her.

And now she had to go and buy Christmas presents for other women's children.

Anna, then Ruth. Ruth again; and then, immediately – within a month – Anna's twins. Farrell felt that the whole world was populated by babies. He wanted to take Grace away to some planet where only adults lived. He couldn't bear to see her unhappiness, month after month, year after year. Every time she bled, it was like a death in the house.

Every month for almost three years now she had hoped, convinced herself that this was it, this time it would happen. The doctors had assured her that they could find nothing wrong. And every month she wept, bitterly, when there was to be no baby. More and more, she cried on her own, coming downstairs with red eyes, a wild, distracted look on her face. She often wouldn't let Farrell touch her. Her sense of failure wrapped her in a black cloud of mourning and Farrell couldn't reach her. In her silence, he felt his old clumsiness return. He was awkward again in her presence, scrabbling around for the right words, searching for comfort. There was no room for him any more. She filled everywhere with her loss; she was sur-rounded by it.

Making love to her was like handling precious china. He imagined that she would shatter, break apart at his touch. She often wasn't present in her own body; only her anxiety moved under him. Her touch was mechanical; her hands plucked at him restlessly, frozenly.

Farrell's guilt grew huge. He knew this punishment was meant for him, not her. He had to protect her from it. It was eating her away.

Something had to give. She still got up in the mornings, went to her shop, made her dolls, smiled at her customers. But she was no longer Grace. Seeing her surrounded by cradles, Farrell was terrified. Sometimes, when he looked at her, she seemed much smaller, shrunken. It was as though she was becoming the child she would never have.

So much of her unhappiness came from Ruth and Anna's arrogant ease at having babies. Anna in particular; the earth-mother. Farrell sometimes hated her. It was unfair, he knew. She was never smug, but in her all-consuming motherhood, she made it look so *easy*. He didn't want to be angry at her. He knew it wasn't her fault. He needed someone to blame, someone else besides himself.

It had always angered Farrell that Grace seemed drawn to those who could hurt her most. She spent hours and hours with her nieces and nephew, growing all the time, Farrell knew, in her conviction that she was unwomanly, a failure at motherhood. Oh, she put a brave face on it, making their toys, designing their dolls, being the perfect auntie and godmother.

But Farrell knew. He was the one to see her desolation, her tears, her terror at being *barren*. He had been shocked the first time she had thrown the word at him. It was such a grim, unforgiving word. A word of biblical proportions.

Last night, when she'd begged him to tell her what was God punishing her for, Farrell knew he had to take action. He'd lain awake until the early hours, listening until Grace's breathing settled into the rhythmic patterns of oblivion. It had taken her a long time to fall asleep; her

157

restlessness had made his heart ache. He knew where all this pressure was leading. He couldn't let that happen to her; he had promised never to let that happen to her again. He shared her memories of locked wards and cruel voices as though they were his own.

This morning, she'd been sad, but composed. She'd hugged him silently for a long time before she got up. She was going to finish her Christmas shopping.

'Do you want me to go with you?'

'No. You go on into the shop until Anna gets in. At this stage, it's only people collecting orders, so you shouldn't be too busy. I need the day to myself.'

Farrell's chest tightened every time she said something like that. But today, he needed time, too.

Once she had left, he phoned Anna.

'Anna? Farrell here. Grace is taking today off to go shopping. I'll look after things. You have the day off yourself . . . yes, yes, I'm sure. No problem. Thanks anyway.'

He made his way at once to Blackrock, his mind speeding, racing ahead. He had it all planned. It was so simple, it had to work.

He spent the first two hours making telephone calls. He wrote down the substance of each call beside the number dialled. By eleven thirty, he had what he needed, enough to make a decision.

He locked up the shop just before five. There were only a few dolls left to be collected the following morning. The Christmas rush was almost over. Farrell took the train into town and got off at Tara Street. He pushed his way towards Henry Street, battling against the streaming shoppers now leaving the city centre.

The ILAC library was warm, peaceful. Sitting on one of the hard chairs, he was reminded of all the other times he had sought refuge in the city's libraries, on all those Saturdays before Grace.

Now, he had a bigger purpose. Farrell made his way to the medical textbooks, selected three of the fattest he could find, and consulted the index. He put two back, and selected two more. He looked around at the tables. There was plenty of room. Christmas was obviously not a time for libraries.

He began reading, stopping every now and again to make notes. At half past six, he broke off, and went to phone Grace. He told her he'd be late, that he'd bring dinner home with him. She sounded tired. It didn't matter. Soon, all of this would be over.

As though energised by her voice, Farrell returned to his table and continued his search. By eight o'clock, he had found his answer. This would be the perfect solution, the best, the most important Christmas present he could ever give her. From the list he had made that morning, he chose a name. In his pocket diary, where he wrote reminders to himself, measurements, messages for Grace, he wrote a man's name and telephone number. He stopped for a moment, trying to decide on the best time. He wrote it in, underlining it heavily. Thursday, 12th December at four thirty. Suite forty-one, Blackrock Clinic.

He walked home, enjoying the damp, freezing air. He walked with a lighter step than he had in some time. He was back in control now; he had all the elements of the perfect plan. All that remained was to put the pieces together.

Then, he could make her happy.

The following evening, when he went out to get a video and a bottle of wine, he left his diary open, casually, beside the phone.

Later, as they were going past the telephone table on their way to bed, he'd snapped the diary shut and put it into the back pocket of his jeans, as though he had just suddenly remembered something.

Grace said nothing. He hadn't expected her to. It was an unremarkable act. But he knew she would have noticed, would remember when he referred to it again, later.

He was crafting the lie with precision, neatness. Like a well-constructed dovetail joint, it fitted together smoothly. There would be no ragged edges.

It was difficult, putting in the time until Thursday came. They were due to go out that night and buy their Christmas tree. He was crowded by memories that evening. Their first Christmas, their first tree, then the first Christmas they were married. He had the strange sensation now that he could grope beyond those memories. He foresaw happier times. He was going to make it right, once and for all.

From the corner across the road, hidden in the shadows, he watched and waited until Grace got home from the shop. He knew she would be surprised that he was not there before her. Surprised, and then worried.

He went to the pub down the road and drank two whiskeys slowly, steadily. He waited until he judged the moment right. Then he walked home and quietly let himself in.

She was out into the hall instantly.

'Farrell! Where were you! I was beginning to get worried!'

It wasn't his imagination. She was much smaller, frailer.

Please God, let me be in time.

'Sorry, love, I got delayed.'

Deliberately, Farrell kissed her briefly, and moved away from her, straight into the kitchen.

'Have you started dinner?'

'No. I'm not long in, myself. Are you all right?'

Farrell kept his back to her. He sensed, tasted her rising panic. It was working. He was playing his part well.

'Fine, fine. How was your day?'

He busied himself at the sink, forcing himself not to look at her.

She was suddenly at his elbow.

'Farrell, what's wrong? You're scaring me. What's the matter?'

It was the first time in a long time that she had shown any concern for him. All of her being had focused on herself, her needs, her baby.

Her tenderness brought tears to his eyes. Perfect.

He'd never meant to lie to her. It was the only time he'd ever lied to her, ever. He turned to face her.

'I can't bear seeing you so unhappy, Grace. It has broken my heart to see you so disappointed, month after month. I really wanted us to have a baby, but it's not going to happen.'

His tears were real. He almost believed in what he was going to tell her.

'I've been to see a specialist. I got the test results today. It's my fault we can't have babies, not yours.'

Grace's eyes were huge, purple.

'And there isn't any hope. There's nothing they can do. The specialist has had a second opinion, an expert from London. He agrees. I'm so sorry, Grace, I've failed you.'

And Farrell began to cry. He *was* sorry. For her, for himself, for the babies they would never have. For all the misery they had suffered for three long years.

And for Martina. Forgive me, Martina.

'Oh, Farrell,' Grace's voice was nothing but a whisper.

She held him and rocked him and told him how she loved him. Farrell heard the strength return to her voice;

he began to feel in his arms again the Grace he loved. She was all he wanted.

She seemed to grow again before his eyes then, nurtured by the freedom he had given her for not being the one to blame.

He allowed her to comfort him. He sat, heavily, at the kitchen table. She covered his face with little butterfly kisses, sliding onto his knee. She twined her arms around his neck. Now she thought only of him. Farrell wanted her to be like this for ever.

'We can be happy again, Farrell. We'll work it out, I promise you. I love you so much.'

He felt her presence had returned. Her body was real, vital flesh and blood.

'Let's go to bed,' she whispered. 'I want to hold you.'

He raised his face to hers.

He was so consumed by her that the lie was already forgotten. This was their new beginning. Let her family think him half a man. They thought that already. He didn't care. Now he was going to forget this. This lie would become transformed, would become part of their new reality, their new happiness. Holding her, having her comfort him, Farrell knew that he had got there just in time.

Farrell woke up early the next morning, feeling that something had changed, had ceased to be familiar. He lay quietly for a moment, watching the digits on his bedside clock shudder and change. He replayed the previous evening, every detail carved and solid in his memory. He had forgotten nothing. He relived in his imagination the moment when Grace had held him close after he'd told her he was the one to blame. He could still feel her, still taste her return to him.

In his memory, the lie no longer existed. Awake last night long after Grace slept, Farrell had felt unease at what he had done. He had felt suddenly cold at the thought of her finding him out. But how could she? He had covered his tracks well. She trusted him, would never check up on him. If, by some miracle, she became pregnant, they would simply accept that all the experts had been wrong.

Grace herself had told him so many stories of people who had given up hope, and had suddenly, miraculously, become parents against all the odds. Stories about desperate couples adopting children, and giving birth to their own nine months later. If it happened to them, they wouldn't be the first. But at least, her obsession, her desperation had been laid to rest. Now she would be able to feel something other than anguish, something else besides the gnawing guilt at having let him, them, down.

Farrell suddenly realised what it was that was so different. The band across his chest had loosened. He could breathe properly. She had been loving and tender all last night. With a great rush of happiness, Farrell realised that he had won her back. Grace was all his again.

He turned around to face her. She was just waking up, eyelids fluttering. Farrell kissed the little blue veins there, and the furrow between her eyes. She woke up smiling. Sleepily, warmly, she held out her arms to him.

'Come here to me.'

Farrell held her, reminded so much of that day in Francis Street when they were just beginning. She felt it too. He knew she did. He looked down into her deep blue eyes, seeing himself reflected there, seeing her love reflected there.

'It's like being given a second chance, Farrell. Let's begin all over again.'

She stroked his hair back from his forehead.

'In a strange way, it's a relief. I feel as if some awful responsibility has been taken away from both of us.'

She kissed him.

'Nobody's to blame, Farrell, not you, not me. It just is.'

Then she began to cry.

'We'd have been good parents, you and I. It's a shame that we never got the chance.'

Farrell kissed her forehead tenderly. Memories crowded. It was a while before he could trust himself to words.

'We have each other,' he said. 'And it's a lot more than most people have.'

She smiled at him through her tears.

'I know. Now that I know there's no hope, I feel I can cope with it. But it's been so hard. And I knew you wanted a baby so much.'

She was trying not to sob. He could feel her body convulse under him.

He was not going to lie to her again.

'Yes, I did. But I want you more, Grace. And now that I have you back, I'm not going to let anything or anyone take you away from me ever again.'

He brushed the tears from her eyes. He had a sudden sense of being cleansed.

She was smiling up at him again, in the way he remembered so well. She hadn't smiled at him like that in such a long time.

His heart felt sore as he looked at her.

She hugged him hard.

'I'm not going anywhere. I'll always be yours, Farrell. We'll put all of this behind us, and make a fresh start. I love you so much.'

They didn't speak any more after that. All his failures, all his sins washed away.

He had won her back. Farrell's sense of being bereaved was finally passing.

After Christmas was a quiet time for both of them. Farrell stayed close to Grace's side, spending almost every day with her in the shop. He watched her carefully, alert for any signs. But her new-found strength did not desert her, and Farrell was content.

They had hardly closed their front door one evening, late in January, when the phone rang. Instantly, Farrell knew who it was. He had a sudden, overwhelming urge to stop Grace from reaching for the receiver. Her father. It had to be. He'd left them alone for a while, now he was creeping up behind them again. His timing was perfect. It always was. Farrell listened, ready for trouble. He tried to make out what P.J. wanted this time.

Grace was hardly getting a word in edgewise. She was tapping her pencil against the message-pad in front of her. Farrell felt his shoulders begin to grow tense; he was almost holding his breath. He stayed sitting, fighting the instinct to leave the room. He had to stay. She was agitated enough already.

'Sure we're interested, but not until much later in the year—'

Then he guessed it. New premises. That's what they were talking about. He hadn't even known that P.J. knew anything about it. Grace had only mentioned it to him once, about a month ago. She must have discussed it more fully with her father. There was a touch of bitterness around Farrell's mouth as he watched his wife. Just as quickly, it was gone.

'No way! We're not anywhere near the stage of signing a lease!'

She raised her eyes up to heaven and looked over at Farrell.

'I'm sure you're right, but we're not ready.'

Farrell began to feel a deep sense of satisfaction that P.J. was not getting his way. He felt his whole body begin to relax. He liked the way Grace kept saying 'we'.

'No.' Sharply. 'No, P.J., we're not going to see anywhere this evening. Well, I'm afraid you'll just have to cancel it. We're busy.'

Farrell had only ever heard her speak to her father like that once before. Her tone reminded him of the night she'd told P.J. that she was leaving home. She had chosen to be with Farrell then, and she was choosing to be with him now, shutting her father out. He was almost ashamed of how viciously happy he felt.

'Fine. I'll talk to you tomorrow.'

Another long pause.

'I don't know. I'll ring you whenever I get the chance.'

Farrell's whole body glowed as she cut P.J. short, refusing to talk any more. She left the phone off the hook and sat down beside him.

'First thing tomorrow, I'm buying an answering-machine.'

She snuggled up beside him and kissed the bottom of his ear. Farrell wondered what he had ever done to deserve such joy. He built the fire up higher, and they turned the lights off, sitting in the orange glow. For old time's sake, Grace made them hot whiskeys.

Farrell was conscious that night of the passage of time. Another new year, another opportunity for happiness. He had to make it work.

We're sorry we're not able to take your call just now, but Grace and I are celebrating. We look forward to seeing you all on Saturday night at eight.

Farrell tests the recording for tone and clarity. When they ring again, as he knows they will, sometime tonight or tomorrow morning, this will be enough. Anna and Peter, Ruth and James, P.J. and Maura. The whole happy family will gather at his celebration.

He wonders what birthday presents they will bring. *Beware of Greeks bearing gifts.* More jewellery, perhaps, or silks; or soft leather bags, like before.

Farrell decides that one more whiskey won't do any harm. A small one, with plenty of water. Moving towards the kitchen, he suddenly realises: the wine! He's forgotten all about the wine.

He goes upstairs again, to the smallest of the four bedrooms. The alcoves are filled, floor to ceiling, with mahogany lattice-work. The bottle racks they'd designed and built together. Sturdy, solid work. The bottles are arrayed according to Grace's system. Red in one alcove, white in the other. Then by country, finally by year. A hardback notebook lists every good bottle they've ever bought.

Some bottles have been here for the whole five years of their marriage. The ones given by P.J. 'for the first christening'. Farrell wonders will he use those. After all, it is a christening of sorts.

Some good Australian Chardonnay that Grace likes, some 1975 Bordeaux. Three bottles of Taittinger, marking their first wedding anniversary. They'll do the trick.

Farrell makes three careful trips up and down the stairs. Nine bottles in all, including some 1972 port for P.J.

He has already polished the silver ice-buckets. He places them at either end of the table, rearranging the flowers in the centre. He sprays the little posies to keep them fresh. He has always been a good pupil. He has been taught well, by the best.

It can't be made better. Farrell walks back into the kitchen again, and takes Grace's keys from the dresser drawer.

It is time to look after the car.

Chapter Six

It was a perfect week. Amsterdam was warm and bright in the early June sunshine. It was just as it had been for their honeymoon, four years earlier. They walked everywhere for the first few days, along endless, glinting canals. In the evening, they took the trolley-buses to restaurants on the outskirts of the city, returning home at all hours of the morning.

For six months now, Grace's health had been steadily improving. She had recovered her substance. Gradually, the skin on her face had become smooth again; her hair had begun to shine. Her eyes had once more become her own, no longer haunted and watchful. She said she felt like a teenager, wild and carefree, the way she should have felt years ago. Instead, her student days had been filled with nothing but dark shadows.

By midweek, she insisted on hiring bicycles. Everyone used bicycles in Amsterdam; they were the only form of transport that moved freely, without restraint. Cars and delivery vans jammed up the narrow canal-side roads with astonishing regularity. Farrell and Grace were amazed at how patient the drivers were; no honking of horns, no shouting out of windows, no waving of fists. The constant tinkling of bicycle bells delighted both of them. It was a sound which could be heard everywhere in the city as cyclists sped past the lethargic traffic.

They found a little shop near their bed-and-breakfast and Farrell hired two sturdy, old-fashioned bikes for the whole day. He grinned when he saw them.

'Upstairs models,' he said to Grace, the term coming at him out of nowhere, part of a long-forgotten childhood store.

'They're huge!'

At first, Grace wobbled a bit, finding it difficult to keep her balance on the old cobblestones. Farrell held on to the saddle while she tried to get moving.

'If you stopped laughing long enough, you'd do it, you know,' Farrell observed as Grace got yet another fit of the giggles.

'I know, I know. I just feel like a little kid again.'

Finally, she got going and sped away from Farrell, waving and laughing as she went. It didn't take him long to catch up with her. They spent that day cycling side by side, stopping off now and then for coffee. By late afternoon, when they stopped for lunch, their faces were glowing.

She looked so young again, in her shorts and T-shirt, freckles sprinkling all over her nose and cheeks.

'That was brilliant, Farrell! It's years since I've cycled!'

She looked directly at him, waiting until she had his full attention.

'P.J. never let me. He thought it was too dangerous for me.'

Outside the café, sitting at a little table in the summer-lovely sunshine, Farrell knew that this was a moment he would remember for the rest of his life.

They stayed in the same, old-fashioned bed-and-breakfast that they'd used for their honeymoon. Their room was right at the top of the tall, narrow seventeenth-century building, up almost vertical stairways which left them gasping. Returning after their evenings on the town, giddy with wine, they half-climbed, half-pulled themselves upwards by the rope at the side of the stairwell, always starting to giggle at the same spot when the effort began to get too much. Then they'd fall, breathless, onto the huge, overstuffed horsehair mattress which Grace insisted must be as old as the house.

All week long Farrell watched joyfully as Grace's energy increased. She was animated, loving, serene. She was full of life; all the old brittleness was now gone.

On their last day, they sipped beer inside a tiny pub with a spiral staircase. The late evening had turned suddenly chilly, and there was a roaring fire.

They sat beside it, holding hands, remembering all the old sadnesses and laying them finally to rest. Grace lit a cigarette. Farrell felt his breath catch. She looked at him.

'Yes, I'm remembering the night we said we wanted a baby. It's OK, Farrell. I'm strong again.' She paused. 'I don't want to open up old wounds, but I have to say this. I know how you feel about adoption. I've always known that it wasn't an option for us.'

He was silent for a long time. He could feel the question in her tone.

'I know you feel that it's like taking other people's children, and you could never accept that.'

He looked up at her.

'It's not that I haven't thought about it, but I couldn't do it, Grace. I just couldn't. I'm sorry.'

'I know. That's why I would never ask you. I just wanted it to be out in the open, clear between us, once and for all.'

He nodded.

'It's OK, Farrell; it really is all over.'

He held her hand more tightly. He was glad it had been said. Now he could tell her what he'd been thinking about. No more looking back; it was time to move forward. The need to leave the past behind was now urgent, keeping him awake at night.

'I've made a decision this week. I want to work full-time with you once we get back. I'll do the odd short contract for Christy; I wouldn't want to let him down. But I won't do any more long-term stuff.'

He paused. He wanted to finish with all that, too. He wanted to spend every moment close to her, by her side.

'I'd like us to spend more time together. I'll concentrate on developing the new lines in wooden toys. I've lots of ideas to show you when we get back. And,' here he paused for emphasis, 'I'd like us to search for new premises together, on our own.'

He almost held his breath. Grace smiled at him and touched his face.

'That's absolutely what we will do. I'm so happy that things have worked out for us.'

Farrell kissed her.

When they stood up to go, the owner of the pub was smiling at them.

'You pay nothing. My present to happy couple for their wedding.'

Grace laughed in delight. Farrell put his arm around her shoulders. He shook the man's outstretched hand.

'You're very kind. But we've been married for almost four years.'

And Farrell held up one hand, fingers splayed.

'We came here on our honeymoon and we always wanted to come back. Amsterdam is a great city.'

'More better, more better! Happy four years!' and he waved them away, nodding his head and smiling broadly.

'Thank you,' said Grace warmly.

They waved and smiled back at the little, balding man standing at the door of the pub, swathed in a massive black apron.

'Happy four years,' said Grace, hugging him as they walked. 'Happy next forty-four.'

When they came back from Amsterdam, there were half a dozen irate messages on the answering-machine. They were all for Grace, urging her to contact her father or she would miss out on the property of a lifetime. She replayed all the messages so Farrell could hear them. They made him angry. P.J.'s voice was all *ownership*, all unquestioning authority.

Almost before they had finished unpacking, Grace phoned her father.

'I'm going to get this over with, right now.'

The set of her mouth was tight, angry.

She held Farrell's hand; he received and understood the unspoken message. She had chosen him again. P.J. would have to play second fiddle; Farrell knew he would not like the tune.

'P.J.? Grace.'

She was silent for a few moments, holding the receiver away from her ear.

'I told you we hadn't made any definite decision. We want to look a lot further afield than Dun Laoghaire.'

Long silence again.

'Well, you shouldn't have done that. Our needs are different now. We may need extra space for a workshop. Farrell's coming in with me full-time.'

Farrell watched as Grace's whole face began to grow angry. Her hands, now occupied lighting a cigarette, were trembling. She cradled the phone on her shoulder.

Farrell had enjoyed imagining P.J.'s defeat until that moment. Now, enough was enough. He would not let him upset her.

He made signs to Grace to hang up.

'I'd rather you left it to us. *No*. We're only just off the plane, for God's sake!'

Grace was now exasperated.

'I said leave it! We'll take care of it when we're ready. Yes, yes, I'm sure you do. Goodnight.'

She slammed down the receiver.

'God – he's getting more arrogant by the day! *He's* spent the last few weeks looking. *He's* found the perfect spot. *He* knows best; I should listen to *him*. You heard what I said?'

She paced up and down the room, tapping the ash off her cigarette angrily, dragging her other hand through her hair.

Farrell nodded. He found it difficult to speak. Staying silent, he was able to appear calm. Inside, there was a great well of bitterness that her father still had the power to upset her so deeply. He had to be careful of what he said to Grace. He knew that the pull from home was like gravity. Once Grace moved out of P.J.'s world, he created an irresistible force to bring her home again. Maybe by sending a sister, or making her a gift of something extravagant, or by subtly manipulating the strings of guilt which still tied Grace to her old home.

When Grace was strong, Farrell felt that God was on his side. But he had to be watchful. When she was vulnerable, he felt again the terrible fear of losing her for ever. He had to keep her busy, distracted from all potential unhappiness. There was nothing else in life which mattered.

And so, he did not criticise P.J. Instead, just after she'd hung up, cutting her father short, Farrell had taken down their maps off the shelf in the sitting-room and became immediately busy. Now he called her over, back to his side again.

'Come here, Grace, have a look at this.'

He drew a circle to represent an hour's journey from home, extending from north County Dublin to south Wicklow. He made a list of towns, targeting all potential locations for their new shop. Gradually, he drew Grace into the web. He had to help her forget, to wipe her father's anger from her memory.

Intrigued, she sat down beside him.

'We don't want to spend hours travelling every day. Everywhere in this radius is easily accessible.'

He pointed to the pencilled circle on the map spread out in front of him. He had another idea, too, one that he was not going to tell Grace about, not yet. If they could combine new premises and a little cottage in the country, he could move her even further out of P.J.'s orbit. It gave him a great surge of joy to imagine making that a reality.

They spent the rest of the evening making notes of estate agents, property advisors, surveyors – anyone who could help them make an informed choice. He was ready to agree to anything, anywhere, as long as Grace was happy.

For the rest of that summer, P.J. was silent. Farrell and Grace decided to take the month of July off work, to carry out their search together. Anna would run the shop in Blackrock, sharing the opening hours with Ruth. Farrell hadn't been so sure at first that that was such a good idea; but he knew it was wiser to say nothing. He did not want Grace to feel his anxiety. He would have closed the shop completely for July, but Grace still wanted to keep a presence there.

'Anna will do a good job. I've left stuff ready for her. Ruth can do the administrative side.'

Farrell stayed silent. Grace looked at him.

'I'd be afraid to close down completely – I don't want to lose my customers again, ever.'

That first week, they travelled north County Dublin, starting with Howth, working their way through Portmarnock, Malahide, Skerries, Rush, even as far as Balbriggan.

They talked to everyone – pub owners, shopkeepers, tourist information officers. They looked at all the available premises, even the most unlikely ones. Farrell was glad to see her so absorbed. After the first week, they had almost reached a decision. P.J. still did not call, Grace did not phone him. Farrell never mentioned his name.

'I think it has to be somewhere in Wicklow,' said Grace. 'Somewhere on the way from Rosslare, to catch the tourist traffic. This is too far off the beaten track for the main holiday trade.'

She looked up at him from under the broad brim of her hat. Freckles were already darkening across her nose. The heat was intense.

Farrell nodded agreement.

'I've been thinking the same thing. We'll have another look at the map tonight.'

He propped himself up on one elbow, shading his eyes from the glare of the sun. He felt relaxed, content. He looked around him, lazily.

The beach at Skerries was filling up with small knots of people. Children were running from the waves, squealing as the cold water clutched at their ankles. A father hoisted his son onto his shoulders, running into the sea and back out again, playing chasing with the waves. The little boy shrieked with delight, both hands holding on tight, wrapped around his father's head. When he'd had enough, the child slid down into his father's arms, nestling against his chest. Farrell saw the man kiss the top of the boy's head and then ruffle his hair. Struggling back down to the sand, the child grasped his father's hand and pulled him over to where they had been making a fortress out of sand. They both hunkered down, intent on their building.

Farrell could not draw his gaze away. His eyes locked on the intimate scene in front of him. His head began to feel strangely light, voices came to him from the water's edge as though from a great distance. From out of nowhere that he could name, a sudden half-thought, half-memory stunned him with its violence.

A sunny day, a beach somewhere, cold water. He could hear a child screaming. Himself. Farrell's head began to pound as something pushed its way to the front of his mind.

'Farrell! Are you OK?'

Grace was looking at him in concern. She saw the same glazed look he had had the day she'd found him standing, rigid, by the Christmas tree.

'I'm fine. Just a bit queasy. I think I'll take a walk.'

He stood up unsteadily, fighting off the crowding, panicking sensation that had a grip of his throat.

'It must be the heat,' she said.

He barely nodded in reply. Grace let him go.

He stumbled down the beach, struggling to see beyond the black lights which were shifting back and forth before his eyes. His whole body began to slow, to grow cold; he had no strength to fight the dark, suffocating memory which gripped him, tightening like a vice around his heart.

He sat down weakly, and hugged his knees towards him, resting his damp, sweating forehead on them. Images of the O'Gormans' shed roof superimposed themselves on the blue summer's day.

Then, suddenly, he had the strangest taste in his mouth. Banana and jam sandwiches; salt water. He felt a strong, fat hand pushing on the back of his neck while his nose, mouth and ears filled with water. The salt stung as he opened his eyes; grainy, blurry pictures swam before him. Fighting for breath, his head was pulled roughly upwards, his hair hurting.

'You'll do what you're told, when you're told!'

The weight inside Farrell's chest suddenly seemed to gather strength, pushing its way upwards until he gasped, helpless in its grip. His eyes watered, his vision grew greyer and dimmer as the noise inside his head changed to a shrill buzzing. His chest heaving, Farrell fought for even one clean breath. Instead, his whole body went into violent spasm and he lunged forward, vomiting, gasping, his arms flailing in an effort to right himself.

Suddenly, his mother's gentle hand was on his arm.

Confused, Farrell looked up. Of course it wasn't her.

'Farrell?'

His face was grey, his lips bloodless.

'Come on, I'm taking you home.'

Grace's face was anxious, shadowed by the brim of her hat.

His heart was still thumping painfully. He wiped his mouth with the tissues she handed him. He tried to focus on where he was, who he was. Trembling, he kicked sand over where he'd been sick. It took him some time to regain control. Out at the edge of his vision, he was aware that Grace was looking at him, strangely.

He began, deliberately, to pull the pieces of himself back together again. He was Farrell, he told himself, a grown man. His father and mother were dead. It was summer, 1996. He was on a beach with his wife. Gradually, the black dots disappeared from in front of his eyes. The thumping in his chest and head began to subside. The beach regained its normal shape. Was it over?

Grace had slipped her arm through his and was walking him towards the car.

'You look really pale. Do you feel any better?'

He nodded.

'A bit.'

He couldn't tell her that he was terrified. He had never before felt so completely enmeshed in his own past. He had been transported there before, yes, by shadows, ghosts, sudden flashes of memory. All that, fleetingly, between sleep and waking. But nothing like today.

He was silent all the way home. He closed his eyes, and Grace did not disturb him.

He began to remember the day more clearly now. A steady pulse-beat was growing behind his temples. He could feel himself begin to sweat again. Jesus, would this ever go away. He suddenly saw himself, etched clear and sharp, like a picture on glass.

A tall, gangly kid in a white T-shirt and a pair of shorts that had seen better days. What age had he been – eight, nine? It didn't matter. Farrell stopped wondering; he allowed the rest of the memory to flow in the swirling darkness behind his closed eyes. The images were razor-sharp, almost violent in their clarity.

They had taken the bus to Dollymount Strand, one summer Saturday. His mother and father, Eoin and himself. He couldn't remember whether his mother had been pushing the pram or the go-car. It wasn't important and if Jody and Patrick had been there, they were no part of his memory of that day.

His father had been in jovial mood; he was carrying a string bag with a flask of tea and a large grease-proof parcel of banana and jam sandwiches. His mother had carried a bottle of red lemonade and some packets of Perri plain crisps; their favourite. They loved the tiny little pillows of salt they gave you inside the bag, so you could sprinkle as much as you wanted for yourself. Of course, they always finished them, greedily licking the salty paper afterwards, Eoin's eyes blue-glinting with mischief.

He remembered them all walking across the wooden bridge. His father had stopped to talk to two men who were fishing. The tide was in full. Eoin and himself were dying for a swim.

They'd run to the sand dunes, pulling their togs from

the string bag. They took turns changing with the big, stripy towel wrapped around their waists. Then they'd raced each other to the water's edge, gasping at the sudden coldness. Early summer, his father had said. Water hasn't had time to heat up, he'd said. But they'd got used to it soon enough.

After lunch, he and Eoin had dug trenches and made a fortress, running back and forwards to the sea filling the empty lemonade bottle with water for their moat. Vinny's mother and father were happy that afternoon.

And then, just before going home, they were allowed to have one last swim. Farrell could see it all unfolding; he remembered every detail. Together at first, they swam out from the shore. Even as he began to pull away from Eoin, Vinny knew that he was going too far, that the water was too deep. But he wanted to show off how well he could swim. He heard his father's voice calling him, of course he did, but he chose to ignore it. Now, all those years later, he could still feel the surge of defiance, the power he'd felt, ignoring his trousered father by the water's edge. *He* couldn't swim.

He wouldn't listen to Eoin's voice either, urging him to come on, they'd better go back. He was on his own. He began swimming further and further away, parallel to the shore now, splashing and swimming underwater, knowing that this was foolhardy, knowing that he was making his father mad.

Eventually, he had to come in. His father was waiting for him, anger deepening every line of his face. Vinny had felt the surge of a new, stronger, defiance. As he approached his father, he was filled with a soaring, dizzying sense of his own power. He knew no fear; whatever was coming, he could take.

Without a word, his father grabbed his eldest son roughly by the arm and half-dragged, half-carried him back into the sea. Farrell remembered his overwhelming sense of surprise that his father would get his trouser-legs wet.

It had all happened so fast. Vinny hadn't had a clue what was coming next. He didn't even have time to brace himself. The next thing he knew, he was face down in the water. He opened his mouth to cry out, and was choked by a gush of sea-water. He tried to breathe through his nose then, and panic set in. Stronger than any other sensation was the weight of his father's hand, pressing him down, down, down all the time. Farrell remembered that a hazy, peaceful feeling had started to fill his head when suddenly, he was pulled roughly upwards by the hair.

His father's voice was loud, angry, booming past his full ears, hammering into his head.

'You'll do what you're told, when you're told!'

He was thrown onto the hard sand then, chest heaving, arms flailing. Something sweet and slimy crawled up his throat, cutting off air, panicking him. Banana and jam. Gasping and slithering, rolling and bucking in blind panic, he was sick all over himself.

When it was over, he drew one full, shuddering breath and believed that he was not going to die, after all. But the feeling of needing to fight for air didn't go away for a long time. The back of his nose and throat was raw-tasting, burnt and bitter.

He lay there, flung at the water's edge, struggling for breath, convulsing like some strange, white, stranded fish, until his mother's touch on his cold arm brought him back to himself.

'Vinny, Vinny,' she whispered. 'Why do you always go looking for trouble, son?'

That day was the first time that Vinny knew it for sure. It wasn't just a feeling any more. It was a thought, with words around it, traced clear and sharp in his mind. Like one of the pages in his atlas, his pure hate was a country with well-defined borders. It existed separately from everything else in his life. He had come to know it that day, had even voiced it to himself. He hated his father enough to kill him. He hated the strength of his will over everyone, the way he made even his own wife afraid of him. Nobody should have that sort of power.

'We're home,' Grace said, patting his hand.

Farrell opened his eyes. He felt suddenly, absolutely, exhausted.

'I think I'll go to bed for a while.'

'Of course. Go on ahead, I'll unpack the car. Sleep as long as you like.'

Farrell made his way upstairs, pulled off his shoes and pulled the duvet over his head. Instantly, he slept.

He woke at some stage, much later that evening. The bedroom curtains were drawn; it was dark. Grace was not yet in bed; there was music playing softly downstairs. Farrell decided to try to sleep again. He didn't want to face her, didn't want to drag the memory back to the surface. It was gone, buried. He didn't have the words to put a shape to it so someone else could understand.

He willed himself back to sleep.

The following morning, he was still tired. His insides felt sore, as though they had been shaken up roughly; everything still felt somehow off-centre. Grace brought him breakfast in bed.

'How are you feeling?'

'Great,' he answered. Only a white lie.

'Do you feel like driving to Wicklow, or will we leave it until after the weekend?'

He could see that she really wanted to go. His heart turned over as he looked at her; she was so lovely. Hair tied back, skin just coloured by the sun, white T-shirt, navy shorts. He thought again how young and vulnerable she looked.

The food was helping. The bedroom felt normal; breakfast was normal. He was beginning to feel better. He aimed for enthusiasm.

'Absolutely. We'll head off in half-an-hour, just give me time to have a shower.'

Her face brightened. She leaned over the tray and kissed him on the forehead.

'You look much better. Sure you're OK? Sure you're up to this?'

He gave her the thumbs up and she went off, singing.

'Hello? I'm interested in talking to someone about the stone cottage you have for sale? Yeah, that's right, about five miles north of Enniskerry.'

Farrell waited, holding onto the phone tightly. They had seen nothing all day, nothing that even approached the kind of place that Grace was looking for. She had grown more and more silent since early afternoon. He had begun to feel panicked, picking up on her mood instantly. He had tried at first to be cheerful, reassuring, but yesterday's memory had made him feel acutely sensitive to everything around him. Even the tips of his fingers felt tingly. He could almost reach out and touch her disappointment. It was a visible presence between them, shimmering away like the heat-haze on the road ahead. Memories of Blackrock had begun to haunt him again; he could see keys dangling tantalisingly in P.J.'s hand, as he stretched his arms out towards his lovely daughter. Farrell knew that if he didn't make it up to her this time, somehow, the chance would slip away from him for ever. He was already on borrowed time; he had to make his move quickly, decisively, cutting off all P.J.'s options, forcing him into retreat. All the estate agents would be closed in an hour. Please, let it not be too late. He couldn't bear to let her down again.

As he waited for his query to be answered, his hands grew a little shaky. His forehead began to feel hot. He spoke to himself, sternly. It was just nerves, nothing more. He tried to concentrate instead on the solid feel of the concrete floor under his feet. A crackle of papers came across the phone line. He looked again, closely, at the grainy black-and-white photograph in the local newspaper, folded on the shelf in front of him. He drew little crosses around the picture with his pen while he waited. Giving his hands something to do had stopped their shakiness. Gradually, he began to feel cooler, more in control. He had a good feeling about this place; he didn't want anyone else to beat him to it. This time, he would get there first.

'Great. Can we meet today? Sure, seven is perfect. John O'Neill. I have that. My name's Farrell.'

He wrote the agent's name, quickly, in his diary.

'That's fine, Mr O'Neill, I'll see you then.'

Farrell replaced the receiver, his hands suddenly sticky. But he was filled with a sense of elation. The cottage was not yet sold; he still had a chance. This was everything he'd been looking for. He could see himself making it all real. Grace's workshop, a summer home, thousands of miles away from P.J.'s expectations of him. As he turned towards the door of the hotel, a pulse-beat jolted, just above his right eyebrow. Yesterday's sensation of distance, of greyness, suddenly began to fill him again, pushing its way up under the surface of his happiness. Horrified, he stood quietly, breathing deeply. Not now, he told himself, staying absolutely still; not now. After a few moments, the thumping sensation receded. Gratefully, he put his diary back in his pocket and went to join Grace.

She was still where he had left her, sitting by the window in the little coffee-shop, reading the newspaper. The wave of relief which flooded him made him stop abruptly, in the middle of the narrow street. If anybody was watching him . . . he looked around, over his shoulder, just to be sure . . . they'd think he was mad. He moved quickly, crossing to the footpath. Before he pushed open the coffee-shop door, he had a moment of complete clarity. His thoughts were ordered, rational. This emotional see-saw was not right, could not be right. Surely it was not normal to be besieged by such an army of emotions, each feeling marching into the space created by the one before, each one taking hold of him, exploding in his head and chest, taking him hostage. Panic, joy, terror, elation – he experienced nothing that was not extreme. He no longer controlled his own feelings; instead, they marshalled him. As suddenly as the window of understanding had opened, it darkened, leaving him confused, watchful again. She was waiting for him on her own, sipping coffee.

What had he expected? Even P.J. couldn't materialise out of thin air, could he?

'You OK?' Grace asked him.

He nodded. At least she couldn't tell by looking at him.

'Fine. I was just checking out what O'Neill's have for sale.'

'Anything interesting?' Grace was folding the news-paper as she spoke, hardly glancing at him.

Farrell fought the instinct to tell her. This was his oppor-tunity to surprise her. He wanted it to be right.

'Maybe. We'll call into a few places on the way home.'

'OK.'

He was relieved that she was satisfied, that she didn't push him. Yesterday's soreness was still with him. His throat was hot and tender, as though burned again by sick and sea-water.

On their way home that evening, almost casually, he said to Grace: 'Take the next right here. There was a sign for a little stone cottage. We might as well take a look.'

Grace followed the signs from the main road. When they pulled up outside the cottage, his excitement was almost unbearable. Even before he pushed open the little rusting iron gate, he knew. He felt a surge of the same powerful instinct he had had when he saw Meadowbrook Grove for the first time.

The cottage was dark, uninviting even in the sunlight. The ground was uneven; tin cans and broken roof-slates hid in the grass, making Grace stumble, more than once. But Farrell saw what she couldn't. He could make this perfect, too.

'Come with me.' He pulled her after him, striding around the outbuildings. 'I want to show you something.'

She had to almost run, to keep up with him. 'Slow down! You're hurting my hand!'

But he wasn't listening. He was driven by the need to be right, to be first.

'This is it, Grace. This is the one. We could make this into a real little gem. Look.'

He pointed to one of the outbuildings. His hand was trembling. Grace had pulled away from him a little. She was looking at him intently; her face was flushed. Good. He had her attention; she was hooked.

'Craft shop, workshop, studio, whatever.'

Then the second one, more dilapidated than the first. It didn't matter.

'Coffee-shop.'

He could see it all before him. He turned her to face the cottage.

'The Farrells' summer residence.'

Grace gasped. She was still looking up at him, her mouth slightly open. Farrell's words raced ahead, desperate to convince her, to win her over. He didn't want her to speak, not yet.

'This is exactly what we need. And look at the garden – look at what we could have at the back of the cottage.'

He pulled her along behind him again, wanting her to want it.

'Farrell, I want you to slow down; I want you to listen to me.'

He turned around to her in surprise. He had never heard her use that tone of voice before. There was an undercurrent of exasperation, almost of anger, to her words.

'I don't think this is suitable at all. For one thing it's much too isolated.'

Farrell felt the impact of her words as a physical blow. His skin seemed to grow colder, thinner, an inadequate covering for his shocked body. He didn't recognise her face, her expression. This was not the Grace he knew. A sudden thought illuminated everything for him. Isolation had nothing to do with her disapproval. It was something very different that made her look at him like that. *Her father hadn't found it for her.* He waited for her to speak again, to make some excuse.

'And for another, it's in dreadful condition. I thought we'd agreed that we were looking for something–'

At that moment, a car pulled up at the gate, tyres scrunching on gravel. They both turned towards the road. A door slammed and a tall, balding man with a clipboard appeared suddenly in front of them.

'Mr Farrell?'

The man pushed the gate open and walked towards Farrell, hand outstretched, broad friendly smile.

'I'm John O'Neill.'

Farrell saw the way Grace looked at him then. Her glance immobilised him, made him speechless. This was to have been so different. This was where she was to have told him how good he was at surprises, how she couldn't wait to see inside the cottage, how she knew he could make it lovely. With difficulty, he shook hands with the estate agent. Grace took over, filling in the awkward spaces for him.

'I'm Grace Farrell,' she said. 'Pleased to meet you.'

'Have you had a look around? It's a really lovely situation.'

He began to pull a sheet from his clipboard, struggling with his car-keys and sunglasses.

'Here, let me help.'

Grace took the sheet from him, and Farrell suddenly recovered. Maybe there was still a chance, maybe he could still convince her. She was at ease, polite, chatting to John O'Neill. Maybe all was not lost.

'It's a little bit off the beaten track for what we had in mind. But maybe we could have a look inside anyway?'

'Of course. No harm in that!'

Farrell suddenly hated both of them. The man's cheerfulness was patronising, his ordinariness grated on Farrell's nerves. And as for Grace, he knew she was only doing this to save face. He felt empty inside, numbed by disappointment and humiliation.

'It's an executor's sale, so it's quite keenly priced for this area.'

He opened the front door, glancing at Farrell. Perhaps he sensed something.

'I'll give you a few minutes by yourselves. Give me a shout if you want to ask anything.'

Grace smiled at him. 'Thank you.'

As she turned to walk through the front door, Farrell again had the strangest, coldest sensation that this woman beside him was not his wife. She was someone he no longer knew, walking away from him into the cool, wet-wool-smelling interior of the cottage. When she turned to him, he thought her face had hardened; there were lines and shadows he had never seen before. But when she spoke to him, her voice was still gentle, still the one he knew.

'I'm sorry if you're disappointed, but this is really not for us.' She looked around her, rubbing her arms. 'To be honest, it gives me the shivers.'

He said nothing.

She reached out for his hand. 'Are you OK? Say something, will you?'

But Farrell's eyes were locking onto the huge fireplace in front of him. The grate was enormous; you'd need to have plenty of logs stored for the winter. Grace's voice suddenly sounded very far away. He watched himself as he stretched out his hand to light the fire-lighter that had been magicked into the empty grate before him. His forehead began to sweat. His hand shook a little as he piled the sticks on top of the weak, yellowish flame, wigwam-style. The twigs spattered and crackled, sending wispy trails of wood-smoke curling outwards and upwards.

Then his nostrils were filled with the hot steam-smell of clothes drying, by the fire. He saw it all clearly; the old wooden clothes-horse, full of vests, pants, nappies. Patrick was on his mother's knee. A milky, new baby scent came from the two of them. The white enamel bath sat on the old rug in front of the fireplace, full of soapy water. They were all together again, now, in this room.

'Get me a nappy from the folded ones over there, Vinny.'

Farrell saw himself walk across the room to the chair which held the pile of aired nappies. He searched for the best one. They were mostly thin; some of them were unravelling. But they were all perfectly white and clean.

'Now, empty the baby's bath, there's a good lad, so we can put the horse around the fire again.'

The boy laughed. He thought horse was a very funny name for it.

It was Saturday night. He and Eoin had had their bath, sharing the hot water. They always looked forward to Saturday nights after Jody and the baby were put to bed. They sat at the table and their mother made them their weekly treat. Cadbury's drinking chocolate, scalding hot, with extra chocolate powder sprinkled on top. Just for the three of them. She always bought a quarter pound of sweets as well. She counted them all out on the table, so that it was fair.

The sucky sweets were his favourites. Glassy ones, she called them. Traffic-lighters, said Eoin, grinning every time. Green, red and yellow. They made them last a long time.

She had them in bed long before their father came home.

Sometimes, on those nights, he stumbled home alone. More often, he brought others with him, all roaring and singing at first, then fighting and swearing until early morning brought sudden, brittle silences. They were always the nights that ended badly.

She tucked both of them in, stroking their foreheads, kissing their cheeks. Then she went back downstairs to wait. They liked the bedroom door open, the landing light on until they went asleep. They slept that night, comforted by drinking chocolate, soothed by the damp, warm smell of clothes drying by the fire.

There was a peculiar stillness in the room. Farrell swung around to see Grace staring at him.

Panic set in. Jesus, where had he been? Her face showed that she knew he had been absent from her. How long had he been standing there, with one foot in the past? His head felt cloudy, as though full of steam from the damp clothes around the fire. Except that there were no clothes, no fire; the room was still cool, dark. The bright, warm corners of his memory faded as he tried to focus on his wife.

'I'm sorry – what did you say?'

'There's something wrong, Farrell. What is it?'

He was silent. How could he explain the feeling he had of being separated from his present self, watching as his life was being lived elsewhere, by someone else? The last two days seemed like another existence. These memories, images, visions, whatever they were – things he had never thought of before – were crowding him out. It felt as though there was no longer any room for him in his own body.

He forced himself to smile at her, squeezed her hand.

'I was miles away. Sorry. This place reminds me of somewhere I've been before, that's all.' Then, as though as an afterthought, as though reluctantly admitting to a weakness: 'And I still feel a bit out of it after yesterday.'

He watched with relief as her face relaxed a little.

'Come on then, let's go home. We probably should have left all this until after the weekend.'

He nodded.

'Yeah. Maybe. Still, I'm glad we came. It's been interesting to see what's available.'

He smiled at her, surprised and relieved that she believed him. To his own ears, his voice had a slight sharp edge to it, an iceberg-tip of unease. But Grace didn't seem to notice. He couldn't tell her what was happening to him. He didn't know, himself. Something was dragging at him, pulling him back to a time when he did not exist for Grace, nor she for him. He did not want to revisit angry rooms, to shiver on bathroom lino and leap from shed roofs. He had left all that behind a long time ago, had escaped through small back gardens and rolled in the hilly freedom of a city park. He wanted never to go back. If Grace knew, she would take him there; she would make him remember. She, his refuge, would become part of what he once was.

Then, he would have nowhere to go.

She took his hand in hers.

'Let's go straight home,' she said softly.

The ease between them was not broken on the journey home. Farrell felt exhausted again, but waited up until Grace was ready to go to bed.

He didn't want her to suspect again that there was anything wrong.

Grace would be twenty-eight in five weeks' time. Farrell wanted to do something special for her birthday, particularly now, after her disappointment over the cottage. Immediately after the weekend, he left messages for Anna and Ruth on their answering-machines, asking them to contact him as soon as they could, that he was planning a surprise for Grace.

He was going to throw her a party, the best one she'd ever had. He was paying the piper this time; P.J. could whistle any tune he liked. He'd invite her parents too, of course. He'd have to. Despite all that had happened, Farrell knew that she still craved their approval. This party, their thriving business, the visible signs of their success together – weren't these all a way for her to say, See? Didn't I make the right choice after all?

For him, P.J. would be something to be endured on the night. And he would do it for her, would make the effort willingly. Now it was really urgent to get Anna and Ruth to accept his invitation; P.J. would just have to fit in. The thought pleased Farrell deeply. He plotted and planned silently all week. He was impatient to get Grace out of the house so that he could tie up all the loose ends.

Early on Thursday morning, once Grace had gone to see her suppliers, Farrell phoned Anna in Blackrock. He felt ridiculously excited, nervous even. He hoped that she was in the shop first, rather than Ruth. Anna was really the only one of them that had ever made any effort to make him feel comfortable.

She answered immediately, and Farrell was relieved.

'Bábóg Toys Ltd. Good morning.'

'Anna! Glad I got you. Can you talk?'

'Hiya, Farrell. Sure, go ahead. We're not busy. I got your message, but I haven't been able to get back to you without Grace finding out. How are things?'

Farrell was taken aback. Her tone was relaxed, not in the slightest bit curious. He felt a stab of disappointment. He had hoped for a little more enthusiasm for his surprise party.

'Fine, fine. I'm ringing about Grace's birthday . . .'

Before he could finish, Anna burst out laughing.

'I know *that*!'

Then he felt embarrassed. Her tone was almost dismissive. He plunged ahead, unsettled by her laughter.

'Well, I was hoping you'd be free on the eighth of September? It's a Saturday. I'm organising a surprise party for her birthday.'

There was a sudden, complete silence that he couldn't fathom.

'I mean for everyone – there'll be about twenty of us altogether. I've contacted Ruth as well,' he added hurriedly, unnerved by the stillness at the other end of the line.

'And what did she say?'

Anna's voice was strained, quiet. No more laughter.

'I haven't managed to speak to her yet. I've left two messages on her machine.'

Farrell felt the perspiration begin to bead across his forehead. What was going on? Had they fallen out? Had something happened in the last week that neither he nor Grace knew anything about?

'This is embarrassing.'

Farrell felt his knees weaken. What was she going to tell him? A dread began to build deep inside him. Behind it, underneath it, twisting upward, he could feel the first faint rumblings of anger.

'Didn't P.J. contact you?' she asked finally.

Farrell tried to keep the harshness out of his voice.

'No. P.J. has never contacted me. What's going on?'

'I thought you were ringing about the party for Grace . . .'

Anna's voice trailed off, as though she had lost her way.

'I am ringing about Grace's party, *my* party on the eighth of September. Now what party are *you* talking about?'

Farrell's tone was now blunt, emotionless. But he knew. P.J. was at the back of this.

'P.J.'s party on the fifteenth. I can't believe he didn't ring you . . . Maybe he couldn't get you . . . I don't understand it . . . He insisted we leave it to him, that he'd get in touch personally . . . Farrell, I don't know what to say.'

Farrell could hear the distress in her voice. He didn't blame her. But still. Blind, black anger threatened. He kept his voice normal.

'No one called me. I have no idea what you're talking about. But perhaps you'd better fill me in.'

'He's booked Jury's Hotel for Saturday the fifteenth. The invitations have already gone out. Ruth and I both got a big party for our twenty-firsts, but Grace didn't. She was . . . unwell at the time. He said this was his chance to make it up to her.'

Anna's voice was recovering some of its normality. This was an embarrassment to her, nothing more. Her tone now implied belief in some rational explanation; this was an unfortunate misunderstanding, it could be nothing more than that.

Farrell's knuckles were white. He was beginning another of those cold, distant sweats.

'I haven't time to discuss it now. Maybe you'd let me know the arrangements so I can do whatever it is I'm supposed to do.'

Anna responded gently, to his words, rather than his tone.

'Of course I will. And Farrell, there must be a reasonable explanation, I'm sure. I'll get back to you when I talk to P.J.'

Farrell laughed shortly.

'I don't need an explanation, Anna. I can work this one out for myself.'

And he replaced the receiver very, very gently.

For several minutes, he stood absolutely still in the kitchen. The walls receded and advanced as the pulse-beat in his head grew louder and more insistent.

Moving towards the kettle, he forced himself through the motions of making a pot of tea. But he could no longer connect with the familiar ritual. He didn't feel as though he was *in* these actions; they were happening somewhere else, in another time and space where he didn't belong.

He felt anger; but more intense than his anger was the most profound feeling of hopelessness he had ever known. He would never be able to hold on to Grace. It was as though a long-denied truth had finally, irrevocably, asserted itself. He suspected that she was already quietly moving away from him. She had looked at him strangely a couple of times over the last few days. She hadn't liked the cottage. She had definitely been quieter since the weekend. And now this. Her father's party. His life with her was nothing more than an illusion. Their home, their business, their love measured up to nothing against the enemy. He, Farrell, had been playing games, believing he could win, while the enemy had bided his time, moving with deadly strategy.

Suddenly cold, Farrell crouched on the kitchen floor, plugging in the blow-heater. The day was bright and hot, but his whole body was shivering. It took him a long time to warm up. He didn't know how long he crouched there, his head bent low. When he tried to move, he was stiff, pins and needles darting as he tried to straighten his legs.

He saw his skinny feet encased in grey, thin socks, felt the chilblains that he'd scratched until they were raw and weeping. He was trying to get warm beside the paraffin heater. The coal had run out again. The blue and yellow flame was small, but comforting. The smell of paraffin and warm lino filled Farrell's head and chest. It helped him to breathe more easily. He tried to see the name on the heater. It was suddenly very important to be sure of something, anything. *Aladdin*, that was it, in scrolled writing, pseudo-Arabic script.

He had lit the heater very carefully on his twelfth birthday to try and warm the kitchen. Mrs Casey had given him some money earlier to fill the can with paraffin. Mr Deegan had filled it to the brim, and then, inexplicably, had given him a threepenny bar of Cadbury's chocolate. Dark blue and gold wrapper. Farrell had saved it to share with Jenny later.

Mrs Casey had shown him how to trim the wick that day. She had also made a cake and the six of them had sat down at the kitchen table to celebrate his birthday. Eoin, grinning as usual, Jody the silent one, Patrick hungry as ever. And five-year-old Jenny. Black-haired, blue-eyed, laughing up at him with a big trusting smile.

Pain began to seep into the warm spaces inside Farrell's chest. He began to grow hot, his palms sweaty. A sudden noise brought the kitchen back into focus. He was staring into the plastic grille of the blow-heater. He reached out, listlessly, to turn it off. A headache began just behind his eyes.

It's only a party, said a voice, Mrs Casey's voice inside his head. But Farrell knew it was more than that. He knew that this was one of those moments against which the rest of his life was going to be measured.

Chapter Seven

Farrell was glad that Grace never found out about his plans for a surprise party. He couldn't bear to have her pity. He didn't even want to think about her birthday now. The heart had gone out of everything.

More and more at night, he was woken by awful dreams, remembering nothing except their awfulness. Heart racing, body drenched in sweat, he had to get up and open the bedroom window, breathing in large gulps of air to stem the feelings of suffocation. Sometimes, Grace woke. He never told her what was wrong, insisting instead that he was fine, not to worry, just a bit of a nightmare. He used one excuse after the other until, eventually, she stopped asking. He couldn't help pushing her away; it was easier than having her beside him, losing her little by little.

He sensed her looking at him more carefully, puzzled, studying him when she thought he didn't notice her. But he always noticed. That was what she didn't realise. He was keeping a close watch, always on the lookout for signs, for the presence of P.J. Unable to stop himself, he had followed her twice when she went shopping. On each occasion, she had done exactly as she'd said she would. But he was not reassured; she was just being careful. He had to be more clever, more watchful if he were to catch her out.

He bought her a delicate gold necklace with a sapphire centrepiece, to match the engagement ring he had bought her almost four years ago. He was unhappy with his purchase, dissatisfied. All he could see was Grace at a window, dressed in black, her father's diamonds at her pale throat, while he paced Merrion Square, collar turned up against the cold.

He persuaded her to wear her Donna Karan on the night of her birthday, saying they were going somewhere really special. A surprise. Her wide-eyed smile, her curiosity, gave him no pleasure. It was like being with someone else.

They arrived at the hotel exactly on time. Farrell pulled open the door of the bar and quickly ushered her inside. There were a few people on stools, a few more scattered around the tables. Farrell bought them both a drink and led the way, as he had been directed, towards the furthest corner of the bar. He waited while Grace lit a cigarette and then gestured her towards an empty table.

Before she had time to wonder what was happening, a great roar of 'Surprise!' suddenly erupted and Grace literally took a step back. People crowded around her, swarming out of the woodwork. Her face drained of all colour, her mouth opened and she looked almost fearful. Farrell, watching it all, felt very detached; he wondered who had ever dreamt up this form of celebration. He wanted no part of it. He stood well out of everyone's way, sipping at his pint. He could see over all the heads; she never even looked around once to find him. When she finally turned in his direction, her face was white, shocked.

On their way to the private suite, she held on to his arm.

'You knew about this!'

He nodded, trying to smile at her.

'And you never said a word!'

She kissed him, still holding on tightly to him.

'I'm relieved. I knew you were keeping something from me, and I was worried. Is this really all it was?'

She was fingering her necklace, smiling up at him. He

was filled again with a mixture of painful emotions. So many memories, so much hope. His heart quickened. She was looking at him so lovingly. Perhaps they could get over this; perhaps *he* could get over this.

He nodded and kissed her head lightly.

'Of course.'

He wanted it to be true. His chest began to expand with hope. He was reminded of the early days in Merrion Square. She had chosen him then, she had chosen him since, maybe she would choose him again. If he could just keep her by his side tonight . . .

She leaned very close to him and her hand touched his face. The expression in her eyes intensified his feeling of optimism. She was about to say something. His heart began to thump wildly. Suddenly, Ruth was upon them, pulling at Grace's sleeve.

'Come on! P.J.'s waiting for you!'

She pulled Grace away by the hand. It only took a moment. By the time Farrell had taken a tentative step forward to follow her, she was gone, swallowed up by the wall of people surrounding P.J. The bitter taste in Farrell's mouth was real; the now familiar taste of defeat.

He saw P.J. strutting about everywhere on his little short legs; he was difficult to avoid. He kept rubbing his hands together in delight. The proud father. *My daughters*. He gathered the three of them around him, holding onto Grace's arm, while Anna and Ruth stood close by.

'Bobby! Over here!' P.J. gestured imperiously into the crowd.

Farrell watched it all from the safe distance of the bar, towering over the heads in front of him. He was reminded, painfully, of his own wedding. There must be easily two hundred people here tonight. All the men around P.J. were well-groomed, Italian-suited, cigar-smoking. Their sleekness reminded Farrell suddenly of performing seals. A man, obviously Bobby, kissed Grace's hand, then Anna's, then Ruth's. His old-fashioned courtliness seemed absurdly out of place, a mockery. Farrell wanted to go home.

Instead, he watched the people in front of him with distaste; he saw how the contours of the different groups kept changing as they opened and closed constantly, admitting some to their inner circle, discarding others. They looked like monsters, disgorging the bodies that were not to their taste. The vast majority of the guests were here for reasons that had nothing to do with Grace. *Networking*, wasn't that what they called it?

There was a sudden surge towards the buffet table. Farrell ordered another whiskey. The steady hum of conversation had risen to a roar by now, and still Grace did not come looking for him. He wanted to smash his way across the room, out the door, and run back to somewhere, anywhere, to a place where he could belong.

Then he caught sight of her. P.J. had gathered his three *girls* around him, Anna and Ruth on either arm, Grace sitting on a chair in front of him. A photographer fussed about them. Then Maura joined the tableau. Only then did Grace begin to look around her, searching for him. Even from across the room, Farrell could feel the intensity of her gaze. He put his glass back on the counter deliberately, averting his eyes from hers. She was at his side in a moment.

'What are you doing? Why aren't you with us?'

He shrugged. He couldn't speak. At that moment, he had too much to say.

She took his hand. 'Come on. They're waiting for us for a photograph.'

The whiskey had stilled something inside him for the present. He walked across the room with her, to where they all waited for Grace. She arranged herself again, among her sisters, her parents. Finally, the photographer finished with the happy family portrait. There was a call from Peter, amid much laughter, that the in-laws get a look-in.

'Right, lads, your turn.' The photographer moved Grace's chair and indicated to the three men where they should sit with their wives.

P.J. turned away from Farrell at once, turned right around until he had his back to him. While the shot was being set up, P.J. addressed not one word to him, never once glanced in his direction. His attentions to James and Peter were pointed, deliberate. Peter was slurring his words already, but P.J. was slapping him on the back, all hail-fellow-well-met. P.J.'s voice had acquired the tone Farrell hated – a jokey, matey tone, one that was used between real friends. His fat hands pushed against Peter's shoulders, keeping him down, down, forcing him to stay still.

'We'll have to get you to do what you're told, young man!'

Farrell felt suddenly breathless and had to look away. James sat beside Ruth, grinning idiotically. Farrell needed to get this over with. He sat, stiffly, where he was told, beside Grace, directly in front of Maura. P.J., now standing behind Grace, placed his hands lightly on her shoulders. Farrell could sense that she was getting upset. Her father's rudeness, his own silence were conspiring to make her unhappy. Her hands, folded on her lap, were no longer steady. He felt a sudden stab of remorse, for making her suffer. He felt locked into his own behaviour; he was helpless. There was nothing he could do to change it.

Suddenly, it was over. Released, Farrell went back to the bar, leaving Grace to her sisters. He felt he would be sick if he hung around any longer. His stomach had already started to feel uneasy, perspiration was dampening his shirt collar, making it feel tight, itchy. He pulled at the knot of his tie, but his hands were useless. He took slow, deep breaths, leaning over the counter, steadying himself, hoping they would all leave him alone.

After a couple of minutes, Anna was at his elbow.

'I know it's no consolation, Farrell, but I think my father is behaving like a pig.'

Farrell turned around to face her. Her face was angry, her hands pulling at the fringes of a beaded shawl. He'd been right. She was the best of them. A glance in Grace's direction showed her walking, stooped, towards the Ladies. Ruth was with her. Farrell felt nothing; a calmness had now descended, his insides were empty.

'Don't worry about it, Anna. Your father and I understand each other. He's hated me from the moment he met me, and I can say in all truthfulness that I feel the same about him.'

'Right now, he deserves it. You don't. He has no right to treat you like that.'

Before he could reply, Peter came looking for his wife, swaying slightly. Farrell felt his familiar contempt for the man.

'Look after her, Farrell,' Anna said quickly and left.

She had made him feel better. He bought another whiskey and drank it quickly. He began to mellow a little. He still felt angry at P.J., but none of this was Grace's fault. She had felt the distance between them, had worried about it. Surely that was hope for the future. Farrell tried to rise above the strange coldness he was feeling towards everything; he tried to see beyond the dark edges of his vision which made everything seem unfamiliar, at one remove from reality. Grace was walking back towards him, smiling now, her hand outstretched, wanting him to dance. But he could see that she'd been crying.

'Will you dance with me, please?'

'Sure.'

Farrell was afraid that she would somehow feel different to him, that he wouldn't recognise her body. But she felt real, solid in his arms again, and he felt the wall inside his chest begin to crumble. He could focus on her now as Grace, his wife, no longer as one manipulated by the enemy. She hugged him. The tightness in her face eased as he held her close; he was able to look at her once more.

'You did a really good job of keeping all this quiet. It must have been some strain.'

He understood what she was asking him. He had to trust her again.

'It was very hard. This is rather more public than I would have liked.' He held her closer to him. 'Tonight is your family's celebration. I have ideas of my own for us, for something very different.'

Sweet, painful memories of Francis Street, of Amsterdam crowded and prodded at his heart. If he could just be alone with her . . . His memories made him feel hopeful again. He wanted her to choose him again, just once more. He needed the time and space with her to resist the force of gravity he felt all around him. What P.J. offered her was always tempting, tantalisingly close to hand. But he could give her more; all he needed was another chance. He would *not* lose her.

'Do I get to guess what you have in mind?'

He shook his head.

'No way. It will be my surprise; I think you'll like it.'

For a whole month after P.J.'s party, Farrell found it imposs-ible to forget. Everywhere he looked, he saw him. The man invaded even his sleep. He began to be suspicious, too, of Anna, wondering if she were, in some way, in league with the enemy. For days after the party, he couldn't shake the image of her as a traitor, a spy in the camp.

Memories of her past kindness, her friendship, now jabbed at him, making him see betrayal everywhere.

Grace was watching him again, still unsure of him. The optimism he'd felt as he'd danced with her on her birthday had slowly dissipated over the following days. He didn't know how to reach out to her any more, to pull her back. Tentatively one evening, late in September, she'd mentioned the photographs of the party. It was the first time that they had spoken of that night.

'I know he behaved badly, but I think he was really trying to keep Peter in line, making sure he didn't embarrass anyone. I don't think he was getting at you.'

Farrell smiled. He was aware that it wasn't a real smile; he couldn't make it reach his eyes. The room fell silent between them. Papers were strewn all over the studio table. Grace was looking up at him from the computer screen. Her expression was defensive, anxious. Farrell called out the next set of orders, and Grace typed, her fingernails clicking across the keys. He did not answer her for some time. Eventually, the tension became unbearable. He had to release it.

'Let's drop it, Grace. I don't want to talk about it.'

Farrell's neck felt stiff; his whole body went rigid every time he remembered. Every time he thought about standing there beside P.J., a suffocating feeling from another time, another place, invaded him, made him feel stranded in his own life. Perhaps words would have helped, but he could not form them. They choked and died before he could give them shape. The only real thing to do was to forget, to make it all into something which had never happened.

He could feel the distance opening up between himself and Grace, and sometimes, at night, it terrified him. Lying beside her in the breathy darkness, the warmth of her body made him more keenly conscious of his own loneliness.

He felt acutely how far they had strayed from one another. He had tried all the ways he knew to close the gap, but nothing worked. He cooked for her, careful, complicated dishes which she seemed to eat without tasting. He cared for her, thought about her ceaselessly. He even planned little surprises for her, which he couldn't carry through. Like the time he'd discovered a pair of tiny diamond and sapphire earrings, on one of his many restless afternoons browsing in antique shops. He'd bought them at once, shocked by the memories they released. They were a perfect match for her engagement ring; he would give them to her straight away, that night, and they would bring her back to him again. He could imagine her delight, her smile, her arms twining around his neck. But she hadn't come home until very late. She and Anna had gone for a drink after work, she'd said, and now she was tired. She was going to bed straight away. Her small, pale face had made Farrell unhappy, then. He'd kept his hands in his pockets, fingering the little box with his gift inside. It was the wrong moment. He put the little box away, at the back of his wardrobe. There were so many wrong moments, these days.

She was beginning to grow silent, too, just like him. She no longer chattered about the things she did each day. In the absence of her words, he was losing the ability to form his own. It was as though he needed her to feed him his lines; without her, the power of speech was deserting him.

Lately, he had started to forget words, the names of ordinary things. In the kitchen, preparing food, he would suddenly stop, overwhelmed by the unfamiliarity of what he was doing. He would pause in the middle of some mundane task, and a sense of being absent from himself would surround him, making everything grow still. At these times, he felt like someone else. It was a dreamy state, with a sleep-like paralysis which made him feel heavy, helpless.

He never knew how long it lasted. He always came back to himself again by being able to name where he was, who he was, whatever it was he was doing. *I am in the kitchen; I am Farrell; I am chopping onions, slicing mushrooms, washing lettuce.* The sense of relief was always enormous. He would practise the words over and over again, until the sweating palms and the thumping heart recovered, until his surroundings became familiar again.

Sometimes, when he tried to reach out to Grace, whole sentences stuck in his throat, although he would have formed them carefully in his mind beforehand. He was afraid that she would discover his sudden weakness. He began to avoid her. She did not come looking for him. Day by day he watched helplessly as the silences between them grew longer and deeper.

At least his woodworking skills had not deserted him; he could still carve and transform. As a result, he began to work, physically, harder than ever. New designs, new additions to old designs, larger-scale models, and finally, an enormous hand-carved chess set which he hung in the shop in Blackrock, on an oaken shelf suspended from the ceiling. It immediately became a talking point. Everyone who came into the shop wanted to know who had made it, how much it was. Could they not buy it? Were there miniatures available, then? Could they order one specially for Christmas?

Making the set had exhausted Farrell. He had put everything into it. It became a refuge, a solace, somewhere where he could transform the pain of losing Grace into something beautiful. When he'd finished, he felt drained of all emotion. He would never make another. It was a one-off; unique.

Whenever he was in the shop, though, he still liked to

handle the pieces. He could connect with the intricately carved figures of knights and rooks, bishops and pawns. They were his; in his hands they felt warmly familiar, his friends. He had once enjoyed the silent strategies of chess with Mr Casey. Now, he would not play the game any more. He had met his match, more than his match. Still, the polished perfection of the final pieces gave him pleasure. At least something was finished, complete. No more loose ends.

But making the set had made him conscious of other things. Was this the sum total of his lifetime's work? Had he nothing else to show for having been alive for so long? He was puzzled at the advance of time, felt it was slipping past, outside his perception. Another autumn almost over. Forty-four years of age. How much longer had he left? Both his parents had been dead before their forties. Sometimes, it felt as though he was living on borrowed time. The days were getting shorter now, darkness falling earlier and earlier. He climbed the stairs to the studio very quietly one evening when he'd come home and found no sign of Grace.

She was there, tidying up the studio, sweeping the wooden floor, straightening rugs.

He watched her from the doorway for a long time before he let her know he was there. She jumped, her hand flying to the base of her throat.

'Farrell! You gave me a fright!'

He mumbled something. Immediately, she stretched out her hand to him.

'Come here,' she said gently. 'Sit down. I have to talk to you.'

He sat.

'I know there's something wrong. I can feel it.'

He couldn't answer her. He waited for her to continue.

She lit a cigarette. Farrell saw that her hands had begun to shake.

'I know you were angry with P.J., and probably with me, too, but that party wasn't my fault. I didn't ask for it. And now I'm being punished for it.'

She began to cry. Something began to disturb the numbness in Farrell's chest. Something was beginning to dissolve, slowly. Warmth began to trickle downwards from the base of his throat. Gradually, the studio came into focus; the ordinary surroundings ceased to be distant. There was a sense of things merging. Farrell felt as though he was stepping across the threshold again into a familiar reality. He was filled with love as he looked down at his sobbing wife. He was able to see her with extraordinary clarity, etched brightly against the dark window. He heard the word; punished. Horrified, he looked at Grace's suffering; suffering that he had caused. Something finally came free inside, and he felt he was recovering, suddenly regaining consciousness. His words no longer felt obstructed; there were no obstacles between them. He was able to take hold again of the power of speech. His head filled with an abrupt, white noise and it took a moment for him to regain control.

'Grace, Grace.'

He knelt on the floor in front of her, folding both arms around her until she rested against his chest.

'I'm sorry, I'm so sorry,' he whispered. 'The last thing I would ever want to do is punish you. You're all I've got; you're everything to me. I love you.'

He tilted her face towards him.

'I've just felt so . . . lost. Your family seemed to be taking you over. I felt there was no room for me.'

'I can't take the distance between us, Farrell. We've been through so much. I want you back.'

Grace clung to him, burying her head in his chest. The

sensation of long, deep distances between them began to lessen. He was flooded with a feeling he was beginning to recognise: things shifting, shuddering back into the ordinary, like a television screen recovering its horizontal hold. He began to feel at home in his own body; his thoughts became his again.

The previous few weeks began to seem like a dream. Ever since the day on the beach in Skerries, when he had been assaulted by memory, Farrell had had a strong sense of being sidelined in his own life. Even as he knelt beside Grace now, he began to see that time as something apart, an episode from which he could recover. If he could only shape his understanding of it, put boundaries around it, keep it safe. Holding her close, still not daring to look at her, he began to speak, forming the sentences slowly. He knew now that the words would flow. His mind felt clear.

'I'm sorry, Grace. Things have felt very strange over the past while. I've felt absolutely terrified of losing you. I couldn't even speak to you about it.'

She looked up at him, her face tear-stained.

'Do you remember our first Christmas together? The day I went out to get milk and you thought I wasn't coming back?'

He nodded, still able to feel the pain of it.

'I did come back, and I'm still here. Doesn't that count for anything?'

Too many memories surged at once, together.

'I've lost everyone that I was ever close to, Grace. I think it's made me . . . over-anxious. I'm sorry; I'll really try to keep this under control.'

He couldn't tell her of the sheer terror he felt every time he even thought of P.J.; he couldn't tell her that at times he felt someone else was living inside his body. He couldn't tell her of the distances he often felt between himself and the rest of the world. She would be frightened, would think that he was mad. Then, he would certainly lose her. No; this had to be played carefully, close to the chest.

'Why don't you talk to somebody about how you feel? I'll help you through it, Farrell, it needn't be like this.'

Grace was pulling a tissue from her sleeve, wiping her eyes with the back of her hand.

Farrell didn't look at her directly. Talk to someone? After what she had told him about doctors, locked wards, people put away? What if they found something wrong with him, took him away from her for good? He would be abandoned, stranded on the shoreline of some illness from which there was no recovery. No. He didn't want that sort of help. He would handle this on his own. The now-familiar greyness had begun to invade his head again.

He pretended to be thinking about what she was saying; instead, he was trying to breathe deeply, quietly, to still the wild rocking of his heart.

'Maybe I will. Let me think about it.'

He knew his smile must be all right, because her eyes lit up, and she smiled back warmly, stroking his face once more with a gentleness that made him ache all over again.

They didn't speak about it any more that night. They were both feeling cleansed, at ease with each other. Farrell knew that he had a difficult task ahead of him. He had to be wary, striving at all times to be what Grace expected, hiding any strange absences from her. Maybe all that was over now. Maybe, now that he had her back, it would never happen again.

Christy's phone call came as a welcome distraction a few days later.

'Farrell? The very man. I've been trying to get a hold of you for ages.'

'We've been very busy in the shop. I haven't been home a lot.'

It was good to hear his voice. This call from the outside, from beyond himself and Grace, suddenly reminded Farrell that there was a normal, ordinary world going on all around him, where people left for work in the morning and came home again in the evening, unburdened by dread. It was a curious relief to hear Christy.

Maybe Grace was right. Tentatively, after that night in the studio when they'd finally discussed the party, she had suggested to him that they should begin to look beyond themselves, create a circle of friends, have some separate interests. He had been feeling so close to her then, so happy within himself, that he had accepted the idea without the paralysing fear of losing her. The fear had come later, deep into his night-time terrors. All week he had swung from one extreme feeling to the other. Christy's voice, solid, ordinary, made him feel he was back on centre again.

'We've a job on up in Dundalk, starting next week. An old house, total refit. They want all the old woodwork and plaster restored, windows done – you know the sort of thing. It's just up your street. Are you interested?'

Farrell hesitated.

'Gerry is coming as well, and Paddy, for the plasterwork. We're all going to stay over, for the first week, at least. It's too far to travel back and forwards every day. Anyway, they're offering a *very* generous allowance for overnights. I figure it'll be well worth our while. We should get a really good run at things next week; the weather's going to be good.'

A week. They had never been apart for that long. Ever. And he didn't need the money.

'Are you still there?'

'Yeah. I'm thinkin', Christy. I've a lot on at the moment,' he lied, playing for time.

'Yeah – but this is one of the jobs you used to love, really got your teeth into. I've praised you to the skies, Farrell, and I really don't know anyone better. Even if you don't need the readies, come for the craic. We haven't even had a pint in ages.'

Farrell was tempted. Christy was holding open a door; and he had been feeling strange lately. Grace's talk of doctors had terrified him. He'd had to make huge efforts to make sure she saw the Farrell she expected, the one she thought she knew. Sometimes, the strain made his head ache, the familiar pulse-beat strafing him without mercy. Maybe a change would do him good.

'I'll have to talk to Grace.'

'You do that, and get back to me. Will you ring me tomorrow?'

Farrell promised he would.

Seven days. Maybe this would show Grace that he trusted her. And he had to admit, even to himself, that he would love to work on a big scale again. The smallness of the toys had begun to oppress him lately. He'd felt as though he was living his whole life in miniature.

Grace was enthusiastic.

'Of course you should go; keep your hand in. We've more than enough to keep us going in the shop.'

Having spoken to her, he felt committed. And the draw of the work of transformation was strong. He phoned Christy the next night and said yes.

Grace drove him and Christy to Dundalk on the Sunday night. Gerry and Paddy had arrived the day before; they were already installed in a small house on a vast housing estate. Farrell had felt uncomfortable as they'd followed Christy's directions, turning right and left in the foggy darkness. The bit of paper that Christy held in his rough hands had made Farrell's insides lurch more than once. The look of these houses was all much too familiar. He was grateful it was night-time, that no freckled children were playing ball against the high wall of a cul-de-sac. He kept looking out the window, his face averted from Grace. It was easy to pretend he was fully occupied searching for number 186.

'This is it!' Christy shouted suddenly and Grace pulled over. She dropped them at the gate, kissed Farrell on the cheek and waved goodbye to Christy. Farrell had a fleeting sense of her washing her hands of him, leaving him to it.

Inside the house, the rooms were familiar too, cramped and shabby. Christy was apologetic.

'I know it's no great shakes, but this way the lads save most of the accommodation money. Tax free.'

He shrugged.

Farrell smiled.

'Don't apologise, Christy, it's fine. I don't imagine we'll be spending much time here anyway. I'll share a room with you anytime, as long as you change your socks!'

Christy laughed with him, dispelling the awkwardness he had suddenly felt at the contrast between their two lives. Farrell had left them all behind, long ago. He had a posh wife, real money, a fancy house and car.

Farrell understood the moment of awkwardness between them, was glad when it passed. Like putting on an old overcoat, he assumed the attitudes which made Christy feel comfortable. He suddenly clapped his hands, rubbing them together.

'How about a pint?'

Christy brightened at once.

'Yeah, why not.'

There was the comfort of old friends between them, although Farrell would never really have regarded Christy as a *friend*. But now there was a substance to him, a constancy which Farrell envied. He began to be reminded very much of Mr Casey. With a pang, Farrell realised that for all the distance he seemed to have travelled, his roots were as near the surface as ever. He had hoped to plant them deep with Grace. It had not happened. Every time he had tried, they had been wrenched roughly upwards by fat, remorseless hands. Like the way his father had grabbed him by the hair on the beach that day when he was eight.

Gerry and Paddy were already in the pub, involved in raucous political debate. They were dragging deeply on their cigarettes, hunched intently over their pints, the table in front of them crowded with empty, cloudy glasses.

'Ah, Jaysus, I don't want to get involved in that, do you?'

Christy had to almost shout, his mouth close to Farrell's ear.

Farrell shook his head.

The pub was jammed. The closing-time noise level was immense. They moved quickly to a table just vacated by a young couple, out of sight of Gerry and Paddy. Watching the young man and woman go, hand in hand, Farrell felt suddenly depressed. He had let all possibilities of family slip through his fingers, all through his life. He had never gone back to see Peter Casey after his mother died; his own brothers and sister were gone for ever; he had no children of his own. Grace was all he had. And no matter what she said, he felt that losing her was only a matter of time. He had thought he'd be able to keep all this under control, that the ordinariness of work and company would keep his fears in perspective. But here, away from her, he only became more convinced that she was stealing away from him for ever. She had accepted his week away with alacrity. She had driven off without even a backward glance. Was she glad to be rid of him? What had she planned?

Jealousy took hold of Farrell's throat. He wanted to get very drunk, to drown what was now real, inevitable.

He turned slowly to find Christy staring at him.

'Are you all right, man? I thought you were sick . . . you looked a bit peculiar.'

Farrell snapped back to the present.

'Sorry, Christy . . . I was miles away . . . I thought I recognised someone over there.'

Farrell gestured vaguely in the direction he was facing. Christy nodded.

'I've ordered a double round – they'll stop serving soon.' Farrell stood up and grinned at him.

'I'd better do the same, then. How about a couple of chasers to take the harm out of it?'

Christy gave him the thumbs up. Farrell hoped that he'd been convincing; he didn't want Christy watching over him. He made his way to the bar, signalled his order and returned to the table.

It had been a very, very long time since Farrell had been drunk.

Now, he thought, it was time again.

Christy's alarm dragged Farrell into consciousness at seven o'clock. He had been just below the surface of wakefulness all night; there had been no rest. Now, he felt hot-eyed, heavy-headed, angry.

None of the men spoke over breakfast. Gerry and Paddy drank tea and smoked cigarettes; Christy made them a large pot of porridge. Farrell felt his stomach heave as he looked at the lumpy, greyish mass put in front of him. He left the table abruptly and ate several slices of toast, standing by the open window. He wondered what Grace was doing.

As he worked through the morning, he began to feel better. His head cleared, his stomach settled. He began to enjoy the planning of the restoration work; the old house, partly destroyed by fire, challenged him, spoke to him. He became absorbed, all the heavy mists of last night dissolved.

Whiskey is the devil, his mother's voice said to him, out of nowhere. He decided not to drink it again; they had finished a bottle last night, back in the house after the pub closed. It was a good while since he had drunk whiskey. He didn't even like it much. His father's, P.J.'s drink. But he was drawn to it more and more. It made him feel powerful, in a way. It made up for long years of feeling insignificant.

By lunch-time, Farrell had a fair idea of the materials he needed. He shouted up to Christy, already on the roof, that he was off to order timber.

'Bring us back a cheese roll from the shop on the corner, will ya?'

'Make that two!'

'Three!'

The calls came from different areas of the house, disembodied, invisible. Each of them trapped in its own space, hemmed in by brick, plaster, precarious floorboards.

'Get your own, ya shower of lazy bastards!'

Farrell grinned up at the redbrick façade, shading his eyes from the sun.

He headed off in the direction of the town centre, Christy's map in his hand, pretending not to hear the shouts of abuse hurtling down on him.

The midday air was chilly but bright. He walked briskly in the direction of the builders' suppliers. In the exhilaration of fresh air and sunshine, Farrell felt an unaccustomed stirring of hope. Why was he so sure that P.J. would lure Grace away from him? He'd tried often enough to put Farrell down, but Grace was still there, still married to him. Maybe he did need to let go, to lighten up a bit. He'd call her later on, just to talk. She'd know by the tone of his voice that he was fine. Things would be easy between them then. They could look forward to being together again. Having decided this, Farrell felt suddenly, dizzily happy.

McConnell's Building Supplies was very busy. He took his place in the queue, idly looking out at the shoppers passing up and down the street. A dark-haired woman paused outside the window, straightening the blanket over a little boy strapped into a buggy. She had an older child beside her, and was keeping a firm hand on his reins. She was clearly pregnant again. Farrell watched as she tucked in the baby, pushing the wispy strands of hair off his forehead, up under his knitted blue balaclava. She wiped the older child's nose, stroking his face affectionately. Farrell was fascinated at the ease with which she cared for her children.

She turned away to walk up the street. Farrell couldn't take his eyes off her. There was something disturbingly familiar about that big-bellied walk. She turned around to say something to the child beside her, and in that split second, Farrell recognised her. An enormous stillness descended, gathering in around him, filling in all the empty spaces.

It was his sister. It was Jenny.

His heartbeat began to quicken. The curve of her face, the dark hair, the smile. It was Jenny. It had to be. He had to see if she had blue eyes. Then, he could be sure.

Farrell left the shop quickly. His legs moved weightlessly, effortlessly. He was aware of nothing, except her heavy figure, drawing him after her. He followed the woman up the main street, keeping a safe distance for now, keeping her well in sight. He didn't want to frighten her. He'd wait until the time was right, until she recognised him. He had no doubt but that she would know him. She was so familiar to him.

He had no idea how long he walked. He saw only her, heard only the beating of his heart.

She turned to the right, into a housing estate. Farrell began to walk more quickly. He would overtake her, look back at her, and then he could be certain. It didn't take him long to catch up with her. His legs were long; she was obviously tired, walking more slowly now, occasionally placing one hand on the small of her back, pulling herself up straighter as though dislodging something which caused her discomfort. With a shock, Farrell recognised that gesture, too. This wasn't Jenny, this was his *mother*. As he gained on her, the little fellow in the buggy grinned at Farrell, pointing a chubby finger. Farrell almost stopped dead with shock. Eoin. He'd know that grin anywhere.

He tried to still the noise in his ears. Tentatively, he reached out and held onto the woman's arm. She looked around in surprise. Her eyes widened. They were blue. It was Jenny, he was right.

Farrell couldn't help himself. He opened his arms wide.

'Jenny,' he said, taking a step nearer her.

He heard someone scream. She started to struggle in his arms.

He was very surprised. She had always wanted him to take care of her. He held her tighter, to quell the shock of her recognition of him.

'Jenny, it's me. It's Vinny.'

Other sounds began to intrude. Farrell's stillness suddenly shattered. The children were screaming. Jenny's face was terrified, her mouth open. She had pushed him away. He was just about to step back towards her again, when strong hands grabbed him, pinning his arms behind his back. He didn't resist. He knew it was a mistake. She'd recognise him in a minute, and all this would be over.

'Jenny, Jenny, don't you know me? I'm Vinny!'

There was a flash of something like horror across her eyes. She *would* recognise him; she *must*. Farrell felt the tears behind his eyes. He was so close. His shoulders began to hurt. He tried to turn around, but whoever was holding him restricted any movement.

'My name is not Jenny. I've never seen you before in my life. Don't you *ever* come near me again!'

Her voice was strange, the accent unfamiliar. As she spoke, she turned away from Farrell, picking up the older child who was screaming hysterically. Resting the little boy on her hip, she pushed the buggy away, walking deep into the housing estate. She never even looked back. Farrell thought his heart would crack.

Someone was speaking, insistently, in his ear.

' . . . Do you understand me, son?'

The pressure on his shoulders was suddenly released. A surprised little group of people had gathered. Women clutching toddlers against their hips, youths in school uniform, the occasional shirt-sleeved man. Farrell turned to face his captor. A tall, broad, balding man, blue shirt, numbers at the shoulder. There were crumbs on his moustache. The pores on his face looked black.

Farrell took a step backwards. He was suddenly confused. His heartbeat was ringing in his ears, he could feel sweat all down his back. Jenny was gone. He'd have to come looking for her again. But for now, he'd have to pretend that it was all an honest mistake.

'I'm sorry, Guard. I was sure it was someone I knew. My sister. We lost contact a long time ago. I'm sorry, I got carried away. I was sure it was her.'

Almost the truth. A lie in a good cause.

The Garda's face softened.

'You frightened her, son. Don't creep up on anyone like that again. Now, I'm going in to finish my lunch. If I see you around here again, I'll arrest you. Do you understand?'

His voice had a hard edge to it. Farrell nodded. It was best to play it safe.

'I won't be back. My mistake. Didn't mean to cause any trouble. Sorry.'

Mumbling, Farrell turned his back on the curious little group of people, and headed off back down the town.

He lurched into the pub opposite McConnell's and ordered a double whiskey. After the second double, the warmth began to return to his hands, the ice inside had begun to melt. His mother had been wrong. Whiskey wasn't the devil; it was his saviour. He fought the images of Jenny and her children, pushed them away deliberately until another time. Gradually, the thumping in his head and chest subsided. The anxiety loosened; he would see her again, of course he would. He'd be able to make her understand.

But for now, he had to get back. He couldn't let the others know there was anything going on. This was between him and Jenny. He'd go over and order the timber, then he'd pick up the cheese rolls in the shop. Keep it normal. He had the best part of a week to find her again, and he now knew, more or less, where she lived. He mustn't let things slip, not at this early stage.

Christy was waiting for him. Farrell was surprised to see that his face was very angry. He had never known him to be this angry before.

'Where the fuck have you been?'

Farrell took a step back from his rage.

'McConnell's was jammed. I'd to wait ages for the order; they didn't have everything in stock. They'd to send out for stuff.'

Farrell spoke rapidly, pushing Christy's anger away from him. He watched the other man's expression, could see that he was already weakening. He decided to take advantage of the other man's uncertainty; he wouldn't fight back – he'd surprise him with an apology.

'I'm sorry, Christy. I went and had my lunch in a pub

across the road while I was waiting. I probably should have come back here instead.'

'You're gone three hours, you know that?'

Farrell was genuinely astonished.

'What!'

He looked at his watch for the first time.

'Jesus, I'm sorry, Christy, I'd no idea I'd been that long.'

He handed Christy the bag of rolls.

'You must be starving.'

'We got our own when you didn't come back.'

All the anger had gone now; Christy was looking at Farrell in belligerent concern, about to ask something, working up courage.

Farrell cut across him at once. He didn't want to explain to anyone where he had been, what he had just seen.

'Tell you what, I'll cook a slap-up meal for all of us tonight. On me. I'd no idea I'd been away for so long.'

Christy nodded. Farrell could see that he still wasn't satisfied.

'Yeah, right. When are McConnell's going to deliver?'

'The stuff will be here in an hour. Don't worry, Christy, I'll make up for any lost time.'

There was now a subtle change in Farrell's voice. It did not invite any more comment from Christy. The subject was closed.

Careful. He had to be careful. As Farrell strapped up his toolbox at the end of the day, he knew he was going to have to manage things better from now on.

Farrell walks out to the driveway. It is a quiet neighbourhood, always has been. The streets are now dark and silent. Curtains are closed, blinds are down. The occasional house still blazes out into the street, windows bare, television screen flickering bluely.

A respectable neighbourhood, where everyone keeps himself to himself. Two cars in every other driveway, flowers in every garden, doors and windows properly painted. Lately, for intense, fleeting moments, Farrell has begun to miss his old neighbourhood, noisy kids on the streets until all hours, women in and out of each other's houses, babies everywhere. He has begun to feel more acutely the sense of not belonging, of not being home. But then, he has always felt that, everywhere. Except with Grace, for a time.

Grace's car is still new-looking, polished, chrome gleaming. Only a year or so old. She had accepted it from her father, as Farrell had always known she would. It is satisfying, now, to have been right all along. P.J.'s car; his favourite model, his brand.

Farrell cleans out the ashtray, shakes the mats, wipes down the dashboard. He picks up the odd piece of paper off the floor, takes out the maps and Grace's address book.

It must be returned to him in perfect order. Farrell will have nothing less.

He opens the lid of the boot about a foot, and it stays. Farrell silently praises German workmanship. He wants to leave this as a marker, a sign to P.J. He wants the anxiety, the puzzlement to begin *before*.

Farrell wants to imagine his enemy asking questions that he will never have answered. For once in his life, Farrell wants to have the last word.

The car is almost invisible from the road. Only someone deliberately approaching the front door will see the open boot, the silent message to the enemy. Farrell has to take his chances that he will not be burgled tonight, of all nights.

And if he is, well, let P.J. figure that out, too. This is Farrell's party; he is calling all the shots. *He who pays the piper calls the tune.* That, surely, is a notion that P.J., of all people, will understand. Not for the first time, Farrell has a flutter of regret that he will not be a fly on the wall. But perhaps to imagine is better.

He leaves the car unlocked. He is nearly finished. Farrell takes a long look around Meadowbrook Grove, the street he once believed was his home, his and Grace's. He walks back into the house, puts the keys in the dresser-drawer and sits down to wait. There is very little left to do. What remains must be done the right way. Like complicated marquetry, all the bits must fit together, however long it takes.

Then, he can rest.

Chapter Eight

Farrell cooked huge helpings of steak and chips, onion rings and frozen peas, ready just as the other three came back from the pub at eight. He was surprised at how little Gerry and Paddy ate. They seemed to exist on endless cups of tea and packets of Major. They went back to the pub almost immediately, and Christy and Farrell cleaned up.

'I'm going out to ring the missus. Back in a few minutes.'

Farrell stopped cleaning up the splashes on the table and looked at him in surprise. Of course. Christy had a wife and a grown-up family. Farrell had forgotten he knew that.

'I'll come with you and give Grace a quick call. Then I'll buy you a pint to make up for starving you to death this afternoon.'

Farrell wiped down the table and the counter-top one last time and dried his hands on the tea-towel. He didn't want Christy to leave without him. He didn't want to be on his own.

Christy shoved his hands into his pockets, and looked up at Farrell.

'To be honest, I was more afraid that something had happened to you. You've had me worried since yesterday.'

Farrell's heart began to thump. He pulled on his jacket, trying to look casual, unconcerned, as he did so.

'Why?'

'I didn't think you looked at all well in the pub last night, and when you didn't come back today, well . . .'

Christy shrugged, looking uncomfortable.

Farrell felt a surge of tenderness as he looked at the man in front of him. Gruff, solid, decent. Just like Mr Casey. Farrell had to make great efforts here.

'I'm fine. Honest. Grace and I have been working too hard lately, that's all.'

Christy looked straight at him.

'Is this week too much for you, then? I don't want you to collapse or anything. If it's all too much, tell me, and I'll get someone else. Who says this crowd deserve the best, anyway?' And Christy grinned.

'You don't need to get anyone else. I'll be fine; I want the change. I'm fed up fiddling about with little bits of wood, to be honest. I want the break. Really. This is just what I need.'

Christy nodded, understanding the need for man's work. Farrell had appealed to just the right feelings. The old ease began to return.

'Right, then. I believe you mentioned a pint?'

Once Christy had phoned home, Farrell tried ringing Grace. There was no answer. He was not going to leave messages on any answering-machine. Her absence made Farrell suddenly angry. Ever since this morning, he had wanted, badly, to talk to her. This evening, while cooking the dinner, he had even toyed with the idea of telling her about Jenny. Not as it had happened, of course, but a much more casual, light-hearted, 'guess what . . .' version. Now he felt let down. Monday night, almost ten o'clock. Where could she be?

The pub was relatively quiet, much quieter than last night. Farrell went up to order pints for the four of them. To still his anger, he drank a whiskey, quickly, at the bar, waiting for the pints to settle. It helped, a little.

Paddy and Gerry seemed to know everybody. Farrell allowed himself to be drawn into the general, meandering conversation. He liked the accents around the table. From

Christy and Paddy's flat, old-fashioned Dublin, to the lilt of northern voices. Farrell was surprised at the conflicting views emerging among them all, the heat of political differences. It was a reminder of just how close they were to the border. Farrell had never thought about that before. It had never made any difference to his life. Ceasefire, post-ceasefire, new ceasefire; whatever.

At least their discussion took his mind off Grace. All he had to do, anyway, was nod and agree every now and again. It was all that was required of him.

Before they left the pub, Farrell tried Grace again. Still no answer. He bought a bottle of Jameson from the barman and he and Gerry drank it before going to bed. It kept his rage real, alive, justified. By the time they'd finished the whiskey, Farrell's anger at Grace, at P.J., at the turn his life was taking, had reached a new level. He felt the beginnings of a new sense of his own power.

He slept.

He and Gerry began work on the top storey first thing on Tuesday morning. Christy and Paddy were already working on the roof. If the fine October weather continued, all the external work would be finished on time. McConnell's had made the second delivery of materials, and Farrell started work straight away on the window-frames. His head was throbbing again, but most of the anger seemed to have been released the night before. He was still prepared to accept a reasonable explanation from Grace.

Gerry's radio was blaring. Farrell couldn't hear himself think. He left his tools on the floor and crossed the landing, avoiding the rotten boards, to where Gerry was sawing new joists.

'Gerry, will you for Christ's sake turn that down.'

But Gerry was standing stock still in the far corner of the room, beside the large sash window. He was looking down, at something under his feet. His stance reminded Farrell, with a jolt, of someone standing over the grave of a loved one.

'Gerry?'

Still he didn't move. Farrell crossed the room quickly and fumbled at the off button on the top of the radio. He turned to Gerry, furious. The man's face had gone dead white; his black hair stood out in ludicrous contrast, like a wig worn by a circus performer. His hands were clenched by his sides.

'Gerry? What's the matter?'

Gerry turned and saw him then. He put his finger urgently to his lips, signalling up to the roof with his free hand.

Farrell nodded. He pulled the radio towards him and turned it on again, a little lower in volume than before. He stooped until his head was level with Gerry's. He had a strong urge to laugh; he imagined telling this to Grace sometime. The name is Bond, James Bond.

'What the fuck's goin' on, Gerry?'

Farrell kept his voice low, to humour him.

Gerry dragged his hand through his already unruly, startled hair. He knelt down, hitching his overalls a little to allow him more freedom of movement.

Farrell watched as he pulled a length of tongue-and-groove board away from under the window. Idly, Farrell noticed that it was newer than the other timbers in the room. Underneath, resting snugly on the hollowed-out joist, was what looked like an oiled rag. Something sleek and black was just protruding, pointing straight at them. Silently, Gerry placed the object in his left hand, drawing away the oiled cloth with his right.

Balanced blackly on Gerry's outstretched, trembling palm was a large, shining gun.

Something flashed behind Farrell's eyes. There was a shock of recognition that ran deep through his body. The germ of an idea began to grow inside him.

'What is it?'

There were beads of sweat across Gerry's upper lip.

'It's a revolver; a Ruger. Standard RUC issue. And it's already loaded.'

Farrell was careful to say the right thing.

'Should we call the Guards?'

Gerry looked at him, horrified.

'You must be fuckin' jokin'. Once you've been inside, they never believe you. I could end up in the shit all over again because of this.'

He wiped his lip with the back of his sleeve.

Farrell ducked.

'Mind where you're pointin' that.'

'It's OK. The safety's on. We could put it back, pretend we never seen it. Or we could take it, throw it away, pretend it was never here. This place has been derelict for nearly a year now.'

'We?'

Gerry looked at him imploringly.

'I don't even want to touch it, man. I don't want any more trouble. And I'd say whoever stashed this is long gone.'

'Any idea how long it's been there?'

'The cloth is scorched, so it must have been here during the fire. I'd say no one will collect it now. You'd be a bit obvious rummaging around here, your arse to the wind.'

Gerry's smile was white, ghastly.

Farrell already knew what he was going to do, had known the minute Gerry had unwrapped the smoky, oily cloth.

'I'll take care of it.'

Gerry's face flooded with relief.

'Jaysus, man, thanks. I couldn't go through all that again.'

His hands were still shaking. Farrell didn't know what had happened to Gerry during his long absences in the past. He didn't want to know now.

'On one condition.'

'What?'

'That you don't open your mouth about this. No pub talk. I swear, I'll land you right in it if it ever gets back to me that you were talking about this, drink or no drink.'

Farrell kept his voice controlled, emphatic. He wanted to make very sure that Gerry got the message. Gerry raised both hands, cowboy surrender. He looked Farrell straight in the eye.

'I swear. As far as I'm concerned, this never happened.'

Something in Farrell's expression made him repeat his promise. His nervousness was extreme.

'Show me how to keep this safe.'

'It's simple. Just make sure the safety is on, like it is now.'

Gerry pulled at something; there was a click and a smooth movement of black metal.

'Now the safety's off.'

Farrell watched closely.

'Now it's on.'

Farrell reached out to touch it. The cold metal tingled like an electrical shock all the way up his right arm to his shoulder.

'They're very simple to use: you just aim and pull the trigger. You don't need to be an expert.'

Farrell looked at him coldly.

'I won't want to use it. I just don't want any surprises.'

'There won't be any. Trust me. I know what I'm talking about.'

Farrell let that pass.

'How do you know it's loaded?'

'I've checked. Four of the chambers are full.'

Gerry was shifting from foot to foot. He was eyeing the door constantly.

Farrell nodded slowly.

'Remember what I said.'

Without another word, he took the Ruger from Gerry, turned on his heel, and crossed the landing to the room where he'd been working. He hunkered over his toolbox and pulled out his white cotton cloth. Carefully, he wound it round and round the revolver, making sure not to disturb the position of the safety catch. Then he placed it in his toolbox, and stood the box in the corner of the room, his jumper draped carelessly over it. Nobody ever went near his things. It would be safe.

As he walked away from it, his calmness began to seep out of every pore. Instead, he felt himself being charged with excitement, his head full of noise, the spaces around him electrified with the needle-sharp sensations of danger.

He would hide it, put it away for ever, of course. But the *knowledge* of it gave him power. It felt like something in his life was finally, irrevocably, shifting towards equilibrium. But he wasn't going to think about it any more, now. He must give nothing away.

Farrell pushed himself relentlessly for the rest of the day. He refused lunch, tea, evening pint. He had loose ends to tidy up. He was making up for lost time.

It was Thursday night before Farrell finally got through to Grace.

'Farrell! I was getting really worried. I thought you were going to ring and leave me a number where I could contact you?'

Her voice was breathless, anxious.

Farrell remembered his promise. Strangely, he hadn't thought of it until now. He hadn't imagined her being concerned, hadn't thought of anything being his fault. But that still didn't take the sting out of her not being there every time he phoned.

'I hate talking to answering-machines, you know that. And I seemed to keep missing you.'

Farrell kept his voice affectionate, casual. There was a slight hesitation, an uneasy pause, before she spoke again.

'Well, I have been out a fair bit. I'll tell you all the news when I see you.'

Guilt. He detected guilt in that admission. But he was newly strengthened now; he could cope with whatever she had to tell him. He finished his glass of whiskey, nursing the warm tumbler as he allowed the silence to grow. He was enjoying this feeling of being totally in control. He liked the way whiskey did that to him. It was a new feeling, this not caring about anyone else. It made his head feel light, free. It was his turn now.

'Money's running out, Grace. Have to go.'

'When will you be home?'

'Sunday night.'

'Do you want me . . .'

And the phone cut off.

No, thought Farrell. I don't want you to collect me. Right now, I don't even know if I want you, full stop. He went to the bar and ordered more whiskey. He drank it while the barman pulled pints for him and Christy. He felt extraordinarily clear-headed. He didn't know what he was going to do next, but he knew it would be something significant, decisive. He felt that he was finally coming to the end of feeling less important than other people. He'd spent his whole life invisibly. He'd had to keep apologising for his own existence, pleasing others, keeping everyone else happy. He shivered as he remembered the Ruger. It would always be his secret; he could draw strength from its sleek, powerful presence.

As Farrell carried the drinks across the room, he put all those thoughts away for later. He must engage with Christy on a completely different level.

He felt exhilarated now, limitless. His new-found sense of his own importance expanded with whiskey and conversation. There were no longer any boundaries to his happiness. He would become a name to be reckoned with. Match that, P.J.

Grace was waiting for him when he got out of the taxi on Sunday night. She hugged him and led him by the hand into the dining-room. He was surprised and pleased. The table was set, candles lit. There was a warm, spicy smell coming from the kitchen.

Grace poured him a glass of red wine.

'Welcome home,' she said, stretching up to kiss him. 'I missed you.'

'I missed you, too,' he said.

It was true. Here, at home with her, some of the events of the past week began to fade, to seem utterly unreal. He felt tempted again to tell her about Jenny; he was ready to tell her everything.

But somehow, he let the moment pass.

'This is one of my surprises,' she said, smiling up at him.

'What?'

'I started a cookery course on Monday night. That's where I was when you rang. And tonight, you're going to sample what I learned!'

Farrell felt immediately guilty, then put out. She hadn't discussed this with him. They always decided together on what they were going to do. He tried to look pleased. But he was aware of his smile as false, brittle. The skin on his face seemed to stretch tightly across his bones. He could feel the dryness in his mouth as he made to speak.

'And what else were you up to while I was away?'

Even to his own ears, the question had a harsh, jagged edge to it. He drained his glass quickly. The wine had an unpleasant, bitter taste after the whiskey he and Christy had had on the train. It seemed to go to his head almost at once, filling him with a reckless, angry lightness.

Grace's face had gone white.

'What do you mean?'

'I tried every night to contact you. I didn't get you until Thursday. Where were you?'

He hadn't meant to behave like this. He watched her face as she grew upset.

'Farrell, please, don't be like this.'

It was the pleading look on her face that did it. It stirred old, old memories. It made him cruel.

'I asked you. Where were you?'

He had never spoken to her like this before. He was filled to the brim with a sense of his own power. He felt as though he was leaving an old, useless self behind. And the dark image of the gun gave him comfort. I'm Farrell; nobody messes with *me*.

'All right, I'll tell you where I was. On Monday night, in the local Tech. On Tuesday, out for a meal in Anna's. On Wednesday, in my parents'. On Thursday, at home. On Friday, babysitting for Ruth. On Saturday, at home. Is there anything else you'd like to know?'

Her face had grown tight and closed with anger. Farrell began to feel sorry, but he couldn't pull back now. He wanted to tell her that he loved her, that he'd missed her, that he'd seen Jenny, but none of it would come.

Instead, irrelevantly, he realised that she wasn't smoking. Hands in his pockets, he looked down at her.

'How come you're not smoking?'

'What!'

She looked up at him, blankly.

'You always smoke when you're upset. And you're not smoking now.'

'What are you trying to say?'

She wasn't angry, Farrell saw instantly: she was afraid. Afraid that he would find out whatever it was that she was hiding? He wouldn't let her know, yet, that he suspected she'd been up to something. Consorting with the enemy. What did they call it? Giving aid and comfort, that was it. Time enough for that later.

He remained silent, gazing down at her.

It was Grace who broke the silence.

'There's something very wrong here. Tell me what it is. What's the matter?'

She was crying now.

He was surprised at how detached he felt from her. Always when she wept, something inside him shattered. He always wanted to make it better. But tonight, all he was conscious of was the empty spaces he could see all around, and in between them. He still didn't answer her.

'Farrell, you're destroying us. Your jealousy will wreck us. I'm tired of it. Tired of feeling anxious every time I have to be away from you, tired of leaving my handbag like some sort of signal that I'll be back, tired of you not trusting me.'

All her anger was gone now; she was speaking more quietly. Farrell could see how small and crumpled her face had become. But although he heard and understood her words, their pain didn't reach him. The stillness had surrounded him again. He realised, with surprise, that he was now invulnerable, impenetrable.

'I'm going to bed,' he said.

He walked out of the room, taking his toolbox upstairs with him.

His legs felt heavy, leaden. But he had just enough strength to get there.

He put his toolbox into his wardrobe, right at the very back. It was too heavy to lift any further. Then he pulled off his shoes. Waves of weariness washed over him, making him sink onto the bed before he was fully undressed.

He slept instantly.

Grace sat among the ruins of the first dinner she had ever cooked. She felt as though her mouth had filled with grit. She had difficulty steadying her hand to light the first cigarette of the day. Not a good time, obviously, to try and give them up. Farrell's jibe had cut her right to her heart.

And she *was* tired, tired of his endless watchfulness, his prickly insecurity. She loved him dearly, but something had to change between them. She wanted only a little more from life than what he offered. She wanted to be able to breathe again.

With Farrell away she had felt free to speak to both her parents, with a confidence she had never known before. It was as though they had finally accepted her as a grown-up; she was aware of having outgrown them as parents. She no longer needed their approval. They were all adults, equals. They'd never mentioned Farrell; the discussion had been about her, Grace. The relief of that had been enormous.

P.J. had been a surprising source of strength. Go for it, he had advised her. He, who had been so dead set against it in the past. Now, he would support her in whatever way she wished.

After all these years. The College of Art. The possibility, no, more than that, the *probability* of a place as a mature student next year. The portfolio, so lovingly prepared in her spare time at the shop, the examples of her craftwork, her design experience – the interview board had been impressed. *A student of exceptional talent.* They had reassured her that she was good. *Very* good. She need never doubt it again.

And, apprehensive as she was of Farrell's reaction, she had desperately wanted to tell him – but not over the phone.

Now, tonight, he was angry – in a way she had never seen him before. She was sure that art college was what she wanted, had never stopped wanting. She was happy in her own strength, sure of the rightness of her decision. But she could not now imagine Farrell even wanting to understand.

It was strange. He had helped her so much, in the early days. And now, when she was so strong, so sure of what she wanted, so serene in a hard-won independence, he was moving away from her, pushing her back behind the boundaries of his anger.

Tonight was the first time ever that she had felt she could not reach him, might never reach him again. She poured some more wine into her glass. So much for a home-cooked meal. She couldn't bear to look at its mute remains.

Grace lit another cigarette and looked around her, at what they had so lovingly built together. She felt very sad.

She didn't know what she was going to say to him in the morning.

When Farrell woke up the next morning, Grace was gone.

He turned quickly to look at the clock on his bedside locker. Half past nine. He had slept long and heavily. His head felt full; uneasy thoughts shuffled around one another. With a shock, he started to remember snatches of his conversation with Grace the night before. He lay back, his hands over his face as he tried to force the details into focus. It was the whiskey; the whiskey had done it. How else could he ever have behaved like that?

He remembered the gun. He took his hands away from his face long enough to check that he had put the toolbox away safely. He had a very hazy memory of having done so. He tried to still his breathing; his heart was thumping painfully against his ribs. What else had he done? What else had he said?

Farrell struggled to a sitting position in the bed. His head began to clear. It was as though he had found a chink in the wall of pain separating himself from the rest of the world. He saw how he must have appeared to Grace. He had frightened her. That he was capable of doing that now frightened him.

He reached for the telephone and dialled the number in Blackrock.

'Bábóg Toys Ltd. Can I help you?'

He felt his shoulders relax. At least she was there. Maybe he could still put things right.

'Grace? It's me.'

He couldn't even say his own name. He was ashamed.

'This is not a good time.'

Her voice was cool, polite.

'I know. I just had to ring to say I'm sorry for the way I behaved last night. I'm really ashamed of myself.'

'I don't know what's going on.'

'I know, I know. I'm sorry for being so difficult. I'll try to explain later on.'

'I have to go now; we're busy.'

Long fingers of panic clawed at Farrell's throat.

'I'll see you later?'

'Of course; about half six.'

'I'll be waiting.'

''Bye.'

Farrell replaced the receiver gently. Mrs Casey's words

from long ago were filling his ears. You don't have to follow bad example. But that was exactly what he *was* doing. Farrell swung his feet to the floor. He felt filled with a sense of revelation. He was being a bully. Just like his father before him. Just like *her* father. And he had wanted to be so different. He began to walk restlessly around the bedroom. He had the sense that he was searching for something. Whenever he felt that he was close, whatever it was slipped away again and his head filled with noise. He began to feel really afraid. He wrapped both arms around himself, anchoring his hands in his armpits for warmth. He was suddenly freezing cold.

Then the sense of space, of a growing distance from himself, began all over again. He shook his head violently, willing it to go away. No matter how he fought it, it was always stronger than he was. His eyes were drawn to the portable television set near the bedroom window. He focused on it, repeating the word, its name, over and over again. It would stop him slipping. But the stillness kept descending, cutting out all the sounds made by his own voice. He stared helplessly at the screen. Its silent gleam fascinated him, immobilised him. He could no longer remember what it was. He was riveted by the convex eye, overwhelmed by its gaze.

He watched as a small boy seemed to grow beside him. He was fair-haired, skinny. Wearing a red jumper with holes at the elbow and Farrell knew who he was. He was Vinny.

And Vinny was excited. He couldn't wait for night-time to come. Everybody on the whole street had been invited to the Caseys'. They were the first family on the street to get a television set. Vinny was secretly proud that he had been the first of all the neighbours to see it. Mrs Casey had singled him out and brought him into their house just before Christmas. She had given him and

Patrick cups of fizzy lemonade and a sticky cake she'd called 'pudding'. Vinny had gazed in wonder at the size and the silent authority of the set, all gleaming mahogany and glass. It had dominated the room, silencing even Patrick's chatter. Vinny couldn't wait for the set to be switched on, to see the miracle of moving images. The day was crawling past very slowly. He did as he was told from early morning, minded the younger kids and kept everyone well out of his father's way. He didn't want to be punished; and he knew his father was just waiting to pounce, to have an excuse to leave him at home, to deprive him of the highlight of the holidays.

Mr Casey had built a large unit in the good room to show off the new set. It had shelves above and below, full of pretty ornaments, and two half-size louvre doors in the middle. Vinny wanted to run his hands over the smooth, polished wood. Everything was shining in the Casey household. Vinny loved its constant smell of varnish, of warm wood. He even liked the bitter, burnt smell of sawdust as Mr Casey's saw cut deeply and smoothly into rough planks; solid, capable hands, shock of white hair, pencil behind the right ear.

Now Vinny waited patiently, waited for the doors to be opened so that the set could be revealed to everyone. He felt absurdly proud, as though he had some special, privileged place in tonight's audience.

It was New Year's Eve, 1961.

Mr Casey waited until all the neighbourhood children were settled expectantly on his floor. The men lounged around, propped up against the walls, talking knowledge-ably about reception, rabbits' ears, VHF. Mrs Casey moved in and out of the kitchen, with trays of cake and lemonade. There was the rattling of cups and saucers, the shrill whis-tling of kettles, the metallic clinking of teapots. The voices and laughter of the women floated high over the sounds they made.

Mr Casey, fiddling with the rabbit's ears, turned to some of the men leaning against the wall and said with a grin: 'There'll be something stronger for us later. We'll not launch the new television station on tea!'

Vinny had never seen him so much at ease, so willing to talk, his blue eyes crinkling with pleasure. The men around him laughed and pulled on their cigarettes. One of them made a response that Vinny didn't catch. Mrs Casey was on her way past with a tray.

'That's enough of that,' she said sharply. 'There are children here, I'll thank you to remember.'

The silence didn't last long enough to be uncomfortable.

Vinny's mother smiled at them all as she carried in a big blue and white striped jug full of milk. The baby, Jenny, was asleep in her arms. She slept through everything. Her three oldest brothers thought she was great but Patrick did not. He wanted to be the baby still. Vinny saw his mother's eyes flicker anxiously above his head to where he knew his father was standing silent, hands deep in his pockets, determined to be unimpressed.

Then, suddenly, someone called for quiet. Someone else switched off the main light. Mr Casey proudly opened the two half-size louvre doors to reveal the huge, gleaming screen which silently reflected all the suddenly elongated children sitting on the floor.

Eoin, Jody and Patrick all sat clustered around Vinny, waiting for Mr Casey to work his magic. Vinny kept an eye on Patrick, who was well past his bedtime. He had a cold and he was cranky. His big brother kept wiping his nose for him, and whispering to him to keep him smiling. The minute Patrick started to act up, he was to take him home, that was the deal. Vinny prayed that he'd be good.

He wanted to see the new miracle of television, the 'coming thing' as Mr Casey called it.

There was a sudden explosion of sound; a black and white picture shuddered into life. Mr Casey kept turning the rabbit's ears. The picture rolled and slipped a few times, jerking back again and again into snowy focus. When it settled, everyone cheered. Vinny stared at the image of Nelson's Pillar which emerged from the gloom. Someone was standing at its railinged base, breath smoking out in front of him, talking excitedly into a large microphone. The grown-ups started talking all at once, putting names to faces, places. O'Connell Street, the Gresham Hotel, Gay Byrne, Eamon Andrews, Donnybrook. It was snowing heavily all the time, but this only increased, rather than reduced, the ardour of the milling crowds in Dublin's city centre.

Vinny thought it was the most wonderful thing he had ever seen. When he looked down again, Patrick was fast asleep. Eoin and Jody were both silent, goggle-eyed at the wonder before them. Vinny began to relax. He'd be able to stay late. No one was going to kick up. Even the adults now fell silent. They ceased calling out to each other the names of the people and places that appeared on the booming screen. Vinny often wondered at that: grown-ups' passion for naming everything they saw, even the familiar, as though reassuring themselves and each other that things were as expected, as they should be. It was important to adults that things were recognisable; this was the sign that their lives were never going to be anything other than secure and unchanging. He felt transported to another world as he watched familiar images of streets and buildings take on a sheen of perfection, a lustre which they lacked in everyday life. Television transformed things, made the ordinary look polished and lovely.

He had no idea how long they had all been sitting there

when Mrs Casey tapped him gently on the shoulder. He looked around, startled. The room had settled into familiarity, as though they all did this every night. He noticed that the men had glasses of whiskey. He was surprised. He had never even noticed it happening.

Mrs Casey was smiling at him.

'You were miles away. Will you give me a hand with the refills?'

He nodded eagerly and followed Mrs Casey into the kitchen. He made his way carefully around Patrick and Jody, who were both fast asleep in warm lumps on the floor. Eoin's eyelids were closing every few seconds, but he was doing his best to keep awake.

'I'll put on the kettle for more tea. Peter and John are making sandwiches. Will you bring around the bottle of whiskey? Pour about that much,' she indicated with a distance between her thumb and forefinger. 'Mr Casey will help you out if you need him.'

Vinny nodded and took the bottle. He knew what she meant. He'd seen before how the men grew insistent where there was whiskey. But it wasn't that sort of night. Everybody was good-humoured, even his father seemed to be enjoying himself, talking to the other men. Normally he surrounded himself with silence, often giving no indication that he heard, or cared about what was going on around him.

Vinny made his way in among the drowsy bodies of the other children. He picked his way carefully, making sure he didn't stand on an outstretched arm or a suddenly shifting leg. He could feel his father's eyes on him, or maybe he was just watching the bottle. Whatever it was, the uneasy creeping sensation was enough to distract Vinny's attention for a split second from what he was doing. He looked up to meet his father's eyes, head on.

At that very moment, Patrick jerked in his sleep. He

flung out his arm, moaning, right into Vinny's path. Vinny wasn't able to stop himself. His right foot came down on Patrick's wrist and the little boy's eyes opened with a howl. Vinny lost his balance and went hurtling over the bodies of the other sleeping children. He watched in horror as the bottle of whiskey sailed over the hearth-rug and exploded against the tiled fireplace, missing the flaming coals only by inches. Suddenly, the room was filled with a tremendous noise.

Vinny wanted to die.

He thought he was going to. His head filled with an extraordinary thumping, but all around him was stilled. He felt as though there were suddenly two of him. One of him watched, silently, as his father handled his body roughly. He watched as his father took him by the ear, felt the stinging blow across his cheeks. He watched as his father marched him down Mrs Casey's hallway and out into the snow. He noticed that his father had not stopped to let him put on his wellies, lined up with the other children's, just inside Mrs Casey's door.

He watched as Vinny was marched home through the snow in thin, grey socks. Up the stairs, into his bedroom at a run. Then the door slammed shut. He lay there, freezing cold, his eyes shut to the humiliation which swam around his bedroom.

Suddenly, the other Vinny's feet began to pain him, changing from icy cold to raw, red, burning. After what seemed like a long time, the door opened again and a sniffling Patrick was carried in by his mother, her eyes reddened. Eoin and Jody followed quietly. The room shifted back to where it should be; sounds began to filter through. He became himself again.

He realised he was sobbing.

His mother put her arms around him. Patrick snuggled up to him, still giving the occasional hiccup.

'Oh, Vinny, Vinny,' she whispered.

He knew what she didn't say. That he always managed to rouse his father's anger. That he always did something outrageous when his father was around, instead of hiding like a little mouse. But he hadn't meant to, had certainly not meant to tonight. And still he had done damage. Now he'd be hearing about it for months, from everyone on the street.

His mother stroked the hair back from his forehead.

'Mrs Casey says you're not to worry. She'll see you tomorrow.'

Her words were whispered, gentle. He could feel her heart breaking as well as his own.

There was a shout from downstairs.

'I'm coming,' she called back.

She kissed them all hurriedly.

'Vinny, tuck them in. I'll be back later.'

And she was gone.

Eoin and Jody looked, unblinking, at their big brother. They had never seen him sob before. He tried to smile, for them.

'It's all right. Come on, into bed quick.'

They did as he told them. Lying beside Patrick, he felt his face begin to throb. His whole body felt the humiliation of what he had done. The uproar, the spilt whiskey, the Caseys' night wrecked. It was too much. He put his face into the pillow and willed himself to shut it out of his mind. It was the only way to get rid of bad feelings. Stay still and silent, and it would feel like it was all happening to somebody else.

Vinny dreamt that the fire in his feet was spreading throughout his body. He felt hot and dry. The flames were not able to get out. They got hotter and hotter and stronger and stronger until eventually they exploded out of every pore, licking and devouring him until there was nothing of him left.

Farrell was trembling, sweat seeping out of every pore, making him feel damp, coldly sticky. He lay down on the bed again until the worst of the shaking had subsided. Why was he remembering all these things, now? What did they mean? The memory of the skinny little boy with the icy feet made Farrell feel very sad. He was normal again now, weakened and afraid, but back in his own body, his own place. He'd have to tell Grace. He needed her help.

He stumbled into the bathroom and turned on the shower. He turned the cold water on full and stood there until his teeth chattered. He never wanted to feel that intense, dry, dream-heat ever again. He towelled himself roughly. As he stepped out from behind the shower curtain he was gripped by such a feeling of exhaustion that he had to hold on. His eyes began to film over. He gasped as the curtain-rail wrenched free of its fixings and he tripped, wrapped in blue and white striped nylon, flailing like a stranded fish. It took him a long time to fall. The wooden floor felt warm under his cheek. The coppery taste from long ago was back in his mouth again.

He closed his eyes gratefully. He slept.

He had no idea how long he'd been lying there. When he woke, he felt strangely alert, as though he was waking up after a long, refreshing sleep. He'd tell Grace he'd slipped. That would be sufficient explanation for the shower curtain and the cut on his lip. He really felt much better, even light-hearted. He needn't worry her with anything else.

It was probably just the strangeness of the last week without her. He'd explain, reassure her that everything was all right. Perhaps he'd even tell her about Jenny; that would help her to understand the strain he'd been under for the last couple of days. He would not alarm her; he'd keep his memories to himself. He was pleased with his decision, went downstairs with an easy mind.

He cleaned up the kitchen, made a quick meal and opened a bottle of wine. When he heard Grace's key in the lock, everything looked absolutely normal.

He went out into the hall to greet her. Without saying a word, he wrapped his arms around her and lifted her off the floor. He knew this always made her feel protected, safe. But tonight she struggled against him. Surprised, he put her down. Didn't she know everything was all right now?

She raised her eyes to his face. He could see that she was about to say something. When she saw his cut lip, his swollen face, her expression immediately changed.

'What's happened to your poor face?'

She touched his cheek with her hand, her eyes full of concern.

Farrell's heart lifted. Good. She would forget all about last night. He would put a shape to it, explain it away for her. It need not be important any more.

'I slipped in the shower. I've been a bit distracted over the last few days.'

'Let me look at it.'

Obediently, he sat down and let her gentle hands probe.

'You should have a stitch.'

Her voice was worried.

He took hold of both her hands.

'I'm OK. Sit down, Grace.'

He loved her name, never tired of repeating it.

She sat.

'I can't tell you how sorry I am about last night.'

She watched him, her face impassive. Even her hands were still.

'I had a very strange experience while I was in Dundalk. I saw my sister, Jenny.'

He stopped. He couldn't help the way his face filled with emotion. He felt the corners of his mouth turn down.

Grace's eyes widened.

'What! Did you speak to her?'

'Yes, but she didn't know me. She said her name wasn't Jenny. She told me to leave her alone, I was never to speak to her again.'

Farrell hung his head.

'That's why I was so desperate to get in touch with you. It really threw me off balance.'

Grace stood up and cradled his face in her hands.

'And I wasn't here for you. Oh, Farrell, I'm so sorry. I could have come up, maybe we could have spoken to her together. Do you know where she lives?'

Farrell was filled with happiness. She believed him absolutely. She didn't even ask — are you sure? She wasn't sceptical or hesitant. The damage was undone.

He shrugged his shoulders sadly.

'No. I met her on the street. She said she'd call the Guards if I ever went near her again.'

'But maybe if I came with you? If we looked for her together?'

Farrell smiled at her. How strange. Losing Jenny had been his means of getting Grace back again. She was enough. He was happy.

'No, I don't think so. We both got very upset. I think it's better not to pursue it.'

'Was she on her own?'

Farrell nodded. He was not going to tell Grace about her children. Two healthy babies and another one on the way.

'Yes. She looked well. Pretty, confident, well-dressed. She's doing OK. It's best to leave well enough alone.'

'No wonder you were upset. I'm really sorry not to have been here when you called. Can you really let it go at that? Are you sure you don't want to look for her again?'

He nodded.

'Yes. Absolutely. And I feel much better for having told you about it.'

And now I have you back.

She hugged him.

'Go inside and sit down. I'll bring in dinner on a tray. We have a lot of catching up to do, you and I.'

She kissed the top of his forehead. He stood up, filled with happiness. It was going to be all right after all. All the catching up was going to be all right.

Farrell was surprised at his own ability to live in two completely different places at the same time. Here he was with Grace, on a normal Monday night in his normal middle-class home, eating good food and sipping a glass of wine, laughing a little ruefully about his cut and tender face. Even his regret at not connecting with Jenny sounded normal, eliciting Grace's sympathy and concern, but no trace of fear. At the same time, he was conscious of covering a great darkness from her. Memories continued to stab at him, causing his heart to pound, his body to sweat. Nonetheless, he was able to arrange himself so that Grace saw and heard only the Farrell she expected. He was able to watch her closely, alert for signs: a frown, an intake of breath, a too-rapid smoking of cigarettes. But there was nothing. She was relaxed; he was in control.

He swore never to let it slip again, never to let last night happen again. He was ashamed that he had made her afraid.

He was, after all, better than their fathers.

It must have been a full week after he came back from Dundalk that she told him.

She had booked a table for nine o'clock in the Chinese restaurant where they had had their first dinner together. Farrell was pleased. It must be a special occasion. She looked lovely. Her dark hair was sleek, her lips and nails painted a bright, glossy red, her short, sophisticated silk dress right in fashion. He was proud of her, proud of what he had made of her. She followed the waiter to their table, her walk relaxed and assured. Farrell noticed the discreet, admiring glances from some of the other diners. He felt a great surge of joy. His wife. He could never match her confidence, her belief in her place in the world, but she was his. She had chosen him above all others. Walking after her, he had a bright vision of the rest of their lives together. He saw them hand in hand, Grace leaning slightly towards him, resting against him from time to time, as they grew older. Nothing would ever change. They would always be together, the same as they were tonight.

She reached for his hand across the white linen.

'Happy memories?' she asked, smiling.

He squeezed her hands, about to explode with happiness.

'Absolutely. We've come a long way.'

The waiter brought the wine to their table. Grace sipped at it, and nodded to him; the waiter poured some for both of them. It was a pleasing ritual, soothing. Like making tea, Farrell thought, and was instantly embarrassed at the thought. Good thing she couldn't read his mind. They read the menu, both deciding at almost the same time to order exactly the same dishes.

They laughed, and Farrell raised his glass.

'To us.'

She raised hers, and looked across the table at him. Yet she somehow managed to avoid looking directly into his eyes. Whatever he saw in her smooth face was gone in an instant, but Farrell recognised trouble. He knew her so well, could read all her expressions. He waited. She lit a cigarette. There was something coming.

'When you were away in Dundalk, something very important happened to me, too.'

He kept his face composed.

'Really?'

There was just a hint of surprise in his voice. He leaned towards her, making his expression interested. Eyebrows raised slightly, eyes open and receptive, mouth smiling. His pulse was already starting to speed up, his palms were already sweaty. He kept his hands firmly anchored around his glass.

'Yes. The National College of Art and Design contacted me about my portfolio.'

Farrell was confused. Art college was years ago, years before him. What portfolio was she talking about?

He knew that puzzlement was written all over his face. He allowed it to settle across his forehead. The freeze of fear was too close, just below the surface.

'What portfolio?'

He had to sip his wine carefully. His mouth was dry.

'Designs and sketches I've been working at on and off for years. But I've been doing a lot more of it lately. When I read that they were accepting mature students, I realised I wanted to try again.'

She stopped. Something in Farrell's face disturbed her. She swirled the wine in her glass. When she looked directly at him, her eyes were pleading. He drew a deep breath.

'Farrell? Are you angry?'

'Of course not. Just – surprised. I thought you would have told me about it.'

She shrugged, spreading her hands to right and left, a gesture of excuse, not quite dismissal.

'I really believed it wouldn't come to anything. I've always felt that I wasn't good enough. But they contacted me last week, while you were in Dundalk. I've been accepted. I'll have to reapply for next year, of course, but they've said it's only a formality.'

Farrell had to make his decision instantly. He knew what he had to do. A lot of things seemed to fall into place once he had decided.

He raised Grace's hand to his lips and kissed it. He smiled, leaning over towards her intently.

'That is absolutely wonderful. No wonder we're celebrating! Congratulations!'

He signalled to the waiter. He used the moment to regain full control of himself. He had promised never to let it slip again. Out of the corner of his eye, he saw Grace's face flood with relief. At that moment, he felt he could almost hate her. It was the face of someone used to getting everything they wanted.

'A bottle of your best champagne, please!'

The waiter looked a little confused. He bowed stiffly, and moved away.

'Now, tell me all about it!'

She was lit up inside; he had made her very happy, she said; she'd been afraid he wouldn't like the idea, she said; she felt so lucky, she said.

Farrell nodded and listened, refilled their glasses, kept a steel grip on himself.

Grace leaving him for art college. His image of a serene middle age together began to disintegrate before his eyes, little swirling black dots all that remained of the picture. Late nights, parties, activities that had no place for him, new friends.

Young men.

Over his dead body.

And of course, that wasn't the end of it. That weekend, she showed him her portfolio, hesitant at first, then glowing with pride as he praised everything she had done. He saw in each sketch, each design, a painful reminder of her talent. Her lines were fluid; even the most restrained sketch had movement, energy.

All day Saturday and Sunday, he made himself think only about her. They discussed the arrangements for looking after the shop for next year. Terms were short, she assured him; she would spend all her holiday-time working in Blackrock. She'd have to cut down on her orders for dolls, but Ruth and Anna were well able to manage everything else, now. With a stab of surprise, Farrell realised that she had been, quietly, unobtrusively, training her sisters to take over in her absence. How long had she been planning all of this? He tried to put the feeling of betrayal aside; now wasn't the time to deal with it.

He went with her to buy an easel, canvases, sketch pads, pastels, oils – the list was endless. They renovated the attic studio together; Farrell installed an extra Velux to improve the natural light. The dolls were put aside, shelved for now, to make room for all her materials. She wanted to work on her painting for a few hours each day, to hone her skills before next September.

Packing the dolls away, Farrell was overcome with sadness. It was like the ending of childhood. It was as though his own child was growing up, moving away from him for ever. Lots of things were being shelved. But he said nothing. He was, he thought, being the perfect husband.

She was so happy he might even have been able to bear it, if it weren't for P.J.

He was finally, ultimately, the one responsible.

Farrell tries to resist the urge to hurry things along. His plans will be carried out calmly, with no trace of panic or fuss. He has always been prepared to wait for what is good.

There is only half an hour left before Grace's birthday. He has been moving around downstairs, rearranging flowers, repeating finishing touches over and over again.

Finally, he sits down beside the *escritoire* that he and Grace had bought shortly after she'd moved in with him. It had given the flat an air of elegance, distinction. They had restored it together, bringing the wood of the solid oak desk back to its original beauty, replacing the damaged shelves in the bookcase with passionate attention to detail. He still remembers the joy he'd felt that she shared his love of precision.

He pulls out the large leather-bound photograph album from among the carefully arranged old books and starts to turn the pages slowly. He smoothes the tissue-paper very, very gently.

There they are. Hundreds of years ago. As though looking down from a very great height, Farrell examines the figure of a tall, fair-haired man, just entering his forties. It could be anyone. He feels suddenly surprised that it is a photograph of himself, rather than any other man. So tall that he looks gauche, uncomfortable in pin-stripe trousers that go on for ever, and a morning-coat. He is holding a ridiculous hat in his left hand.

P.J. paid the piper, P.J. called the tune.

The man is looking down at a young woman on his

arm, who is laughing joyfully up at him. She is carrying a huge bouquet of red roses and ferns, tied with green and white satin bows. Farrell remembers that someone was horrified that the bride would carry anything green. It was supposed to bring bad luck.

Her hair is swept up under a short veil, held in place with a glittering tiara. With no hair to frame it, Farrell sees how childlike, how vulnerable her face really is.

He remembers the moment when that photograph was taken, the look of complete love on her face as the photographer had called 'Hold that!'

A dress of lace and satin, simple and elegant, moulded to the curves of her small body. Farrell remembers how his fingers used to touch behind her back as his hands spanned her waist.

He remembers how completely happy she was, that day. All the guests were there for her. Grace had begged him to think about his brothers and sister, to think about finding them in honour of the day. So recently reconciled to her own family, she had wanted the same for him.

But Farrell had shaken his head. He would not disturb their lives, he told her. It would be selfish. He was absolutely happy as he was.

In a way, he had told her the truth. He *was* happy, would be even happier once he got her completely away from P.J. But she was so much his life now that he did not want his brothers and sister to disturb that. They were best forgotten.

Farrell remembers how he got through the rest of that day. He remembers the cool politeness of the guests, the expression in P.J.'s eyes as he introduced him to cousins, uncles, business associates with fat cigars and clammy palms.

He remembers counting the hours that night, too.

When he led Grace out onto the dance-floor, he was

rewarded for his patience as she pulled his face down to hers and kissed him, in front of everyone. Out of the corner of his eye, Farrell saw P.J. turn away, shrugging his shoulders, making for the bar with two or three others.

Farrell had held Grace tightly. The spoils of war. Victory was never so sweet.

Abruptly, Farrell closes the album and replaces it in the bookcase.

There are other memories, too. Farrell sits completely still, and allows them to flood him.

There is no hurry.

Tonight, he has all the time in the world.

Chapter Nine

Farrell came home from Blackrock late one evening in April, to find P.J. installed in his kitchen. Under his roof. For the third time in five years. So what did he want this time? Farrell had learned all about P.J.'s part in Grace's new life. She had told him all about her father's helpfulness. For the past six months, ever since she'd told him of her decision, she'd been spending more and more time in her old home. Farrell had even had to endure Christmas dinner in enemy territory. But at least the man hardly ever visited them. Now he was here; what gift was he offering now to bring chaos into their lives?

'Guess what, Farrell?'

Farrell was grateful for the need to take off his jacket and hang it over the back of a chair. He smoothed its shoulders and rested his hands on them. It was like leaning on an old friend. He nodded to P.J. and turned to Grace, smiling, his face open, interested.

'Tell me.'

'P.J. is retiring in June. He's selling the business.'

'Really?' said Farrell.

And then he couldn't think of anything else to say. Grace filled in for him.

'Had enough of the rat-race, haven't you, Dad?'

Farrell felt his heart contract. He hated to hear her call him Dad, hated to hear such fondness in her tone. P.J. smiled. Farrell did not like that smile.

'Yes, it's time to hang up my boots. I want to enjoy my retirement.'

Farrell thought the man looked strange; whiter, thinning around the cheeks. The old expression of mockery was dimming. He looked very different from the way he had at Christmas. Maybe he was getting suddenly old, after all.

'P.J. and Maura are going to Donegal for the summer, and then on a golfing holiday to the South of Spain. They'll be gone until the middle of September.'

Farrell's heart lifted a little. That was the best news he'd heard in a long time. Good riddance.

'But back in time for your birthday, chicken.' P.J. leaned over to Grace and pinched her cheek gently.

Farrell moved over, quickly, to the sink. For something to do, he put on the kettle.

He heard his own voice speak, even before the idea was properly formed.

'Then we must have a party here when you get back. We'll celebrate your retirement and Grace's birthday. We'll have a proper family get-together.'

Farrell smiled broadly as he issued his invitation. Looking down at the enemy, he saw a flicker of uncertainty cross the older man's face.

'Why, thank you, son, that's very kind of you.'

Son. How dare he. Farrell's rage began to build slowly.

'Not at all. I'll cook something really special. We'll make it a night to remember.'

Grace returned his smile, her face gentle, grateful.

'There's one more surprise, Farrell,' she said, smiling over at P.J.

He slapped his hands on his knees. Farrell could see that he took delight in whatever it was that was coming next.

'I'm getting a good price for my company,' he said, looking down at his highly polished shoes, brushing imaginary specks off his trouser-leg; all modesty. 'I want my daughters to share in my good fortune. I'm making each of them a gift.'

He raised his hand as Grace was about to interrupt.

'No, I've made up my mind. All you have to do is talk it over with – Farrell here, and decide whatever it is you both want. You can tell him what we've discussed.'

At that, P.J. stood up, clapping his hands together, delighted with himself. Farrell's throat felt tight, hard as stones again. Another gift. He'd been right all along. Things would never change.

He had difficulty hearing what the man said as he was leaving. Farrell made sure to keep his face still, expressionless, apart from a meaningless little smile of farewell.

Grace closed the door and turned to face Farrell.

Her face was shining.

'He's offered me my fees for college, and a car. He said he hoped this would make up for any unhappiness he'd caused me in the past. Something's changed him, Farrell.'

Yes, thought Farrell. He knows he's won. Full circle. *My daughter*. Farrell felt the insult deeply. As though *he* couldn't provide for his own wife. All these years, the success he'd made of the business, this house – vapour, just vapour. When it came right down to it, it all counted for nothing, not even with Grace. She had turned her back on him, allowing herself to be drawn back into P.J.'s web. She had chosen her family. Blood was thicker than water.

'Farrell?'

Grace had been speaking. Farrell hadn't heard a word. The anger which P.J. had stirred, calling him *son*, began to tighten its fist-like hold around Farrell's heart. Something in Grace's face made him snap back to reality. Control. Get a grip.

'So what did you discuss?'

It must have been a good guess. She continued.

'He's giving each of the three of us twenty thousand

259

pounds. Anna and Ruth are taking cash; he's offered me instead, if I want, all my fees paid and his Mercedes. It's only about a year old. What do you think?'

Was she asking him, or did she want him to confirm what she had already decided for herself? He'd have to be very careful here.

'It really is up to you. I mean this in the best possible way, Grace, but he's your father, and it's his gift to you. I want you to have whatever it is you like best.'

'It'll mean that going to college won't cost us anything. I can sell my own car, and that'll help towards Ruth and Anna's wages . . .'

'The cost is not the issue, Grace.' Farrell's voice was curt. 'We can afford whatever we need. *I* can afford whatever we need if you want to go to art college. I'm asking you to choose whatever gift from your father you like best. That's the only issue.'

He sounded stilted and chilly, he knew that. Allowing any emotion to surface would be his downfall. He had to get this over with.

'I want you to enjoy it, too, Farrell,' she said quietly.

Farrell raised his hands in the air. He was careful to keep the anger out of his voice.

'I'm going to say this once, and then we can put it behind us. I don't want anything to do with any gift from your father. I'll be polite and pleasant and not cause any trouble. But I don't like the man and he doesn't like me. This is his gift to you; I don't feel hard done by or left out or anything else. I just don't want it.'

'He does like you, Farrell, and he respects you.' Grace's voice had gone very quiet. 'He said to me how glad he was that we were happy, that I had made the right choice.'

Bollocks, thought Farrell. And then it struck him. The white face, the thinness, the retirement. The man was *dying*. He wanted to have things all his own way before he died. Tidy up everything to his satisfaction, as if people were just loose ends. He was making one last investment in getting his own way, in making others do as he wanted. He expected to live off the interest until he died.

The thought filled Farrell with a savage satisfaction. Now that he really understood what the man was at, he would not make it any easier for him. He could suffer for whatever time was left, just as he had made Farrell suffer for all the years of his marriage, and before.

He left the room without answering Grace. There was no answer to give her.

He sat on the bed in their bedroom and held his thumping head in his hands. Gradually, the pounding grew a little softer and everything around him grew still again. Wearily, he let it happen. He no longer had the energy to fight it. His body felt invaded by heaviness. Unbidden images began to march in front of his eyes. How could this man expect not to suffer? There he was, calling Farrell a nobody, mocking him at his wedding, scorning him at christenings, taunting him with gifts to his daughter. Big belly, fat hands, smell of smoke and whiskey.

And then, from long ago, all the other hurts. The blows to the face, the suffocating panic on Dollymount Strand, the icy walk home on New Year's Eve. P.J. was to blame for all of them.

In the middle of his silent, waking dream, Farrell realised finally what he'd known from the moment he'd first set foot in Merrion Square as a carpenter.

P.J., Vincent. Father. Father-in-law – what did names matter? There was no difference.

They were all one and the same man.

Grace sat in the August sunshine, watching her nieces and nephews running riot in the garden playground Farrell had created for them. Swings, slides, paddling pool for the toddlers. And today, as a special treat, a garish bouncing castle in the shape of a monstrous, grinning clown. Farrell had insisted on it. To Grace's surprise, he had taken over completely and organised this family gathering for the Bank Holiday weekend. He had, he told her, meant to do it a long time ago. She had been touched at his eagerness to please.

Anna and Ruth sat on either side of her. They were all sipping chilled white wine. Farrell had prepared a picnic for them; they hadn't had to lift a finger since they'd arrived on Friday evening. Grace stretched luxuriously. She loved these long weekends. Renting a house for the month, away from the demands of the city, had been a good idea; Farrell's idea. She saw the next few years unfold in her imagination. College, her work, her closeness to her family again. And Farrell.

He had been wonderful lately. Grace believed that he had finally overcome his unreasonable suspicion of her father, his fear of her family. He'd convinced her that he was happy for her to accept her father's generosity; she'd accepted that he didn't want to talk about it again. Ever since, life had been easy, serene.

Childish shrieks drew her eyes towards the corner of the garden. The children were lining up to be thrown by Farrell onto the clown's inflated lap. He threw each child with just the right amount of force; the older ones were daring, the toddlers longing to be brave, but just a little frightened nevertheless. He never got it wrong.

'Farrell is great with them, isn't he?'

Anna turned to Grace, smiling and waving at her children who were showing off for her benefit.

'Wonderful,' agreed Ruth.

'He really enjoys having them here,' said Grace.

She felt a pang as she looked at her husband, was startled

by a sudden rush of love for him. It must have been very hard on him, too. Being childless had felt as though it was her hurt only, for such a long time. Watching him now, she realised how much of it he must have shared. She wondered at how little husbands and wives knew about each other, really.

Her own grief had grown more diffuse over the years. Sometimes, she felt it would have been easier on them if they'd lost a child, together. Instead, everyone's child, every new baby born had renewed her pain in those early years. But it had got easier. She'd finally stopped seeing babies as a reproach. Now, she was even prepared to see that there were compensations. Her sisters' lives were so completely arranged by the presence of their children that their days seemed to be a constant round of demands, responsibilities. She knew that Anna felt sometimes hemmed in, suffocated by the interminable neediness of others. She, Grace, would have welcomed all of that, of course, had she been able to choose. Lacking that choice, she was learning to relish her freedom; her approaching thirties felt like her coming of age. Thinking of her twenty-ninth birthday next month, of the family party Farrell had planned, she had been struck with all the force of her own mortality. She had never thought about age before. Now, she was conscious of enjoying each day, savouring what the future was holding out to her.

The baby-ache had begun to ease from the moment she'd started to work seriously on her portfolio, from the time when she'd had a definite aim in view. At least she'd been able to create something. Her growing, expanding portfolio had been like a pregnancy, in a way; it had taken away the gnawing emptiness of childlessness.

Grace was glad that all those years were over. She took another sip of her wine, and leaned her head back, closing her eyes against the sun. The noises of the children, the desultory conversation of her sisters began to fade. She felt sleepy.

She had been surprised and pleased at Farrell's acceptance of her plans. She felt that they were really fitting together well of late. In every sense, he felt like her other half.

Filled with love, she opened her eyes for a moment, fighting sleep. She watched him. He waved to her, smiling, pretending exhaustion to all the screaming, tumbling little bodies, wiping his forehead with a huge white handkerchief, begging them for a rest, for mercy. Grace laughed out loud and waved back at him.

She thought she had never been happier in her whole life.

August passed slowly. Farrell couldn't wait for September. He was using his time to think, to plan. He had grown much more peaceful once he had made his decision; the images and memories were less vivid now. Instead, their place had been taken by a gleaming, black, smoothly solid piece of metal. The Ruger. Even the name gave him comfort. It was a word that held power, coiled like a dark spring inside it.

Farrell now saw it all as inevitable. From that moment in that house in Dundalk, when he had held its cold body in his hands, wrapping it carefully in a white cotton cloth, he had known what he was going to do. Maybe at one stage, he had had control over that decision. But not any more. The trail of events from Dundalk to Grace's plans for college, to P.J.'s final gift – they'd all led him to the same place. To be honest, even his first day in Merrion Square as a common carpenter had begun to lead him to this same place.

He wanted to kill P.J. He wanted to shoot him in the

face, to explode him, to shatter every bone and sinew of his existence. He was filled with the image; he felt an almost physical hunger and thirst to do it, to act in some way that finally had consequences. He didn't think of it as revenge. He thought of it more as claiming his place in the world, the place he had always been denied. His years with Grace had not been as he'd hoped. He'd always come second. He was still coming second. There was no other way to say – this is who I am, this is what is mine.

The thought kept Farrell company as he spent long, sunny weekends with Grace and her family in their rented house in Wicklow. He was giving her the best months of her life. She was so pleased with his generosity, so touched by his new efforts with her sisters. He had never seen her happier or more grateful. He was satisfied.

He travelled alone back to Dublin a couple of times each week. Just to keep things ticking over, as he put it. He craved the solitary, silent evenings in his own bedroom. He often laughed out loud when he thought about the sheer, limitless power that filled him. When he stroked the gun's long body, it felt as though all his anger was being taken care of. The feeling renewed him, made him feel strong, gave him the most powerful sense of himself that he had ever had.

On these evenings, he plotted. He imagined many different scenes, many different conversations. The final outcome was always the same. P.J. cowering, pleading. Then, a satisfying ending. Catharsis, wasn't that what they called it?

But he still hadn't got his finale quite right. Something nagged. There was a roughness to it, a prickly discomfort, like splinters in your hand.

And then, one night, it came to him. He had been trying to sleep since midnight. The bed felt huge and empty. He had drifted off a couple of times, coming back to wakefulness with a sickening lurch, his stomach falling as though he had just jumped off a cliff.

Grace would never forgive him. He'd almost forgotten that she was the reason; but she'd never forgive him, never love him again. Even in death, P.J. would stretch out his fat, grasping hands towards her and reclaim her. Either way, she would never be his again.

Of course. How could he have been so stupid. That way he would lose her for ever.

Suddenly, the room was filled with light. A clear, three-dimensional vision shuddered into life before his fascinated eyes. As he watched, he knew what was coming next. He saw P.J., Grace, himself, a whole tableau of figures like some symbolic, mythological painting in one of Grace's books. It was as though he had written each scene himself. It had its own rightness, the smoothness of joints all fitting into place. At first, its appropriateness appalled him, shocked his heart into skipping a beat. But the more he thought about it, the more perfect the design became.

It was the best way to punish Grace's father, all fathers.

Take their child away from them.

Just as he had been punished. All his babies had been snatched from him. Farrell felt a great rush of happiness as the scene played itself out in front of his fascinated eyes. There was a rightness, a feeling of retribution to this scene that delighted him. The sensation was so strong it left him breathless.

To curtail P.J.'s own life would be a kindness, really. Farrell knew that he was dying. He was sharper-eyed than most when it came to death. Grace and her sisters were merely concerned at how tired their father looked, and comforted each other that retirement would make a new man of him. But each time Farrell saw him, it became more obvious to his keen eye that there was something very wrong. The man was shrinking, little by little. He was losing more and more of his substance. The flesh had begun to hang loosely around his face. He was courteous to Farrell. He thought the war was over.

Farrell exulted in P.J.'s appearance. There had been only brief, occasional visits this summer when P.J. travelled back to Dublin from Donegal for reasons he never discussed. Farrell was pleased at his own ability to reassure Grace that yes, he thought he was looking a little better than last time. Yes, his colour was better. No, he didn't look thinner. The old man's weakness filled him with strength. For the first time in his life, he felt in complete control. No one would beat him into submission again. He was Vincent Farrell, a name to be reckoned with. Even after it was all over, he was the one who would control P.J.'s last few months. He would have decided how, and how much, the man was to suffer. Nobody would ever mock him or dismiss him again as a nobody, as half a man. He was not to be messed with.

And now, finally, September was here. Art college began in a week's time. P.J. would be home in ten days. And then, the party for Grace's birthday. Only three more weeks. She would be all his.

He need never fear losing her again.

Grace was gone from early morning, every day now. She was meeting other mature students, spending hours in the college, the library, or painting well into the night. She was filled with such a sense of urgency and energy that sometimes Farrell wondered if she knew, if she'd read his mind.

He worked with Anna and Ruth in Blackrock. Grace had been right. They were well able to handle everything. Even Ruth, with her accountant's mind, managed to surprise him with her flair for tiny pillows and patchwork quilts. Everything was under control. Farrell was grateful to Grace for this. They didn't want any loose ends.

Late September was cool. Farrell took to walking around Merrion Square in the afternoons, remembering. He should have had happy memories of here, but all he could visualise was Grace in a black dress, another man's diamonds at her white, lovely throat. He passed by their old flat several days in a row. Something was gnawing at him, something he couldn't put his finger on. He could see both of them lugging the Christmas tree up the steps, getting wetter and wetter in the fine, sleety rain. He remembered his face stinging.

Was it here that she had started to grow away from him, or had that happened later? They had been happy in the flat, but he had wanted something more for her. Had the move to Meadowbrook Grove done it? Had it reminded her too much of her roots, of what she was entitled to? Gracious living. Her name said it all. He could never compete, should never really have tried.

Two days before the party, Farrell knew that he had one more place to visit. He took the bus from the city centre, getting off at the Clontarf end of Fairview Park, near the railway bridge. He would walk all of it, all the way back again towards the city centre. The park was prettier than it had been in his day. The railings were newly painted, there were cycle paths everywhere.

The bandstand hadn't changed much, though. Peeling paint, sad empty centre. There was a children's playground nearby, now. Farrell watched the children on the slides and see-saws. He ran some of the bark chippings through his fingers. If the children fell, they wouldn't hurt themselves. He was glad that someone was watching out for the children.

The mothers were all young, energetic. Any one of three or four of them might have been Martina. They all dressed in black; leggings, heavy jumpers, boots. The children, on the other hand, were a riot of colour. He smiled at the strength of their resistance to putting on coats or jackets of any kind. Their faces were that raw, ruddy colour whipped up by an east wind. Their noses were snotty. Some things never change, thought Farrell, remembering Patrick with a pang.

He was filled with a most extraordinary longing to visit his old home. He had never been back, never even passed it by in the days when he'd visited the Caseys. Now the need to go was overpowering, suffocating. Farrell stood up suddenly, drawing in a deep breath. He could feel his heartbeat begin to speed up. To his horror, he felt his stomach suddenly turn and he had an urge to vomit. He sat down clumsily on the bandstand again, almost missing his footing.

'Are y'all righ', mister?' asked a young voice.

Farrell looked up. A skinny boy of about eleven was looking at him, curiously. He wore a red jumper, the stitches unravelling at the elbows and wrists. His track suit bottoms were baggy, mucky at the knees. He twirled his football between his hands, at chest level, and kept peering into Farrell's face.

'Yes, I'm fine. Just felt a bit sick all of a sudden. I used to live around here.'

Farrell surprised himself with the suddenness of his confession.

The young boy just nodded.

'Yeah, well. I'll see ya.'

And he was gone, calling out to unseen others.

Farrell felt lonely after he was gone. The park felt cold, grey. Everything had suddenly lost its colour. He stood up unsteadily. He shoved his icy hands in his pockets and made for the little iron gate. Traffic sounds were suddenly unleashed as he left the quiet greenness of the park behind.

It took him a good twenty minutes' walk to reach the corner of his road. He stopped in amazement. It had changed utterly. There were no kids on the street, no homemade trolleys with steering mechanisms made out of string, no swings on lamp-posts. Instead, everything had been prettified beyond recognition.

Double-glazing, aluminium windows, roller-blinds. Gardens pert and tidy. Pebble-dashing white and gleaming. And silence everywhere.

He was upon his old house before he had time to think about it. The small porch was now glassed-in behind a white-framed door. A little hanging panel of stained-glass threw crazy coloured patterns onto the front door. To right and left, the porch was full of umbrella plants and trailing ivy. There was barely enough room to make your way from the front step into the house. He wondered did the new owners polish the tiles on the front step. Or had that gone out of fashion as well? He could see nothing behind the white glare of net-curtained windows. It was as though the houses had closed their eyes to him. The street had a whiff of hostility to it. This was not his territory any more. There was nothing for him here. He was as much a stranger here as he now felt in Meadowbrook Grove.

Farrell turned away abruptly, before reaching the Caseys' house. He had some memory of Angela and her husband having moved in. He didn't want to see her, didn't want to see anyone any more.

It was all nearly over.

Farrell hailed a taxi just before Connolly Station. He didn't feel like walking any further. Tomorrow, he would shop for the party.

The birthday party that no one would ever forget.

He wouldn't tell Grace the menu for the party. It was to be a surprise. Didn't he always surprise her on her birthday?

'Not even a hint?'

'Absolutely not; this is my party. I call the tune.'

They were sitting together on the sofa on Friday night. Farrell had already been shopping early that morning; she knew the fridge was full of bags, but he wouldn't budge. He was giving nothing away.

It was the first evening at home they had spent together in some time. Grace had become more and more taken up with her college activities, arriving home late most evenings. It didn't matter any more. Farrell had spent the time tying up loose ends in Blackrock. He was pleased at the neatness with which everything was being tidied up. A good, clean sweep.

Tomorrow was her birthday. P.J. and Maura, Ruth and James, Anna and Peter would all arrive tomorrow night as planned. Now that the time had come, Farrell felt an enormous tenderness for Grace as she leaned against him on the sofa, her feet tucked up underneath her. She smelt of shampoo and body lotion. He had run a bath for her when she'd arrived home from college, insisting that she take as long as she wanted.

'You're a pet,' she'd said, kissing him on the chin.

Now she was in her dressing-gown, relaxed, at peace with him. Farrell knew it could never get any better than this.

He stroked her hair as they watched some programme on television. When it was over, he kissed the top of her dark, shining head.

'I'm going to pretend we're a couple of old fogeys. Would you like some drinking chocolate?'

'Your special one? With grated chocolate on top, and the little bits of almonds?'

'The very same.'

'I'd love some, and some biscuits to dunk.'

He bowed as he left the room, walking backwards, leaving the presence of royalty.

She laughed.

'I'm glad to see you know your place!'

In the kitchen, he prepared the hot chocolate. Into Grace's mug, he emptied three Dalmane capsules, making the chocolate thick and sweet to hide any lingering after-taste. He decorated the top with curls of chocolate and little nibbles of almonds. He placed the cup on a doily, a silver spoon beside it. He believed in the importance of ritual.

He shook small, crisp wafers onto a plate and carried the tray inside to the coffee table. She put out her cigarette at once and waved the smoke away with her hand.

'Mmm . . . this looks positively decadent. What a lovely treat.'

He sat down beside her again and picked up the remote control for the television. Flicking through the stations, looking for something worth watching, he kept a careful eye on her face as she sipped. Nothing. She had noticed nothing.

He reached for his cup and a movement of her hand stopped him.

'Farrell?'

'Yeah?'

'Thank you for this party tomorrow. It means a lot to me.'

He smiled at her.

'I know.'

'You've been really generous. This last year has been very special. I just wanted you to know that I love you, I love my life.'

She stroked his face.

What was she saying? Was she forgiving him for what

he had to do? Did she know? The thoughts flashed through Farrell's mind as he looked at his wife. She was smiling at him, continuing to stroke his face. At that moment, Farrell became completely peaceful. He knew that he had made the right decision, the only decision. She was telling him that, too. His body filled with a sense of well-being that he had never experienced before. He felt that, at last, he and she were complete.

It was going to be all right. Everything was going to be all right.

He leaned forward and kissed her softly.

'I love you, Grace,' he said, quietly.

She rested her head on his shoulder, and they didn't speak again. He was glad that they had said all they wanted to say to each other.

Very soon, Farrell noticed a change in the rhythm of her breathing. He looked down at her, cautiously. She was asleep. He was beginning to grow stiff, afraid to move and disturb her.

She stirred a little then, and her eyes opened. They were vague and filmy.

'I'm so tired,' she murmured.

Unspeaking, Farrell stood and gathered her in his arms. She was so small, so light. He carried her upstairs and laid her gently on the bed. He took off her dressing-gown so that she would be comfortable. He smoothed her long T-shirt, getting rid of any wrinkles. Then he pulled back the white sheet, careful of the lace edging.

Turning away from her, he reached up to the top of his wardrobe. The Ruger was there, ready, still wrapped in the white cotton cloth. Farrell's heart had begun to thump now. But the feeling of relief was stronger. It was nearly done. It was nearly over.

He remembered what Gerry had told him. He released

the safety catch and waited until the gun began to grow used to his hand.

Then he turned towards his wife, took one step nearer to her, and fired.

Farrell has finished all his preparations now. He makes his way back upstairs. All the last-minute details are complete – dinner, car, answering-machine. He doesn't think that he has left anything out. He sits down on the top step again, smoking the last of Grace's cigarettes. He reviews all the clues he has left for P.J. He has to leave some element of doubt, something for the man to puzzle and agonise over until the day he dies. He can see the man's bewildered face as he tries to understand what he sees before him. Buy your way out of *that*.

Farrell turns his attention to the walnut bookcase on the landing. He can see all the titles from where he sits. Grace's books on the history of art, guides to the National Gallery, the Louvre, the Prado. Books on craft, on doll-making, on toy-designing. His own books on carpentry, on furniture restoration, on wood finishes.

He reads all the titles, allowing the memories evoked by each one to flood him as he sits on his own stairs for the last time.

He remembers Mr Casey and his own years as an apprentice to an exacting, caring master-craftsman. He remembers Mrs Casey and her sideboard. The memory of working with Grace on the cot for Anna's first baby, Eleanor, is especially vivid. He can see her laughing with pleasure as the simple mechanism works smoothly, changing their creation from cot to child's bed and back to cot again. He can still see the smooth, unhurried movements of her arm as she applies coat after coat of beeswax, delighting in the soft lustre. And, of course, the cradles. He can see her surprise on the night he showed her the cradle and all the toys he'd made for her. The night she'd said she loved him.

So many things have happened in this house, his first real home. He does not think of the home he had when he was Vinny. He does not want to remember any of that now. He has put all of that aside. That all belongs to a different person, a different time.

Farrell stubs out the cigarette in the ceramic ashtray. He gets slowly to his feet, brushing the grey flakes of ash off his trousers. He puts his whiskey glass down on the landing windowsill.

He starts to pull the bookcase towards him. He has forgotten how heavy it is. Solid walnut. Sweat begins to bead across his forehead. Farrell drags the heavy bookcase across the landing until he gets it parallel with the top step. Then, deliberately, grunting with effort, he turns it sideways. It is too heavy. He pulls all the books off the top shelf and flings them downstairs. Some fly open, making a gasping sound as they hit the end of the stairs. Still too heavy. He clears all the remaining shelves until there is nothing left.

Then, he upends the bookcase and, with a brief flutter of regret, hurls it downstairs. It crashes against the wall, splintering loudly, one corner lodging firmly between the wall and the bottom stair-rails. It forms a tall, awkward barrier between the hall and the landing.

Couldn't be better, Farrell thinks. Let him work that one out.

Then he starts to laugh. The beauty of this jigsaw is that there is no solution. There is really nothing to work out, no final, neat answer. He imagines the puzzlement again on the face of the enemy.

Now, this really is three moves ahead. Farrell has always admired the simplicity and symmetry of the chessboard.

He raises his glass to his lips, draining it.

My turn now: Checkmate.

He stares into the chaos below him, feeling suddenly cold, wanting a rug for his knees.

Forgive me, mother.

Forgive me, Martina.

I love you, Grace.

Farrell walks back into the eerie stillness of his bedroom. He switches on the bedside light. He pulls a pair of brand-new pyjamas from the lower dressing-table drawer. He never wears pyjamas, but in the circumstances, some dignity is called for.

He pulls back the sheet on his side of the bed. The blood has crept all the way over to him. No matter.

He pulls the plastic gloves on again and lifts the Ruger from the floor. He feels for Grace's hands. They are cold. Sweating a little, cursing the last glass of whiskey, Farrell wraps both of Grace's stiff, resisting hands around the black metal. They stay.

Still holding onto her, he peels the gloves off, one at a time, and hides them at the bottom of the wastepaper-basket on the floor beside him.

And have you any idea, sir, why your daughter would kill her husband?

He eases himself into position beside Grace. The bed is cold and sticky. There is a smell like copper.

He reaches back and snaps off the light. He waits for a few moments until his eyes become accustomed to the darkness. He tries to imagine the confusion, the questions and contradictions arising out of the chaos he has so carefully constructed.

Was your daughter depressed, sir? Can you think of any reason why she might have committed suicide?

Farrell places both his hands over Grace's. They had once held a glass of champagne like this. And once a glass of whiskey, to comfort him. The memories of those times are gentle now. Perhaps he can warm her hands a little for her.

He settles the gun at his temple, and places his finger over Grace's, on the trigger.

What was your son-in-law's first name, sir?

Answer the man, P.J.

His last thought, just before he fires, is of sunshine in Merrion Square and a heavy door slamming as another man calls her Gracie.

Also available in Vintage

Catherine Dunne

IN THE BEGINNING

'Beautifully written, perfectly paced and very, very moving'
Roddy Doyle

In the beginning there is a family. It is a very ordinary family, just like yours or mine – Ben, Rose and their three children. Then, one morning, without warning, Ben leaves and Rose is left to face life alone.

In the Beginning is the story of Rose and Ben's marriage before he leaves, and of how Rose struggles to re-invent her life when he has gone. Written with an almost artless simplicity, Catherine Dunne's brilliant first novel is at once heartbreaking, inspiring, and very true.

'Dunne has written a page-turner...compelling...edgy, fast-paced'
Mary Morrissy, *Irish Times*

'This is one of the most unusual novels you are likely to read...It is a triumph of the ordinary. When it comes to an end, you feel you've lost your best friend...Startling and unforgettable...compelling'
Justine McCarthy, *Irish Independent*

'Fascinating...extraordinary...This perceptive Irish author exposes deep truths about modern marriage'
Andrew Biswell, *Daily Telegraph*

VINTAGE

Also available in Vintage

Anne Tyler

A PATCHWORK PLANET

'Possibly Tyler's best book yet – which must make it pretty near perfection'
The Times

'Barnaby Gaitlin has less in life than he once had. His ex-wife Natalie left him and their native Baltimore several years ago...taking their baby daughter Opal with her...He acquired an unalterably fixed position as the black sheep of the family. And this family isn't one where black sheep are amusedly tolerated. The Gaitlins are rich and worthy, supposedly guided by their own special angel to do the right thing...*A Patchwork Planet* is thoroughly enjoyable...from this most responsive novelist'
Sunday Times

'I can think of no other writer whose novels I look forward to with such gleeful anticipation. *A Patchwork Planet* is her fourteenth book, but were it her fortieth, it would not be enough for me...a delight from beginning to end'
Observer

VINTAGE

A SELECTED LIST OF CONTEMPORARY FICTION
ALSO AVAILABLE IN VINTAGE

☐ NIGHT TRAIN	Martin Amis	£5.99
☐ LOVE WARPS THE MIND A LITTLE	John Dufresne	£6.99
☐ IN THE BEGINNING	Catherine Dunne	£5.99
☐ ONE DAY AS A TIGER	Anne Haverty	£6.99
☐ MY BROTHER	Jamaica Kincaid	£6.99
☐ THE LAST RESORT	Alison Lurie	£6.99
☐ THE CONVERSATIONS AT		
CURLOW CREEK	David Malouf	£5.99
☐ ENDURING LOVE	Ian McEwan	£6.99
☐ AN INSTANCE OF THE FINGERPOST	Iain Pears	£6.99
☐ SEX CRIMES	Jenefer Shute	£6.99
☐ A PATCHWORK PLANET	Anne Tyler	£6.99
☐ TIMEQUAKE	Kurt Vonnegut	£5.99
☐ THESE DEMENTED LANDS	Alan Warner	£6.99

- All Vintage books are available through mail order or from your local bookshop.

- Please send cheque/eurocheque/postal order (sterling only), Access, Visa
Mastercard, Diners Card, Switch or Amex:

☐☐☐☐☐☐☐☐☐☐☐☐☐☐☐☐

Expiry Date:_____Signature:_____

Please allow 75 pence per book for post and packing U.K.
Overseas customers please allow £1.00 per copy for post and packing.

ALL ORDERS TO:

Vintage Books, Books by Post, TBS Limited, The Book Service,
Colchester Road, Frating Green, Colchester, Essex CO7 7DW

NAME:_____

ADDRESS:_____

_____

_____

Please allow 28 days for delivery. Please tick box if you do not
wish to receive any additional information ☐

Prices and availability subject to change without notice.